KEEPING MY BRIDE

ANGELA SNYDER

COPYRIGHT

Copyright © 2021 Angela Snyder
Cover Art ~ Opium House Creatives

This book is a work of fiction. Names, characters, places and incidents either are products of the author's imagination or are used fictitiously.

All rights reserved. No part of this publication may be reproduced, stored in retrieval system, copied in any form or by any means, electronic, mechanical, photocopying, recording or otherwise transmitted without written permission from the publisher. You must not circulate this book in any format.

This book is licensed for your personal enjoyment only. This book may not be resold or given away to other people. If you would like to share this book with another person, please purchase an additional copy for each recipient. If you're reading this book and did not purchase it, or it was not purchased for your use only, then please return to the retailer and purchase your own copy. Thank you for respecting the hard work of this author.

BLURB

I was forced to marry a monster.

Luca Vitale is the heir to his father's empire.

He has the reputation of being a dangerous monster who can bring even grown men to their knees.

And he's about to become my husband.

Our families have been at war with one another ever since I can remember.

I am the daughter of his enemy, and he will try everything to control me, to bend me...to break me.

When I'm forced to make a deal with the devil himself, one question still remains — will our union be one of love or violence?

Keeping My Bride is a standalone dark mafia arranged marriage romance. It contains adult content for mature readers.

DEDICATION

This book is dedicated to my husband. A little piece of you goes into every book boyfriend I create. I've suffered a lot of loss lately, and you are always there for me, a constant source of love and strength that never wavers. I love you more than anything in this world, and I simply don't know what I would do without you.

PLAYLIST

Meg Myers – *Desire (Hucci Remix)*
Laylow - *Megatron*
Mr. Kitty – *After Dark*
Cigarettes After Sex – *Apocalypse*
Architects – *Dead Butterflies*
Eminem - *Venom*
Cemeteries – *I Will Run from You*
Sharon Van Etten – *Jupiter 4*
Borns – *American Money*
Aurora - *Runaway*

PROLOGUE

Verona Moretti

8 years old

A S SOON AS our nanny opens the back door to the minivan, we jump out and run, screaming at the top of our lungs, towards the huge playground.

"Don't run!" Penelope, our nanny, calls after us, but we don't listen. We never listen.

Dante is the first one to the jungle gym, and I'm mad because he always beats me.

"Beat ya!" he calls out, bragging.

"Yeah, yeah. You have longer legs than I do!" I point out.

He stares down at his legs like he's noticing them for the first time before he smiles up at me with a toothy grin. I watch in awe as he quickly climbs to the top of the jungle gym with no effort at all.

Dante is two years older than me. He came to live with us about two months ago after his parents died. I don't know how they died, and he won't tell me when I ask. And believe me, I've asked a lot.

The first month, he was really quiet and sad. But slowly, I've gotten him to come out of his shell and open up. He actually smiles now, which is something he never did before.

"Verona, look at me!" Dante calls from above me, but I'm too busy searching the parking lot for a familiar vehicle. And when I see the black sedan pull in and park, I'm practically bursting with excitement.

I run over to the swings, our favorite place, and wait.

I peek a glance over my shoulder and watch as the most beautiful boy I have ever seen gets out of the car and walks towards me. Usually he runs to meet me, but today is different. He looks...upset.

I decide right then and there that I'll cheer him up, just like I do with Dante. Dante used to be sad all the time, but he's not anymore. So, I can make my new friend less sad too.

Pumping my little legs, I begin to swing back and forth, waiting for him. We've been friends for a few weeks now, and our nannies always let us play together. Luca is Dante's age, but the two of them don't really get along, not like Luca and I do.

When Luca Vitale steps onto the grassy area of the swings, my smile widens. "Hi, Luca!" I call to him as I swing higher and higher. We always have a contest to see who can swing the highest, and sometimes he lets me win.

He doesn't answer me. Instead, he just glares at me with those strange gray eyes of his.

I stop pumping my legs, so that I can slow down a little. "What's wrong?" I ask him, curious.

"What's wrong? What's wrong is that my dad told me you're a Moretti."

I stare at him, confused. "Yeah, so?" I ask.

"Well, the Vitales hate the Morettis. And so I hate you!" he calls before running over and pushing me off the swing.

I fall onto my hands and knees, scraping both on the dirt and gravel. Big, fat tears form in my eyes as I stare down at the tiny cuts in my skin. But they don't hurt nearly as much as Luca's words.

My eyes are blurry as I watch him run away from me like I have some sort of disease that he could catch.

Dante runs over to me and helps me up, brushing the grass and little rocks from me. "Are you okay?" he asks, his brows furrowed. Dante is like a big brother to me; very protective and always taking care of me.

"I'm fine," I lie.

I watch as Luca says something to his nanny, and then she leads him back to the car. My lower lip trembles and tears fall down my cheeks as I watch them drive away.

"He's a jerk," Dante tells me, reassuringly.

Suddenly, I push away from Dante and run as fast as my legs will carry me. I don't stop running until I'm by myself at the other end of the playground. When I'm all alone, I cry over the loss of my new friend.

I had told my mother that I wanted to marry Luca someday so that I could stare into his gray eyes forever.

Luca Vitale was the first boy I ever loved. And he was also the first boy to ever break my heart.

CHAPTER 1

Verona

Present Day

I SIT QUIETLY in the corner of my father's office. My hands are clenched in my lap as I listen to what he's saying to the other man in the room. Blood is pulsing in my ears so loudly that I can barely make out their words.

Papa is planning out my life at this very moment, my entire future depending on his every word, and I don't even have a say in what happens.

When Salvatore Vitale made an unexpected visit to the house this morning, I should have known my father was up to something.

I've only been back home for a few weeks, and my father hasn't said more than several cursory words to me the entire time. Maybe he knew this was coming. Or maybe it's because of something else.

When I was nine years old, my mother overdosed on sleeping meds and drowned in the swimming pool. I didn't know what suicide meant at the time, but I still find it hard to believe that my mother would have done it on purpose. She loved me. And I loved her. She wouldn't have just left me. To this day, I still believe it was an accident.

After her death, things changed in my house. Papa barely spoke to me. Maybe he simply didn't know how to handle me and my emotions.

All I know is that eventually he deemed it not safe for me to be living at home anymore, and he sent me away to an all-girls boarding school in another state. After I graduated, he didn't ask me to return home. No, he sent me away again to live with a great aunt. And let me tell you, there was nothing *great* about her.

When my grandfather passed away a few weeks ago, Papa finally asked me to return home, although it doesn't really feel like home anymore. So much has changed, and yet my father's attitude towards me remains the same. I feel like a burden to him. Alone and unwanted, just like when I was a little girl.

After all the years of being away from my father, I can't believe he's trying to send me away yet again. It's as if he can't stand the sight of me. Maybe it's because I remind him of Mama. Everyone always says how much I look like her...

My father abruptly stands up from his desk in the large room and shakes Vitale's hand. They agreed on something, and I wasn't even paying attention. I was lost in my own thoughts as my future was decided for me right before my eyes.

"So, we agree that Verona and Luca will be married one week from now?" my father announces.

My teeth sink into my bottom lip as I do my best to keep from screaming out in protest. He can't just barter me like cattle...can he?

Mr. Vitale nods and firmly shakes my father's hand before letting go. And then he turns, meeting my gaze with piercing gray eyes that match those of his son. I open my mouth to speak, but Mr. Vitale walks out of the room before I can say a word, leaving me alone with my father.

My bottom lip trembles as I dare to speak up to my father. He was never a gentle man, even when I was a little girl.

"Papa," I start as I rise from my seat and take a step towards him.

He suddenly raises his hand, stopping me dead in my tracks. "I don't want to hear your complaints, Verona," he says, boredom dripping out of his voice like he didn't just decide my entire future without giving me a say in it just now.

"I don't want to marry Luca Vitale," I protest with as much vehemence as I can. "I-I don't even know him!"

The truth is, I used to know Luca Vitale. But that was many years ago when we were children. He was lovely back then, a good friend, probably my first love even though I was so young and naïve.

But then one day, when Luca found out who I truly was, he hurt me, physically and emotionally, and never looked back. I never saw him again after that day in the playground.

Our families have been at war for as long as I can remember. I don't know much about Luca Vitale other than the fact that his mother died a couple of years after my own mother passed away. I've heard stories about him, though. I've heard about the cruel and heartless man he became. And I want no part of him or his mafia lifestyle. I don't want to find out how ruthless he can be.

"I didn't know your mother before I married her," my father offers.

I knew about my parents' arranged marriage. My mother told me about it not too long before she died. I know she loved my father, but I'm sure that took time. And I know she would want me to marry for love, not for convenience or because of someone demanding it.

"Please, Papa, don't make me do this!" I plead.

"What you want is of no consequence to me, Verona. The wills of the patriarchs of the two families forged this union before they passed away, and there's no backing out of it now."

My forehead wrinkles in confusion as I move closer to his desk and see the papers sitting in front of my father. My eyes scan the top few pages, reading as much as I can before my father snatches them away and walks over to a large safe in the corner of the room. After inputting a code that even I'm not privy to, he tucks the papers safely inside before closing it and locking everything away from me.

"The patriarchs of the family decreed this union in their wills."

Valerius Vitale and Marcello Moretti both died within a couple of weeks of each other. Rivals from when they were children, they never stopped fighting until their dying breath. And now I'm supposed to believe that they wanted Luca and I to marry? That just doesn't make sense.

"Grandfather would never agree to this," I say, confused.

"He did. They did. And unless this wedding happens, neither of the families will get any of the inheritance."

So it all comes down to what always mattered the most to my father — money. If I don't marry Luca Vitale, then my father gets nothing. He will probably lose everything he owns, because my grandfather was a very powerful man with lots of assets.

"But the Morettis have always hated the Vitales and vice versa," I tell my father. "Why would they do this?" I ask, my voice just above a whisper.

My father frowns. "I guess their last wish was to have reconciliation once and for all. And with the two of you married, there will be peace between the two families." He doesn't seem too pleased about the *peace*, though.

I open my mouth to plead again with my father, but he silences me with a glare. "Start preparing, Verona. You have a wedding to get ready for." And with that, he leaves the room.

His departing words are the final nail in my coffin. There will be a wedding. I will marry Luca Vitale whether I want to or not.

All of my life I've been told what to do. I've never had a say in what I want to do, and I hate the fact that I can't even choose whom I want to marry. I can only hope that Luca is not as cruel as the rumors make him out to be. If I have to marry him, I will try to make it work. But one question still remains — will our union be consummated in love or violence?

CHAPTER 2

Luca Vitale

I WOKE UP *early that Tuesday morning, starving. Mama told me my body is going through some kind of growth spurt, and it's like I can't get enough to eat. She always makes me a big breakfast before I go to school, so that I can make it until lunch time without my stomach eating itself.*

With my guts grumbling, I go downstairs to the kitchen. The house is quiet, but I know Mama will be awake. She's always the first one up.

When I walk into the kitchen, I slip on something wet and almost fall. Gripping the counter to steady myself, I look down at the tiled floor and see something dark and shiny. My first thought is maybe it's dirty water or some kind of cleaning product, but it smells like pennies, not bleach.

My feet are covered in the liquid, and I flip a switch nearby to see what the heck I stepped in. It takes a few seconds for my brain to process what exactly I'm looking at.

Blood.

There's blood everywhere.

Why is there so much blood?

And then I hear it. Something scratching against the tile floor. I walk around the center island and see my mother, crawling towards me. Her throat has been slashed, but she's still alive as blood pours out of the wounds in her neck.

"Mama!" I yell, panicking. I rush to her side, falling to the floor beside her. She collapses into my arms, gazing up at me with fear in her eyes. Three deep slashes are on her neck, and I can't stop staring at them.

She's trying to talk, but no words come out. Quickly, I cover the wounds on her neck with my hand the best I can, but I can feel the blood pushing out between my fingers. "No, no, no!" I cry. "Someone help us!" I yell. I don't know if anyone will hear me, but I can't leave her like this.

Mama's eyes drift closed, and I scream for her to wake up. "Please, Mama! Don't leave me! Don't leave me!"

Her body goes limp in my arms, and I sit there, stunned. I hold her tightly to me, rocking her like she used to rock me to sleep when I was a baby.

If only I had been a few minutes earlier, I could have saved her. I could have seen who did this. I could have killed them instead.

I rock her gently, and I cry.

My mother's dead.

She's dead.

She's dead.

She's dead.

"Luca!" my father's voice roars as he barges into my bedroom, effectively waking me out of the nightmare I was having.

I sit up straight in bed. I'm covered in sweat from head to toe, and it takes me a few seconds to realize where the fuck I am. I don't have the nightmare about my mother's death often; but when I do, I always wake up confused and terrified.

My father walks over to the nearby window and rips open the drapes. I squint my eyes against the glaring light and slowly sit up to look at him through narrowed eyes and a growing headache thanks to the rude awakening and my hangover. "Good morning, Father," I tell him sarcastically. "This couldn't wait until noon?"

"It is noon," he hisses.

"Shit!" I grab my watch on the nightstand and realize he's not lying. I slept half the day away thanks to all that booze last night and the great sex that followed soon after with a girl whose name I can't even recall. I don't normally indulge in that much alcohol, but I was feeling particularly sad and depressed last night. Today marks the anniversary of my mother's death, and I just wanted to feel numb last night, knowing that today would be so hard to get through. But now that I'm awake, I realize I went about it all wrong. I'm not numb at all. I feel fucking horrible. And having such a rude awakening by my father is not helping matters.

"You weren't answering your phone, so I had to stop by here in person."

Grumbling, I rub my eyes with the heels of my palms. "What did I do this time?" I ask, assuming that's why he's here — to gripe about something I did or didn't do.

"We need to discuss your grandfather's will."

I swipe my hand down my face and grumble. My grandfather passed away last week. His funeral was the other day, and it was the second saddest day of my life, after my mother's funeral.

"Get cleaned up," my father instructs. "I'll be downstairs waiting for you."

And with that, he leaves me alone in my room. I flop back on my bed and stare up at the ceiling as I wonder aloud, "What does my grandfather's will have to do with me?"

After I'm showered and dressed in my usual attire – a tailored and expensive black suit with a black button-up shirt underneath, I meet my father downstairs in the lobby of my condo building. The car ride to his mansion is quiet and filled with tension. I try to pry into his reasoning for bringing me back home to discuss my grandfather's will, but my father refuses to budge.

And by the time we reach my childhood home, I know something isn't right.

We walk into the house and go straight to my father's study on the first floor. He motions for me to take a seat as he goes to stand over papers spread out over his large, mahogany desk.

"What the fuck is that?" I ask him, curiosity getting the better of me. "A new contract?"

"Something like that," he mutters in annoyance. My father never had any patience when it came to anyone or anything, especially me. "I need you to read over this and sign it right away."

I notice the bold heading on the first page, *Last Will and Testament*, and cock a brow. "This is my grandfather's will?"

He nods once.

Intrigued, I sit down in a chair and begin to read the paperwork. At first, it's all the usual legalese. But then the terms and conditions start coming to light, and my fingers tighten around the papers, clenching them tightly as I read what can only be described as archaic bullshit.

"He can't fucking do this!" I exclaim, rising out of my seat.

My father shrugs nonchalantly. "But he did."

"I am not going to marry a Moretti!" I spit out, cursing the name on my tongue.

"Both of the grandfathers agreed to this bullshit clause in their wills."

Valerius Vitale and Marcello Moretti died within a few weeks of each other. And this is what they agreed to?

"This can't hold up in court. This is ridiculous!" I yell, my voice rising to dangerous levels.

"We need to honor their wishes," my father simply says.

Banging my fist on my desk, rattling everything on top of it, I tell him, "No. No, I will not agree to this. I haven't even seen Verona Moretti in years." Slamming the papers down on the desk, I say, "There's no way she will agree to this."

"She's already signed the necessary paperwork. Her father faxed me the copy this morning," he tells me, causing my world to come to a complete stop.

Shaking my head in disbelief, I walk away from my desk and pace the room. "There has to be another way."

"None of us get the money, the estates, the properties, the mansions, the cars, *anything* unless this comes to fruition."

"Why would they decide this? This is some kind of sick joke!" Valerius Vitale and Marcello Moretti were adversaries, some say from birth. Our families feuded over land, territory, everything for years. And then, when my mother was murdered, everything came to a head. Rivals soon turned into sworn enemies willing to go to war with each other.

And now my grandfather is requesting that I marry one of them?

"I suppose the old men reached a point of peace and agreement in their final days. I just wish my father would have told me about his plans, because I most certainly would have talked him out of it," my father explains.

"This is about peace? There will be no peace if I'm intertwined with the Morettis!"

My father considers this for a moment, but then says, "Maybe this will be the end of the war. We can't continue to go to war if we're *family*. And I think that's what your grandfather was trying to resolve before he died. He didn't want us fighting anymore or tearing each other down at every turn."

A dark chuckle releases from my mouth. "If I have to marry her so that we don't lose everything we worked so hard for, then so be it. But I won't be faithful. I won't ever love her."

"No one said anything about love, my dear boy. We are talking about marriage after all."

I scoff at his words. He can say what he wants, but I know he loved my mother. And the day she was murdered, I saw my father cry for the first and only time in that kitchen while he held her lifeless body in his arms. Sure, their marriage had its ups and downs, like all marriages tend to do, but he loved my mother. And he also had the privilege of knowing his bride before their wedding day. They met in high school, dated, got to know each other, had a chance to fall in love.

Me, on the other hand, I have to marry a girl I haven't seen since I was a kid. There will be no courtship, no easing into this. "How long do I have?" I ask my father.

"One week."

Of course I would be delivered this horrible news on the anniversary of my mother's death. It seems fitting almost. Tragedy upon tragedy. That's what my entire life has been composed of.

"Will you sign the papers?" he asks impatiently.

"Do I have a choice?"

He doesn't even hesitate when he tells me, "No."

"Then I'll sign."

I'll marry Verona Moretti. I'll follow the terms of the will so that my family isn't destitute and out on the streets with nothing. But there's nothing saying I can't take my anger and frustration out on my new bride to be, that I won't treat her like my own little plaything. She will be my wife in name only. And I'm going to make her regret signing the contract. I'm going to make her life a living hell.

CHAPTER 3

Verona

I STAND IN front of the mirror inside the dress shop and stare at my reflection. I don't even recognize myself in the wedding dress. I look so...different. So grown up.

"Oh my god, you look gorgeous!" the shop owner exclaims with animated hands. She's a small, older lady with frizzy blonde hair and huge glasses that make her blue eyes look enormous behind the thick lenses. "I knew this one would look great on you," she gushes.

Tears fill my eyes when I glance around the empty room. God, I wish my mother could be here with me. After she passed away, an empty void filled me, hollowing me out from the inside, and I wonder if I'll ever feel unconditional love like that again.

My father was always a stickler for rules and obedience, but my mother...she was more lenient and understanding. She made me smile, made me laugh. She was like a real-life angel on this earth disguised as a human.

And I miss her terribly, especially today.

"Oh, sweetie, don't cry," the woman says, handing me a wad of tissues out of a nearby box. "Weddings are *happy* occasions!"

I almost roll my eyes. She's so oblivious to my situation that she couldn't even begin to comprehend what I'm going through. This wedding is going to be anything but happy. I'm about to marry a total stranger. Sure, I knew Luca back when we were kids, but we were just that — children. Many years have passed since we've spoken or even seen each other. I have no idea what happened to him after puberty. For all I know, he could look like a potbelly pig. And smell like one too.

Cringing, I tell the woman, "Okay, I'll take this one." There's no sense in trying any other dresses on. None of them will ever feel perfect to me since I'm being forced to walk down the aisle instead of doing it of my own free will.

"Are you sure? It's the first one you tried on. I'm not saying you don't look stunning, but I have many more styles for you to choose from," she says while pushing her big glasses up the bridge of her tiny nose.

"I'm sure," I tell her with a firm nod. It was the first dress that caught my eye, and honestly, I don't even want to try any others on. It's not like I've been waiting for this day. No, this was sprung on me just a few days ago through a contract that I had to sign. And it felt like signing my life away.

If Papa wouldn't kill me, I'd buy a black wedding dress to suit my mood and feelings towards this arrangement. But I don't need him any more distant and angrier with me than he already is. He's the only family I have left. Love him or leave him. And I guess I'm choosing to love him.

"I don't think I'll need to make any alterations," the woman says as she walks around, feeling the fabric and looking for gaps or flaws. "It's perfect, really. It fits you like a glove."

"Lucky me," I mutter sarcastically.

"Now, it's been in storage for a few months. I'll have it steamed and pressed for you. It will be ready in two days. Is that all right?"

"That's fine," I answer.

"I'll be right back with some veil options, and then we can look at shoes," she tells me before disappearing into the backroom.

I stand there, admiring the dress in the mirror. It's a mermaid style dress full of intricate lace detail with a V neck and low V in the back and a short train. It really is beautiful. I just wish I wasn't wearing it to a wedding that I want no part of.

"Wow, look at you," a voice says behind me.

My eyes meet Dante's in the mirror, and I can't help but smile. Dante is the one who drove me here. He's been my best friend since I was eight years old. When I was sent away to boarding school, he stayed behind to work for my father. We stayed connected through letters, and we spoke on the phone almost every night when I was allowed to make calls.

And when I went to live with my great aunt and was back in the same state as him at least, Dante came to visit me every weekend. He never missed a single one.

Dante has been my rock through all of this. Ever since I lost my mother, he has always been the shoulder I've cried on. I don't know what I would do without him. And I hope I never have to find out.

"What do you think?" I ask, turning to face him.

"*Bellissima*," he says with a thumbs up and a wink.

Beautiful. Of course Dante would say that. He always knew how to make me feel better about myself.

"Thank you," I tell him as I turn back to face the mirror. I can't help but let my gaze linger on Dante a little longer than I should as he walks around the store, his handsome face now serious as he looks for any threats to me. A blush creeps up my neck to my cheeks as I check out my best friend secretly in the mirror.

Dante has definitely grown up over the years. Gone is the scrawny kid I remember so well. In his place is a tall, handsome man with dark hair, dark eyes and a kind smile. He filled out well, and working out has definitely paid off. His muscles that I sometimes spy when he wears t-shirts are huge.

When I was a teenager, I used to swear up and down that I would marry him someday. But that was just a fickle dream because, in reality, my father would never allow that. Dante will never be equal or good enough in his eyes, and that hurts. My father has no idea how wonderful Dante truly is. Dante would take care of me. I know he would. Our feelings have never crossed the friendship line into romantic, but I always wondered what would happen.

But now look where I am. Any dreams I had of marrying someone I could actually fall for went right out the window.

The woman comes back, holding several veils in her hands. "Okay, let's see what you like best out of these," she says.

She places the first one on my head, and it completes the look. Now I really do look like a bride. And I can't help the frown that instantly appears on my face.

"Smile, dear," she says with an exaggerated grin. "Just think about how happy you'll be on your wedding day."

The frown deepens, and I wonder if I'll ever have anything to smile about ever again. In a few days, I'll be Mrs. Vitale. And that scares the hell out of me.

CHAPTER 4

Luca

I PACE THE floor in the small anteroom off to the side of the chapel. Verona and I will be married in less than an hour. I'm not nervous, not in the least. I am anxious, however. I don't know how we're going to make things work, the two of us. We're bound by contract to get married and stay married, but we're complete fucking opposites. I mean, at least I think we're exact opposites anyway. I don't even know her well enough to know what her likes and dislikes are.

What I do know is that she was sheltered most of her life, kept away from the family business and affairs for a long time. She hasn't had to pick up the pieces of shattered empires or operate day-to-day businesses to keep things afloat. She never had to get blood on her hands or deal with the consequences. She doesn't belong in my world, and I certainly don't belong in hers.

And yet...here we are.

I never saw myself ever getting married, so it's not like this whole thing has dashed my hopes and dreams like it probably has for her. All girls dream of the perfect wedding, the handsome groom, the happily ever after.

I never had such illusions when I was growing up.

After my mother's death, my father became a bitter, hateful man. He took the brunt of his anger out on me. And if that's what happens when you lose someone you love that much, then I don't want to feel that. Ever.

Marriage was never on the table. I fucked my way through most of the city, never so much as calling the girl again or remembering her name.

And now I'm about to be tied down. Well, technically. There's not a cheating clause in the contract. Trust me, I made sure.

No, Verona will be my wife in name only. In reality, she is still the daughter of my enemy, my family's biggest rival. Her family has been a thorn in my side for years, and this contract is complete and utter bullshit.

I don't know what my grandfather was thinking. Marriage doesn't solve anything. This union won't bring peace. If anything, it will make me hate the Morettis even more than I already do.

Sure, our families have put our differences aside for this wedding, but it doesn't change a thing. Verona is still my enemy. And I don't plan on making her life easy. No, quite the opposite. I plan on making her life miserable. I'm going to make her regret ever signing that contract. If she thinks she's going to be treated like a princess in my home, she can fucking forget it.

The door to the small room creaks open, and my father enters. He's dressed to the nines, just like I am. And when he says, "They're ready for you, son," I swallow hard past the lump forming in my throat.

"There has to be a way out of this," I tell him for the twentieth time today. I keep protesting, but I know my efforts are futile. The contract has been signed. It's done.

"Your grandfather wanted this. We have to respect his wishes," my father says solemnly.

"This is a mistake. I don't even know the girl," I blurt out like a petulant child trying to get out of trouble.

"You knew her once. When you were young."

I shake my head at his words. There was a time when I can remember playing in the same park as Verona. I would even venture to say we were friends back then. But that was before everything happened and my mother was murdered. I was innocent then. Things were different, so fucking different.

"We were kids," I tell my father.

"You loved her then," he remarks, causing my gaze to snap up to meet his.

"What?" I exclaim.

"I remember you running home one day, telling me that you were in love with the girl from the park. Let's just say my reaction when you told us the girl's last name was not a good one." He shrugs his shoulders. "Maybe it's my fault you grew hateful of her. When I told you she was the daughter of our rival, the next day you went to the playground and pushed her off the swings." He chuckles at the memory. "Our families almost went to war back then because of what you did." Then his face suddenly grows serious. "Maybe it was just a foreboding of what was to come later on."

I barely remember the playground incident. "The Morettis are scum," I spit out. "And now I'm being forced to marry one of them."

My father claps me on the back as he leads me out of the room. "It could be worse, my boy," he tells me. "At least she's pretty."

I turn to him quickly. "You've seen her?"

He nods. "She's easy on the eyes, so at least you have that going for you."

I don't know why that makes me feel a little better, but it does. But her being pretty on the outside could be a disguise for a disgusting personality, one that I won't be able to tolerate. "Some of the most beautiful things can be rotten inside," I explain to him.

"That is true," he agrees. He cups my head in his hands and kisses each one of my cheeks. "Good luck, son."

"Thanks," I mutter as I walk up to the altar where the priest is waiting. And as I stand there before the two feuding families packed into pews and divided on each side of the crowded church, I know I'm going to need a lot of luck to get through this.

CHAPTER 5

Verona

I CAN'T BREATHE. I'm standing in the vestibule of the church, waiting to go inside...to be married...and my dress is too tight. It's weird because I swear it fit me just a few minutes ago. But now I feel like I might pass out.

"Relax, Verona," Dante's soothing voice says from next to me.

"My dress is too tight," I tell him, my voice rising to new heights in panic.

"Your dress is fine. You're giving yourself a panic attack." Dante steps in front of me, takes my hands in his and starts breathing in and out slowly. "Do what I do."

At first, my breathing is rapid, but eventually I'm able to get it to slow down to match his level.

"See? Just a panic attack."

I can't help but smile at Dante. He always was so good at calming me down. When we were kids, I used to have panic attacks fairly often after my mother died. He was always there to make sure I was okay.

"You look handsome," I whisper in the quiet room. He's wearing a dark blue suit, and his hair is styled. I don't get to see him dressed up very often.

"And you look gorgeous," he whispers back, his eyes roaming down and then back up until finally resting on my face. A frown pulls down at his lips as he tells me, "He doesn't deserve you."

"It's not about what anyone deserves or doesn't deserve at this point," I tell him with a dismissive wave of my hand. "We're under contract to do this." Tears burn my eyes. "I just can't believe my father would allow this."

"The Morettis and Vitales are all about money," he says, and I can hear the contempt in his voice. When he notices me staring at him, he clears his throat and says, "Well, at least the Vitales are anyway."

I shake my head. "I can't expect Papa to lose everything because of me. He's worked so hard all his life. Grandfather wasn't a nice man. My father had to work his way up in the ranks to even be equal to my grandfather." I stare down at my hands. "This has to be done whether I like it or not."

"Well, I definitely don't like it," Dante spits out.

"What don't we like?" my father asks as he enters the room. He glares at Dante and sternly tells him, "Go take a seat, Dante. The wedding will be starting soon."

I watch as Dante opens the door and disappears inside the church. I catch a glance at some of the pews, the people seated who are waiting. I recognize some of them, while the rest are strangers from the Vitale side of the family.

"Papa, I don't know if I can do this," I say when the door closes, turning to my father.

"You can. And you will," he says, his words uncompromising... and final.

I nod in agreement. I never was able to stand up to my father. My mother was the gentle, caring one of the two. My father was the disciplinarian. I learned from an early age to never question him or else there would be consequences. He was always quick to get his belt to get his point across, and I feared him as a child. I guess maybe a part of me still does.

The string quartet begins to play *Canon in D*, and my entire body seizes up. I can't move. I can't think. I'm about to marry a total stranger, someone I knew years ago when I was a little girl, and there's nothing I can do about it. I can't say no. I can't run away, like my legs are protesting to do right at this very moment.

"Verona," my father whispers at my side. Perhaps he can sense that I want to flee.

I look up at him with tears in my eyes.

"You *have* to do this. For the family."

I nod even though I'm screaming out *no* inside of my head.

The song ends. I can hear someone clear their throat from inside the church, and more tears build up in my eyes as the song starts over.

"It's time, Verona," my father tells me before pulling the veil down over my face.

When I give a final nod, he motions for the ushers to open the intricately carved doors before us. The people sitting on the pews immediately stand, all eyes on me.

My legs are moving, but I can't feel them. I feel like I'm gliding. Maybe I'm moving on my father's sheer will and determination alone.

Through the lace of my veil, I glance at the two families gathered on each side of the room. On the right are the Vitales, and on the left are the Morettis. I can see some of them staring one another down from across the pews. The families have been at war for years, for as long as I can remember.

And now this union, *my union*, with Luca Vitale, is supposed to bring peace amongst us all.

Since our two families are just like the Capulet and Montagues, I guess that makes Luca and I a modern-day Romeo and Juliet. Fitting, since I'm named after the city in which the tragedy took place.

It's unimaginable that a wedding can bring a war to an end, and I have my doubts. All I can do is pray that my husband isn't a monster. I haven't seen him since we were children. When I first met him, he was the sweet boy who gave me candy on the playground when we snuck away from the prying eyes of our nannies. If anyone ever saw a Vitale and Moretti together, it would have been an all-out war, but we were kids back then. We didn't know about any violence or hatred amongst our loved ones. We were innocent.

And then one day, he pushed me off the swing set. It was like a switch had gone off inside of him. And I recall hearing my name come from his lips with disgust and hatred, like he finally figured out who I was, who I really was.

I remember going home, crying, with skinned hands and bruised knees. I never saw Luca after that day, nor did I want to.

And now I'm about to marry him.

If he could be so cruel as a little boy, what kind of man did he ultimately become? I shudder at the thought.

My father stops walking, and I come to an abrupt halt, so lost in my thoughts that I didn't even realize we walked the entire length of the church. My father turns to me and lifts my veil, giving me a kiss on each cheek as he takes the bouquet out of my grip and squeezes my hand in reassurance.

And then he walks away, leaving me alone.

My dress feels too tight again as I struggle to pull in a deep breath. I barely make it up the few steps to the altar where the priest and my future husband are waiting. I haven't even looked at him yet. My future husband, that is. I'm too terrified. I haven't seen him up close since he was a boy.

Taking the final step, I stand next to Luca, staring at the priest and refusing to look anywhere else.

"Face your future husband," the priest instructs me.

And so, I turn...and stare right into the eyes of the devil himself.

I'm so taken aback by his brutally handsome face that I forget how to breathe. I don't know what I expected...but it wasn't this. He's tall. So tall, in fact, that I have to strain my neck to look up at him. He's wearing a black suit that fits his broad shoulders flawlessly. His raven hair is perfectly styled and is in stark contrast to his steel-gray eyes that narrow the longer I stare at him. His face looks like it was carved out of stone, his jawline covered in stubble and so strong and ticking under the pressure of his teeth grinding together as he stares at me with...contempt.

I'm taken right back to that day at the playground. I hadn't done anything to the boy back then either, but he hated me so much in that moment just because of who I was and who my family was. And now the man I'm about to marry obviously feels the same way he did when he was a child.

I snap my eyes shut, blocking his face out. When I open them again, I stare at the priest, hoping that he can see in my eyes that I don't want to do this. I don't want to marry this man, but I don't even have a choice in the matter.

But the priest simply continues with the ceremony, and the next several minutes are a blur as the priest goes on and on with readings from the bible and several prayers.

"Verona, do you promise to honor and cherish Luca in sickness and in health, 'til death do you part?"

My heartbeat is pounding in my ears, and I feel like I'm going to pass out. Glancing around the room, I see my father with a grim look on his face as he gives me an imperceptible nod.

"Verona?" the priest prompts.

"I do?" I answer, but it sounds more like a question.

The priest repeats the same vows to Luca, and he responds with a formidable, "I do." His voice has a deep, rich timbre. And I'm sure whenever he talks, people shut up and listen.

"Verona and Luca will now exchange rings as a symbol of the promises they've made here today and their ongoing commitment to each other."

I begin to panic because I don't have a ring for Luca. But suddenly, my husband-to-be is thrusting a ring into my hand. I stare down at the simple black band that will serve as his wedding ring.

The priest continues on with, "These rings were made from precious metals forged in fire, a symbol to your unbreakable bond for this marriage." He looks to me, "Verona, place Luca's ring on his finger."

Luca holds his left hand out to me. The tattoos peeking out under his sleeve and covering the top of his hand catch my attention as I work the band up his thick ring finger. He immediately pulls away from me, like my touch burned him somehow.

"Luca, place Verona's ring on her finger."

I hold out my left hand, and Luca's large hand practically engulfs my small one as he thrusts the diamond ring onto my finger.

I don't even have time to study the ring before the priest says, "I now pronounce you husband and wife." He turns his attention to Luca and says, "You may now kiss the bride."

Luca leans in, and I think to myself, *I'm finally going to have my first kiss*. But instead, he veers off and places a cold, inconsequential peck to my cheek.

He might as well have slapped me in the face, because that's what his rejection feels like. A blush burns my cheeks as I stare out at the crowd. I'm so embarrassed by what just happened.

The church falls silent. There are no cheers of encouragement or well wishing. In fact, I'm surprised no one's been shot yet.

Luca wraps his hand around my arm and roughly forces me to move with him down off the altar and towards the front of the church. Tears are in my eyes as we walk down the silent aisle. I don't feel like a bride at all. No, I feel like a prisoner being taken to jail for a life sentence.

CHAPTER 6

Verona

AFTER THE CEREMONY is over, my father, Dante and I return to my father's home to pack my things. I will be moving in with Luca Vitale, my new husband, tonight. The thought of sharing a room with him...or a bed makes me nauseous.

And the sickness stays with me, gnawing at my gut, as I pack.

"You don't have much here," Dante remarks as he pulls a few hangers from the closet and brings the clothes over to me. He carefully lays them out on the bed.

"I've never had much," I admit. The clothes I obtained throughout the years were mostly school uniforms from the boarding school. Those are long gone now. I threw them out as soon as I graduated. And when I went to live with my great aunt, we spent a lot of time thrift store shopping. I rarely was allowed to buy anything, but I accumulated some things over the years.

The only thing of value in my entire closet is my mother's old dress that I snuck away with me to boarding school. Papa doesn't even know I have it. Not that he would care, I don't think. I've kept the dress with me for years, and it got me through some of the worst days of my life. Having a small piece of my mom with me always kept me sane.

I fold the dress carefully along with the rest of the clothes and put them inside the suitcase.

"This isn't going to take very long," Dante admits with a sigh.

"You know, we could always pretend like it's taking a long time," I suggest with a grin.

He smiles back momentarily before a frown appears on his handsome face. "Fuck, V, I'm going to miss you."

Tears fill my eyes when I think about Dante not being around. It's been nice the past couple of weeks having him around on a daily basis. Our friendship has really grown lately, and I'm going to miss him horribly.

I wrap my arms around him, and he holds me tightly. We don't normally hug or touch, but this feels nice. It feels right.

"Maybe I could talk to your father. Maybe he would let me go," he whispers into my hair.

My mood brightens at his words. I pull back and look into his dark eyes. "You could be my...bodyguard," I say. "I will need one."

"Bodyguard? I like that," he says with a chuckle. "I just don't know if your father —."

"Leave that part up to me. I'll make it work," I promise him.

Dante goes back to the closet, and I sit down on the bed. The wedding ring on my finger feels foreign and heavy, and I take a moment to study it. There's a large pear-shaped diamond in the center, surrounding by tiny round diamonds. On the white gold band are two infinity symbols encased in diamonds on either side of the center stone.

Infinity. Eternity. *I'm sure it will only feel like eternity*, I tell myself, sulking.

"How do you only have two pairs of shoes?" Dante yells from the closet, making me laugh. "I thought girls were supposed to hoard these things?"

"Just shut up and put them in my suitcase," I tell him with a grin.

~

AFTER A FEW HOURS of pretending to pack my things, Dante and I go downstairs to my father's office. He's sitting behind his desk, looking through some paperwork. He glances up over the rim of his reading glasses when we enter.

"Dante is going with me. I want him to be my bodyguard while I live with Luca Vitale," I announce, holding my chin up high.

I expect a fight from my father, but instead he says, "All right. Fine."

"Then it's settled." I turn to Dante, overwhelmed with joy.

"If Luca Vitale actually lets him stay, then he can stay," Father says, bursting my bubble.

I didn't even think about Luca protesting to this decision. Chances are he will say no, but I'm willing to fight for Dante to stay. I will do whatever it takes and not back down from my new husband. We've both had to make sacrifices for this marriage, and my friendship with Dante is not one I'm willing to part with.

I'll need someone on my side in that house. Maybe even someone to protect me from my own husband.

CHAPTER 7

Luca

I'M IMPATIENTLY WAITING for my bride to arrive at my new home...or I guess *our* new home. My father gave me a mansion as a wedding present, saying that my bachelor pad was too small for a *family*. Even thinking about having children with a Moretti makes my blood turn cold. I don't know why my father would even suggest such a heinous thing.

He's taking this marriage contract way too seriously, and it's starting to piss me off.

I hated moving from the city to a rural town in New Jersey, but we're not that far from NYC. Only about forty minutes or so. Besides, it's not like there are houses with properties of this size available in the city. The sacrifice will make it all worth it in the end. I can create a nice, secure compound here on the acres of land my father purchased.

Along with the new home, I had to hire on a housekeeper and

some kitchen staff last minute, so the skeleton crew will have to suffice until I can hire on more people to take care of this huge place.

I stare around the foyer, which is probably bigger than most people's apartments alone. The crystal chandelier screams decadence upon entry, even though the rest of the house does that entirely on its own.

I've only been living here for a week, but the place feels strange, cold...and lonely. And I'm sure Verona's presence won't fix any of that. I already have her bedroom picked out. It's down the hall from mine only because I didn't have a choice. It's the only other room in the same wing with the master bedroom. The other wing is allocated for the staff's living quarters since I'll need full-time staffing to keep up with this massive home and property.

If I had it my way, Verona wouldn't even be under the same roof as me. But some things are beyond my control. The contract clearly stated that we must live together, and so I must abide by the rules...for now.

Benito enters through the front door, drawing my attention to him. He was busy arranging my cars and security's vehicles in the attached ten-car garage.

Benito is my first-in-command and my most trusted and, well, only friend. We grew up together. His family is mafia as well, but a different kind of mafia — the kind that kills and cleans up messes. Benito has killed more people than I could ever count, and I'm not sure if even he knows the exact number.

"She's not here yet?" Benito asks.

I shrug in response. "Her father said she needed to get her things from his house."

"Must be a lot of stuff," he comments.

"Spoiled little princess," I scoff, disgusted.

An alert sounds on his phone, and he's quick to check it. "They're here."

"You already installed the motion detectors?" I ask, impressed.

"Yes, of course. That's the first thing I did, along with the security cameras, when your father bought the property. Well, that and swept the entire place for bugs." He glances at me. "It's clean, by the way."

"Good to know," I say with a nod.

The front door opens, and Verona stands there with a man I recognize as Dante. I remember when we were kids, Dante and Verona were as thick as thieves. It took me a while to win over Verona's attention, but I did time and time again to Dante's dismay. He was in love with her back then. Probably still is.

My eyes narrow as he meets my gaze. He carries in a battered, brown leather suitcase behind Verona, and I stare at it. "Do you need Benito to help you with the rest of the luggage?" I ask him.

Dante cocks a brow at my question. "What other luggage?"

I look to my new bride. She's no longer in her white wedding gown. Instead, she's dressed casually with a pair of leggings and a large, oversized sweater, leaving *everything* to the imagination, unfortunately. "This is all the luggage you have?" I ask her incredulously.

She nods, suddenly looking shy and nervous.

Grabbing the suitcase from Dante, I flick open the lock and dump the contents on the floor. I glance at the pile of clothing and frown. Looks like I'll have to do some online shopping after we're done here.

"What are you doing?" Verona exclaims, desperately trying to refill her suitcase of her personal belongings...which isn't much.

"Vitales have a reputation to uphold, and I won't have my wife looking like a homeless person in rags."

She glares at me from on her knees on the floor, and I like the idea of her kneeling before me. Maybe if there weren't people here, I would make my new bride take my cock into her mouth and show her husband some respect.

"They are not rags!" she yells, breaking me out of my dirty thoughts.

I watch as she repacks her suitcase and locks it back up before standing and ruining my fantasy of her kneeling to service me.

"I'll order you new clothes," I tell her. "Benito will show you to your room." Then, I turn my back on her to head to my new office.

"What about Dante's room?" she asks, causing me to turn back around quickly. "Dante is staying here, as my bodyguard," she informs me.

"The fuck he is," I hiss. I stare at the tall, dark-haired, dark-eyed man that I once knew as a boy. "That's not part of the deal."

"I'm making it part of the deal," she says, jutting her chin out and up like she's suddenly royalty in this house with a say in what goes and what doesn't.

A dark chuckle releases from my mouth. "I won't accept any kind of deal from a Moretti," I tell her. "You're staying. He's going."

"No."

"No?" I test her.

"If he goes, then I go," she says so stubbornly that I want to take her over my knee and beat the defiance out of her in that moment.

And just the thought of her bent over my knee has my cock jumping in my pants. I wonder what kind of panties she's wearing under all those clothes? I wonder if she's wearing innocent, white, cotton underwear...or a black, lacy thong that emphasizes her ass cheeks. Fuck, I want to find out.

"Do you have a bodyguard here for me?" she questions, effectively ruining my filthy musings.

"Not yet," I answer. Honestly, the thought of protecting her hasn't even crossed my mind, but she is right — she is my wife now, and protection is a must. Although, if anyone would take her from me, I wouldn't give them a cent in return. They could keep her, for all I care. She would be out of my hair and the marriage contract would still be valid since it was something beyond my control.

"Then it's settled," she says. "Dante is staying."

I walk over to her and stare her down. She's so petite, especially without heels on now. At the church, she was a few inches taller, but now I tower over her little frame.

"He can stay until proper protection is hired," I concede through gritted teeth.

A smile graces her pouty lips, and I hate to admit that I like seeing it on her pretty face. Turning and walking away from them before I do something stupid like smile back or try to kiss those bee-stung lips, I throw over my shoulder, "Benito will show you both to your rooms."

CHAPTER 8

Verona

I HAVE MY own bedroom. I was not expecting that. I thought I would be in the same room as Luca and forced to consummate the marriage on the first night. I'm relieved, but at the same time I'm confused. Does he not want to sleep with me? I never questioned the idea of how our marriage would work. I figured it would be like all arranged marriages. Eventually, you just make it work like a normal, loving marriage. That's what my father and mother did anyway. They slowly fell in love, and their bond was fiercer than any I have ever seen.

Do I want to fall in love with Luca? The possibility seems so far away, like some distant universe, that I can't even really consider it. But anything is possible, right? Eventually, if we get to know each other, everything will gradually go on a natural course towards love, true love.

I glance in the mirror as I unpack my things and catch my reflection. Maybe Luca isn't attracted to me. I did put on the most casual clothes I own. But after being in that heavy wedding dress for hours and feeling like I was suffocating the entire time, I needed a break. Plus, my feet were killing me from the high heels.

Popping open my suitcase, I stare at my meager belongings and grimace. Luca made me feel so embarrassed earlier when he called my clothing rags that belong on a homeless person.

No.

I shake my head, straighten my spine and go to the walk-in closet to begin hanging up my favorite pants, dresses, skirts and shirts. I'm not going to let him make me feel like I belong under him, like I'm not good enough.

Even though my father is wealthy, I haven't been privy to his money in a long time. After graduating from boarding school at eighteen, I went to stay with a great aunt in upstate New York. She was in her seventies, strict and cold...and even cruel sometimes. I never knew why she agreed to take me in since she acted like she hated me most of the time.

The only thing I can think of is that my father offered her money in exchange for keeping me. But I never saw a single red cent. No, my clothes were mostly hand-me-downs and thrift store finds. God, my great aunt loved her thrift stores. And she knew how to pinch a penny so hard she could make it bleed.

After my grandfather died a few weeks ago, I was suddenly beckoned by my father to return to my childhood mansion. I didn't understand it then, but now I know why — my grandfather's will, and the marriage contract that coincided with his passing. I was simply a pawn in a game that I never knew I was playing.

My father knew the entire time and didn't say a word. No, I was blindsided instead, just like I have been my entire life when it comes to family matters.

And did I get a say about whether or not I wanted to marry Luca Vitale?

Of course not. I've never had much of a voice when it came to my father, but I mean, what did I expect when I haven't even been around him in more than a decade?

The father I remember growing up was kinder, gentler. The man he became after my mother killed herself turned cold and bitter.

Shivering, I wrap my arms around myself as I stare at my progress. My fingers run over the familiar fabrics and stop at the last dress. It was my mother's. The dress is soft and ivory with vibrant flowers. I hold the fabric close to me and sniff. Sometimes I swear I can still smell her even though I've worn it and washed it many times. It's my favorite thing that I own, and I could never part with it. It's the only thing I have of hers, unfortunately.

Sighing, I release the dress and stare around the walk-in closet that's bigger than my old bedroom at my aunt's house. My clothes don't even take up one rack of the many dozens that are in here.

No matter. Maybe I can get Dante to take me shopping soon at a thrift store. I have some money, but not a lot. Maybe I can find something more *suitable* for the wife of a mobster.

Another shiver moves through me as I wonder how much power Luca Vitale actually has. How does he make his money? Is he in arms dealing, drugs, or…human trafficking? I pray and hope not the latter, but I have no idea.

For his family to afford a place like this, maybe they have their fingers in all sorts of pies across the city. I thought my childhood home was immaculate and vast, but it doesn't even hold a candle to my new home.

Home.

I glance around the room and frown. It doesn't feel like home to me. And I have to wonder if it ever will.

CHAPTER 9

Verona

AFTER DANTE AND I are settled in our separate rooms, Benito offers to take us on a tour of the mansion and property. I try to memorize the rooms, which include a gym, a vast library, two formal living rooms, a den, an enormous dining hall, a billiards room, and a huge state-of-the-art kitchen. Lastly, we pass Luca's private office, which is off limits. Benito didn't have to tell me that, but he didn't so much as even knock or open the door when we passed, so I know it's not a place I'll be welcome in anytime soon. In fact, I'd wager money that the door is locked and only Luca is privy to the key.

Benito then takes us outside. The hot summer sun is beating down on us as we walk across the large patio with outdoor furniture. And then we stop at…the swimming pool.

Instantly, I can feel sweat beading on my face, but it's not because of the heat. It's because the pool looks so similar to the one I had at my childhood home.

"You're welcome to swim anytime you want," Benito suggests, perhaps noticing my discomfort.

I shake my head vehemently. No, I won't be swimming or getting anywhere near that water.

"What? The pool isn't big enough for you?" comes a strong, demanding voice from my right.

I can't tear my eyes away from the water, but I would know Luca Vitale's voice anywhere. A cold shiver runs down my spine as he approaches.

"Can't swim?" he asks, but I can't even answer him. I'm glued to where I'm standing, unable to move or speak. Suddenly, Luca grabs my arms and turns me towards him. "I could always throw you in and find out."

Terror runs through my very bones as I snap out of my traumatized state and beg him with tears in my eyes, "No, please, no!"

He has a serious look on his face, and I'm so scared that he'll actually go through with his threat that my fight or flee instinct kicks in. Quickly, I tear out of his grip and run back into the house like my life depends on it.

I don't stop running until I'm safe and sound in my new bedroom. Panic seizes my lungs, and I go to the bathroom to splash some cold water on my face to try to calm down.

Every time I'm near a body of water, I'm instantly brought back to that horrible day in my childhood that scarred me for life.

My mother overdosed on sleeping pills and decided to end her life by drowning in the family's swimming pool. I'm the one that found her body floating face down in the water. I knew how to swim back then, so I jumped in and desperately tried to save her. I almost drowned in the process, because I was only nine years old and not strong enough to pull her out.

I remember the burning sensation of the water inside of my lungs and how hard I coughed, but it still felt like I was drowning.

And it still feels like I'm drowning to this day every time I think about it.

It was a traumatic experience that I'll never get over. I haven't been able to go near a body of water without sheer panic setting in.

After several minutes, I'm able to calm myself down. I know I'll have to explain my dramatic reaction to Luca, but a part of me isn't ready to tell him yet. I feel like it's too personal, like he'll know an intimate part about me when I know next to nothing about him. I figure over time we'll get to know each other, but I have a feeling Luca will always be an enigma, keeping his most guarded secrets close to him, never letting them out. And maybe I should do the same.

CHAPTER 10

Luca

I WATCH ON the security monitors as Benito takes Dante and Verona on a tour of the property. For some fucked-up reason, I want Verona to like it here. But I watch her indifferent reaction to each room, and it pisses me off. I don't know what I expected really. The girl grew up mafioso royalty and in opulence. She's used to this. It just doesn't impress her.

The three of them pass by my office, and Benito doesn't so much as try to reach for the doorknob, which is what I expected of him. He knows my boundaries, and this room is off-limits to everyone except myself, him and whoever we are having a meeting with. This office will be my sanctuary, the place I can go to when I need to clear my head or escape the world for a little while. Once I have the keypad installed, no one will be able to bother me here, and I like knowing that fact.

Standing, I leave my sanctuary and follow them silently outside.

"You're welcome to swim anytime you want," Benito offers Verona.

She emphatically shakes her head like the very idea of getting in my pool disgusts her. And the look of what can only be described as revulsion on her face sets me off.

What the fuck is her problem? Is the pool not good enough for her? Is it not clean enough? I hired a pool guy. And if he didn't do his goddamn job, heads will roll.

"What? The pool isn't big enough for you?" I ask, stepping forward. I walk over to the edge and inspect the pool and the attached hot tub situated in the middle of a huge pad of stamped concrete. It looks clean to me, and it's the standard size, if not bigger than other pools, so what is her deal?

I turn to her. "Can't swim?"

Instead of answering me, Verona stands there, not moving or speaking. Angrily, I grab her arms and turn her towards me. "I could always throw you in and find out," I threaten. I'm not truly serious... or maybe I am. I don't know. This girl has me so riled up that I am tempted to throw her in and give her a lesson in respect.

Tears fill her eyes as she stares up at me and begs, "No, please, no!"

And while I normally like it when women beg, this is not turning me on. I can hear the tremor in her voice and see the fear in her eyes. But why?

Before I can even ask, she tears out of my grip and runs inside the house like her ass is on fire.

Standing there, feeling confused, I turn to Dante for answers. Even though it pisses me off, I understand he knows Verona much better than me. "What's her fucking problem?" I demand. I know for a fact that her family had a swimming pool. I remember her bragging about it as a kid. I didn't have one, so it always made me jealous.

"You don't know?" Dante asks with a cocked brow.

I shake my head, internally seething because he obviously knows something I don't. "What is it?"

"Her mother drowned. Verona is the one who found her floating face down in the pool. And she almost drowned trying to save her mother."

My eyebrows crease in confusion. I knew Verona's mother died when she was young, but I never knew the details. "How old was Verona?" I have to ask.

"Nine."

Fuck.

Suddenly, Verona and I have a lot more in common than I had originally thought. At least my family wasn't responsible for the murder of her mother, though. I can't say the same for her family and my mother.

Curling my hands into fists, I give him a nod before I turn and make my way back into the house and towards my office.

Verona is terrified of water. And while normally I would use that little tidbit of information against someone, I know I never will with her. Her fear of water runs much deeper than simply not knowing how to swim. She was traumatized that day. Probably never got in the pool or any body of water after that.

That's what death does to children. It scars you so deep that you never forget, always remember...and you never, never forgive.

CHAPTER 11

Verona

LATER THAT NIGHT, I'm requested downstairs for dinner with Luca. I'm surprised when I enter the dining room and it's just the two of us. I frown, hoping that Dante had something to eat at least.

Luca is still wearing his suit from the wedding, making me feel completely out of place in my comfy top and yoga pants. His tie is missing now, though, and the top few buttons of his black shirt are undone. I'm starting to think that this might be how Luca does *casual*.

I approach the table and see bowls of a cream soup and a variety of grilled sandwiches with different kinds of cheeses and meats.

"It's nothing fancy," Luca says when I sit down to the right of him at the long dining table. "I haven't hired a professional chef yet."

I nod in understanding. I didn't expect anything extravagant, but I don't tell him that. I think the less I talk around him, the better.

We eat our meal in silence. The sandwiches are really tasty. The soup is a little bland, but I eat it anyway since I'm hungry. I've never been one to turn down food. My aunt was never the best cook, and the boarding school meals were atrocious, so I grew accustomed to eating whatever was served to me. It was either eat or starve, and I obviously didn't want to starve.

After I'm finished, I wipe my mouth with the linen napkin and turn to my husband. "Luca, about earlier..." My voice trails off, but he holds up a hand, stopping me.

"I know. Dante told me everything," he says.

I furrow my brows at that. Dante had no right to tell Luca. I was going to tell my husband on my own eventually. Dante didn't need to share my traumatic childhood since it's not his story to tell.

Benito enters the room to announce there's a delivery.

"Yes, upstairs. You know which room," Luca says cryptically.

"Do you always get deliveries this late in the evening?" I ask him.

He turns to me and says with a smirk, "Only when they're absolutely necessary."

I stare at him for several seconds before looking away. A server brings out dessert, which consists of different kinds of cakes and pastries. They all look good, but I only take one piece of mint chocolate cake, my favorite. With everything being so new and my nerves on edge, I hardly have an appetite. I'm not even able to finish the delicious cake.

Luca frowns at my plate before he meets my eyes. "Not up to your standards?" he questions.

What is it with him and thinking everything is beneath me? I'm not some stuck-up prude like he clearly thinks I am. "I'm full," I simply answer.

He nods, but I can tell he doesn't believe me. "I'll try to get a chef and kitchen staff hired this week, so that the housekeepers aren't doing the cooking and cleaning."

Well, if the housekeepers are cooking, they aren't doing a terrible job. I've had better, but I've also had much, much worse. And if this is what I have to eat every night, then I'm fine with it.

We sit in silence as I sip my water and Luca nurses a small glass of dark liquor. It isn't until Benito enters the room to let Luca know the delivery was taken care of that Luca tells me I'm free to return to my room for the evening.

I stare at him, blinking. I figured on our wedding night, of all nights, that he would want to...

"What?" he snaps as he glares at me, like I'm wasting his time.

"Nothing. I..."

"You what?" he asks, standing and towering over me.

I shrink in his presence. I don't know what I was thinking. Do I even want to sleep with a man like Luca? The answer is a clear and astounding no. I need to get my ass to my room before he changes his mind and forces himself on me. "Goodnight," I tell him before leaving the room.

I decide to wash this stressful day away with a hot bath. I soak for what feels like hours before I'm finally calm enough to get out. I towel dry my hair and then wrap a white robe around me as I walk into the bedroom.

I go to the closet to change for bed and stop dead in my tracks. The once almost empty closet is now filled with clothes. New, unfamiliar clothes.

In awe, my fingers breeze over the soft, expensive fabrics of the racks of new shirts and dresses. I check the tags, and sure enough, they're all in my size. It makes me wonder if Luca guessed or if he snooped in my closet when I wasn't in my room and checked the tags of my old clothes.

Speaking of my old clothes...I go back to the rack I had them on. My heart sinks as I realize my stuff is gone. All of my clothes are missing...including my mother's dress.

"No, no, no, no," I chant as I search rack after rack, searching for the beloved dress.

After I've searched the entire closet and torn my whole room apart and come up empty, I find my feet moving before my brain can even catch up. Logical reasoning is completely thrown out the window at this point, as I leave my room and go the short distance down the hall for the door that Benito told me earlier was the door to Luca's room.

My tiny fists bang against the wood, rattling the frame. It takes him several seconds to answer; but when he does, I instantly regret my decision to confront him.

No longer in his suit, Luca is shirtless with a pair of dark gray sweatpants hanging off of his hips, his hair dripping wet from a recent shower.

"May I help you?" he asks, agitated.

"M-my stuff!" I blurt out, stammering because I'm so upset. "What did you do with my clothes?"

"Let me guess," he says while crossing his arms across his chest, his muscular biceps on display, "You don't like your new clothes."

"I don't care about the new clothes!" I yell. "I care about my old ones!"

He rolls his eyes. "For a princess such as you, I would think you'd be happy to be rid of those ugly rags."

"They weren't rags!" Tears burn in the back of my eyes, but I refuse to back down or show any weakness. "I want them back. Now!" I demand.

"Now?" He uncrosses his arms and takes a step forward, towering over me. "Those clothes belonged in the garbage, and that's exactly where they are."

I swallow hard against the lump in my throat. If I lose my mother's dress, the only thing I have left of her, I just don't know what I'll do.

He steps even closer to me and leans down to whisper in my ear, "If you come to my room in the middle of the night again, it better be because you either want to sit on my face or get on your knees."

A hot blush creeps up my neck and cheeks as I lower my gaze to the floor, all the anger and fight in me quickly depleting. I've never had a man talk to me like that before. I was always off-limits to anyone who dared look in my direction. But I have a feeling Luca isn't used to being told no.

"Trash doesn't go until Tuesday. Maybe you can still save your rags," he remarks, fueling my anger and making it instantly spark back up again.

Furious, I turn away from him and go down the hall and steps. I run to the kitchen, searching for any garbage bins where my clothes might be.

Benito is sitting at the kitchen island, eating a sandwich with a glass of milk. "Something I can help you with?" he offers.

"My clothes. What did you do with them?"

He stands, leaving his half-eaten sandwich sitting on the counter as he leads me outside to a row of garbage cans at the back of the house. "Luca told me to throw them away."

"I know," I tell him with a sigh before I open one of the garbage can lids. I find a black plastic bag and rip it open. The smell of rotting food hits my nose, and I turn away in disgust. "Do you know which one you put them in?"

Benito goes to the next one and opens it. "Maybe this one." He pulls out some bags, and underneath all the trash are my old clothes.

"Oh, thank god," I exclaim before I dig into the pile and pull out my mother's dress. I bring the fabric to my chest and press it against me. It reeks of garbage, but I don't even care. I'll wash it tomorrow and bring it back to life, just like always.

I catch Benito's confused expression. "It was my mother's," I explain to Benito. "It's the only thing I have left of her," I whisper.

"Ah," he mutters in understanding.

Hurrying into the house, I hold on to the dress for dear life. I'm still fuming by the time I make it back to my room. Luca thought he could just take my things and throw them away as if they meant nothing. I wish I knew what he cared about so that I could throw that away. But a part of me thinks he doesn't care about anything at all.

CHAPTER 12

Luca

WHEN I WAKE up the next morning, I watch the security camera footage of Verona rooting around in the trash like a fucking raccoon. My lip curls in disgust as she rips open trash bag after trash bag until she finds her old clothes.

Hitting a button, the camera zooms in on her face, and I can see the absolute relief flooding her features when she finds what she's looking for. An old dress? It just looks like a regular garment; nothing special about it. But obviously it holds some kind of significance to her. Maybe it's vintage Gucci or something.

Benito knocks before entering a code into the newly installed keypad to my office. I pause the footage and look up at him when he enters.

"Enjoy your time dumpster diving last night?" I ask him with a smirk.

"It was her mother's dress," he tells me.

My brows furrow as I glance back at the laptop and see Verona's elated face frozen on the screen. "I see," I mutter. I'm not one for sentimental things, but I do have an old music box of my mother's that I keep locked away. The song it plays reminds me of her. Perhaps this dress is just like the music box. Something to keep her mother's memory alive whenever she needs it the most.

I give Benito a dismissive wave. I don't want to talk about the past or Verona or the fucking dress she dug through the trash for. "Any news about the deal?" I ask. That's really what I'm interested in.

"Constantine isn't budging," he answers.

That angers me. Constantine Carbone has been a thorn in my side long enough. His mob is a rival in notoriety and size to my own family, and he's been rising through the ranks just as fast as me. We've always competed against one another, even if we have completely different interests at heart.

For me, I value the drug market, arms dealing, laundering money.

For Constantine, he deals mostly in the flesh trade. Human trafficking. And more specifically, the trafficking of minors. His acquisitions are earning him a lot of money, making him more powerful by the minute and also more dangerous.

I've been trying to put a stop to his new acquired taste in unlawful activities, but he won't even accept my offers to give him territories in exchange for him stopping the trafficking of children.

I don't have a soul...or a heart. In fact, I like to think the darkness swirling inside of me spills out from time to time whenever needed. But there's something about what he's doing that gets under my skin, and I can't let it keep happening.

"Offer him the west territory as well," I tell Benito.

Benito stares at me for a while. "That's our biggest territory. We will lose a lot of business and money if we do that."

I narrow my eyes at my most trusted and only friend in the world. "I don't give a fuck."

"Your father would never allow it."

"Last I heard my old man is stepping down and putting me in charge. He won't have a say soon enough."

"Very well," Benito says before leaving my office.

I push away from the desk, fuming. First, my wife defies me at every turn, and now Benito is beginning to question my motives as well. What the fuck is going on in my world?

My legs carry me across the room to the safe that is housed behind a very expensive painting on the wall. I punch in the long code and open the door. Inside is everything I value in this world. Money and my mother's music box.

I reach out and grab the small box, turning the delicate switch on the back before setting it down. The familiar, soothing music begins to fill the room, and I can instantly feel myself calming.

Yes, I can understand why Verona wanted that dress so badly. And a very small part of what can only be described as a guilty conscience gnaws at me that I ordered her belongings to be thrown away without asking her permission first.

After the song is finished, I lock up the safe once more with any new, foreign feelings I have developed towards my wife. It's dangerous to care about someone in my world, and I can't afford to care about anyone or anything, let alone a Moretti.

CHAPTER 13

Verona

THE NEXT MORNING, I wake up early, too early. In fact, I can't remember the last time I was up before the sun. I take my time, stretching and relaxing in bed for a little while before going to the bathroom to start getting ready for the day.

After my shower, I go to the closet and sort through all the new clothes. It's not that I'm not happy to have such nice, expensive things. It's just that the things I owned were perfectly fine in my opinion, even if they weren't good enough in his eyes. And now that he went through all this trouble of buying me new things, I feel like I owe him something. And I hate feeling that way.

After several minutes, I finally decide on a cute, blue summer dress. It fits me perfectly, and the material is so soft that it almost feels like silk against my skin.

I blow dry and straighten my hair and put on a little makeup. I'm just trying to kill time really. But when my stomach growls loudly, I decide it's time to go downstairs. I don't think the staff will have breakfast ready, but no matter. I can make something for myself. I'm completely capable of handling things on my own...right?

Trepidation follows me the whole way downstairs and into the kitchen. I wouldn't consider myself spoiled, by any means. I would be more likely to say that I wasn't given the opportunities that most people have in life. I wasn't able to try new things or learn how to do even the most menial tasks.

My great aunt wouldn't even let me step foot inside her kitchen. I swear she loved her appliances a whole hell of a lot more than me. No, scratch that. She didn't love me at all. I guess I could say that maybe she loved her appliances more than her cats. Her cats were her babies, and they were the only ones who ever received any kind of affection from the cold-hearted woman.

The kitchen is quiet and empty when I enter. I flick on some lights and stare at the pile of dishes in the sink from last night's dinner. I guess the housekeepers figured they'd tackle the dishes in the morning.

A smile graces my lips as I decide to give them a hand. I'm sure they'd be happy to have a little bit of workload off their plates for the day. Besides, they have to clean every room of this huge mansion, and I'm sure that's time-consuming and tedious enough.

I walk over to the dishwasher and stare at all the buttons. I've never used one of these before, but the description of what each button does is plain as day, so I don't think it will be too hard to figure out. Getting to work, I rinse off the dishes in the sink and carefully load them into the racks.

When I'm finished, I stare down at the door where it indicates that's where the soap should go.

Looking around, I find a bottle of dish liquid sitting near the sink. Grabbing the bottle, I squirt the liquid into the large detergent dispenser and close the little lid. Then, I add a generous amount to the pre-wash side as well.

Satisfied, I close the front of the dishwasher and press a button to start it. "All done," I say to the empty room, smiling. It's not rocket science, and I figured it out on my own.

I'm feeling pretty proud of myself by the time I go to the fridge and grab a yogurt and a cheese snack for a quick breakfast outside on the patio.

I watch the sunrise as I eat, loving the way the sun slowly heats my skin in the cold air. After I'm done, I scoop up my trash and take it inside.

But as soon as I step foot into the kitchen, I know I messed up. Big time.

CHAPTER 14

Luca

AFTER I SHOWER and get dressed for the day, I immediately go downstairs. I'm hungry. No, I'm fucking starving. I'm hoping the staff has breakfast ready; but when I reach the dining room and hear loud shouting, I'm thinking breakfast is the last thing on everyone's minds this morning.

The shouting grows louder with each step. And when I push through the kitchen door, I step knee deep into...bubbles?

There are fucking bubbles everywhere. The whole room is filled with them!

My eyes search the room, but everyone is busy yelling back and forth in Italian. Verona stands across the room with tears streaming down her face while my staff calls her every name in the book.

Dante snaps back in Italian to them while Verona simply stares at him in awe, so I'm assuming she doesn't even know the language. Surprising, given who her father is. But then again, maybe not.

Maybe he didn't want his daughter privy to his private meetings. He probably wanted to keep her in the dark.

Dante pulls Verona into his arms, rubbing his palms up and down her back, soothing her. My blood fucking boils in my veins at witnessing the intimate contact.

"Verona!" I roar. The entire room is suddenly quiet, and Verona pulls back from Dante's embrace like she was just burned.

Her big, honey-colored eyes widen as she stares at me. I can see the fear in her gaze; and for some fucked-up reason, it turns me on.

"Come with me. Now!" I demand, turning on my heel, leaving the room full of bubbles behind me.

I walk straight to my office, not stopping to see if she's following me. I know she'll follow like the good, little, obedient wife that she is.

I stop at my office door, giving her a chance to catch up. Blocking the keypad with my body, I punch in the code and then open the door, stepping inside and holding the door open for her to enter. I feel like the lion that has just caught the lamb. She is my prey. But the sick fuck in me wants to play with her a little first before I destroy her.

I walk behind my desk and stand there as I watch her timidly move to the front of it. I sit there for several long seconds, watching her squirm. And then very calmly, I ask her, "Why is my kitchen full of bubbles?"

Her long, dark lashes are still wet with tears as she stares at me with those honey-colored eyes. "I-I-I put the wrong soap in the dishwasher," she says, looking to the ground with embarrassment.

"And why were you running the dishwasher?"

"I woke up early, before everyone else," she explains. "There were so many dirty dishes. I...I just wanted to help," she says with a shrug.

"Never used one before?" I ask her, already knowing the answer.

When she shakes her head, I roll my eyes. Pretty, little princess never had to lift a finger at home, I'm sure. So why would she attempt it here and try to destroy my house? Is she deliberately trying to fuck things up here? Sabotage me?

I round the desk and stand behind her. Grabbing her by the neck, I force her to bend over until her face is pressed against my desk. Her breathing picks up as she places her palms on the expensive oak next to her head.

When I release my hold, she stays in that position with her face down and ass in the air for me, on display. She's so short that she has to stand on her tiptoes to stay bent over the tall, oak desk, and I love how she fidgets, trying so hard to be a good girl for me. And fuck, her obedience makes me hard. I have to step away from her, so she can't feel my arousal.

"Do you have any idea what my staff was yelling at you in there?" I ask her, curiosity getting the better of me.

"No," she says, releasing a shaky breath.

"I'm surprised your father didn't demand you learn Italian. Maybe he wanted to hide things from you."

She doesn't respond to that.

I pace behind her. She's wearing a short, blue dress, nothing special, but the material has ridden up, giving me a tempting peek of her ass. I can see the bottom of her perfect globes and the material of her lacy, light blue thong between them. I smirk, knowing she doesn't have much choice in underwear since I only ordered thongs. I can't help but wonder if she ever wore thongs before now.

"What do you think your punishment should be for fucking up my kitchen?" I ask her.

"My...my punishment?"

I can hear the unease in her voice, and it makes my cock twitch in my pants. I'm sick for getting off on her fear, but I can't help it. I've wanted her to suffer for a long time now. Her and her entire fucking family.

My hands itch at the need to take my belt out of the loops and beat her until she can no longer walk. But I know that if I start hurting her, I might not be able to stop. I don't trust that I won't take it too far.

I curl my hands into fists at my sides. I'd rather take my frustrations and hatred out on her father. But since he isn't here...I guess she'll have to take the brunt of my anger.

Walking over to her, I brush my hand over her backside. She jumps at the touch and then slowly relaxes. I like how much she fears me. How much she doesn't trust me.

"Count, Verona," I tell her while flicking up the back of her dress to expose her completely to me.

"What?" she asks right before I bring my hand down on her delicious ass.

She cries out in surprise, but doesn't give me what I want. "That was one," I say as I lean down to whisper into her ear.

"One," she says in agreement.

I slap her other cheek, and she cries out, "Two!"

My hands have a mind of their own as they caress her flesh between spanks. Her ass is turning a delicious shade of dark pink, and I still want more. I spank her over and over again, relishing the pained cries coming from her mouth.

The light blue thong grows darker between her legs with every spank. This is turning her on. Who knew Verona would be a little slut for pain? And, fuck, I can't help but wonder how much wetter she can get just from me spanking her.

"Please!" she cries out suddenly.

I lean down and whisper into her ear, "Does that mean you want me to stop or that you want me to continue?"

She closes her eyes, effectively blocking me out as a shiver runs through her.

Standing and moving away from her, I say, "Go to your room." I want her to feel like an ill-behaved child. "Somebody else will have to clean up your fucking mess."

With tears in her eyes, she slowly stands, fixes her dress and runs out of my office. My cock presses painfully against my zipper, and I grind my palm down against it. I need a fucking release, but now isn't the time. I have shit to deal with thanks to my new wife trying to be *helpful.*

Taking a few minutes to compose myself, I finally tame the beast in my pants so that I can take care of the situation in the kitchen.

When I walk in the door, the staff is still arguing loudly. They haven't even begun cleaning, because they're too busy fighting over who should be the one to do it.

Benito and Dante look at me and instantly shut up. I look at the five housekeepers and tell them, "*Sei licenziato!* Get the fuck out of my house."

They all look at me and then at each other, thinking they misheard me.

"You're fired!" I tell them this time in English. "No one disrespects my wife in my own home."

I watch and wait as they all leave the room. Benito and Dante stare at me, waiting for what happens next. "Benito, hire some new staff. I want them to start today. And make sure they sign the NDAs."

"Yes, of course," Benito says, walking out of the room to get started on the task.

And then, with a grin on my face, I tell Dante, "Clean up this mess," before I leave the room.

If Dante thinks he holds some kind of power over me because he knows Verona better than me, then I'm going to have to put him in his place every fucking time he tries to overstep his boundaries. Most men would get their hands cut off for touching another man's wife. He's lucky I'm letting him keep his hands long enough to clean up the mess Verona made. Next time, he might not be so fucking lucky.

CHAPTER 15

Verona

I RUN TO my room and shut the door, locking it behind me. I'm out of breath, but it's not from running. No, it's because I'm utterly and ridiculously turned on. I've never been so turned on by a man in my entire life.

Luca spanked me. He *spanked* me.

And I liked it.

I'm so confused...and wet. My thong is soaked completely through. I can't help but wonder if Luca saw how wet I got for him.

I walk over to the mirror and glance over my shoulder, lifting the skirt of my dress. My entire backside is red and aching. I can still feel the way his large hands caressed my sore flesh between each spanking.

I bite my lip to keep from groaning out loud. Turning in front of the mirror, my fingers skate their way down my stomach and under my dress and material of my thong. My fingertips slide into my arousal, and I begin to play with my clit.

I close my eyes and imagine my husband with his hand between my legs, fingering me. I've never had so much as a boyfriend, so I have no idea what it feels like to be touched by a man. Especially not one as possessive and demanding as Luca Vitale.

Just the thought of his hands on me has me racing to the edge of pleasure. My fingertip caresses the little bundle of nerves until I'm crying out softly and coming so hard I almost see stars.

When I open my eyes, I stare at my reflection. My cheeks and neck are flushed, and I look...different. I feel different. I've never pleasured myself thinking about a specific man before. I want Luca, but I don't think he wants me. We haven't even consummated our marriage yet, but I worry if our first time would be out of hate or out of love, because I have the feeling my husband doesn't like me very much.

It's like my very presence annoys him. I don't know if that will change over time or maybe after we get to know each other better. But considering the fact that Luca barely talks to me, I don't know if we'll ever really get to know each other. I don't even know much about my husband other than the fact that he's ruthless and cruel at times. And he's always controlling and demanding. That's a given.

Shaking myself out of my inner thoughts, I go to the closet and grab a new thong to put on. Then, I leave my room and make my way downstairs. I know Luca told me to go to my room, but he can't expect me to stay in there like I'm grounded. Besides, I'm responsible for the mess in the kitchen, and I should be the one to clean it up.

When I enter the room, I see Dante with a mop and bucket, vigorously scrubbing the floor. No one else is around, and my brow furrows as I realize Luca tasked Dante to do it by himself.

"Where is everyone?" I ask.

Dante turns, and his scowl softens a bit when he looks at me. "Luca fired them."

"Fired them? Why?"

Dante shrugs his shoulders and goes back to mopping the floor. The bubbles have since dissipated, leaving only a soapy film over the tile.

"Let me help," I tell him.

"No, it's fine," he says quickly with a shake of his head.

"I want to help," I say, walking over to him.

"I said no, V!" he snaps suddenly.

I take a step back. Dante has never so much as raised his voice at me before, so I'm taken aback by his attitude.

"I'm sorry," he immediately apologizes. "It's just been a very stressful week, and I'm taking my anger out on the wrong person."

Nodding slowly in understanding, I tell him, "I'll just keep you company while you do this then."

He smiles at that. "Okay." After a few moments of silence, he asks, "What did Vitale do to you when he ordered you out of the room?" He stops mopping and looks at me, concern mixed with anger written all over his face. "Did he touch you? Did he hurt you?"

"No," I quickly lie. I have no idea why I'm lying for Luca, but I feel like if I tell Dante the truth, he would try to hurt Luca, and that could only end in disaster. "He just...he told me to go to my room."

A smile forms on Dante's handsome face. "And yet here you are." He shakes his head. "Always so rebellious. Even when we were kids."

"I'm not rebellious!" I protest.

"Anytime you were asked to do anything, you always wanted to do the opposite."

I frown as I think about my childhood. "Maybe that's why my father sent me away," I offer.

Dante shakes his head. "No, you know why you were sent away."

He's right; however, I don't know if I ever understood the full reason. I was only told it wasn't safe for me at home. It was not long after my mother died. I was shipped off to boarding school in another state with a suitcase full of my things.

"You were better off," Dante tells me. "The things I saw and did as a kid..." His voice trails off as he stares off into the distance like a barrage of bad memories are hitting him.

"I wish we could have just run away together," I whisper, coming closer to him. I wrap my arms around him and inhale his familiar scent of soap. "We spent so many years apart." After I finished with boarding school, I went to live with my aunt. Dante and I kept more in touch then, and he even came to visit me every weekend. When I came home for my grandfather's funeral, my father appointed Dante as my own personal bodyguard. I trust him with my life.

The mop falls from Dante's hands as he wraps his arms around me. I feel him smelling my hair, and it makes me laugh.

"Do I stink?" I joke.

"No. You smell really good."

The hug starts feeling too intimate...and awkward, so I pull away from his embrace. Dante and I have never had more than a friendship, even though I've suspected for years that he wanted more. My father would have never allowed it, though. And now that I'm married...well, that's all off the table now. I could never be with Dante, not as long as I'm married to Luca Vitale.

I walk to the fridge and open it up, inspecting the contents. "How about I make us lunch?" I suggest.

He stares at me for a few seconds, and I can see the longing in his eyes that shouldn't be there. "Sure," he finally says before returning to mopping.

CHAPTER 16

Luca

BENITO COMES TO me later on that day with video footage on his phone of Verona and Dante in the kitchen together. When I see her go to him and wrap her arms around him, I'm so angry I can't even speak.

"Do you think something is going on between the two of them?" Benito asks.

I watch closely as Verona pulls away from Dante and tries to play the whole thing off, looking nervous. "Not on her end. But him..." I study the forlorn look on his face when she walks away from him. "He's in love with her. I knew it from day one. Hell, I knew it when we were all kids."

Dante was probably never allowed to act upon his feelings at the Moretti household. Her father probably would have had his head on a stake.

But here...no, here he must feel safer. But if he thinks I'm going to allow him to try to steal my wife away from me in my own goddam house, he's got another thing coming.

"Keep an eye on them," I instruct Benito.

He nods in agreement. "I don't trust Dante."

"Me either." I stare at the tiny screen, studying my wife floating around the kitchen, making the two of them lunch like *they're* the ones who got married. "Before we went to war, the Morettis and Vitales were in business dealings together. Partners you could even say, although probably more out of convenience than by choice. Dante's parents were traitors to the two families, and so they were killed for the insolence. For some fucked-up reason, the Morettis took in Dante, raised him as one of their own."

"Do you think he harbors some ill will towards the families?" Benito asks.

"Wouldn't you?"

Benito considers it for a second before nodding. "I wouldn't be able to rest until they all suffered."

"Which is why we can never trust him. Even if he was a child when it all happened, I don't believe his thirst for revenge ever totally went away." Maybe he's planning on trying to take Verona away from me as part of his vengeance. Over my dead fucking body. "He can never be trusted."

"Understood."

Benito is halfway to the door when I call out to him, "Thank you for the information."

"Of course," he says before leaving my office.

Benito is keeping a close eye on my wife. That's a good thing, because right now I can hardly stand the sight of her. She is the daughter of my enemy; therefore, she is my enemy too. I will never be able to love her. Maybe one day I'll be able to tolerate her presence, but it's doubtful. All I feel towards my wife is hatred. There is not a shred of doubt in my mind that her family was responsible for the murder of my mother. And so, for that, I will never be able to forgive their crimes.

Opening my laptop, I bring up the security camera footage from around the house and outside. I scan through the screens until I find Verona. She's in the library, reading. Her long legs are crossed over the arm of the chair as she relaxes with a book in her hands.

My eyes skim over her legs, and I can't help but think about this morning when she was in my office, bent over while I spanked her like the naughty, little girl she is.

I close my eyes, and I can still remember vividly how wet she grew between her legs when I spanked her. Fuck, that was so hot, and my dick jumps at the memory.

Growling, my eyes snap open, and I try to shake the dirty thoughts out of my head. I don't need to be fantasizing about Verona. No, what I really need is a fucking release.

Scooping my phone from my desk, I enter my passcode and then find the number I'm looking for. It connects after two rings.

"Vitale, what's up?" Marco asks on the other end.

"VIP, tomorrow night," I request. Marco's strip club is as classy as an establishment of that type can get. I've frequented it many nights with my team, and we're always taken care of by Marco and his girls.

"Yes, yes, of course. I'll make the appropriate accommodations for you and your guests."

"Thank you, Marco," I say before ending the call.

You know, they say the best way to get over someone is to get under someone else. And that's exactly what I'm going to do. I'm going to get Verona out of my system one way or another, even if it means cheating on my new bride.

CHAPTER 17

Verona

THE NEXT MORNING, I wake up early again...but not to run the dishwasher this time. After the whole *bubbles incident*, as I'm calling it, I'm desperate to do better. If I'm going to be stuck in this marriage, I'm going to at least try to get along with my husband. And I want him to at least *like* me. Is that so hard to ask for?

And so, when I see Benito, Luca's second in command, walking down the hall the next day, I corner him. Benito towers over me, and so I have to look up so far it almost hurts my neck. "Hi, could I, uh, talk to you for a second?" I ask, feeling intimidated by his size alone... not to mention the tattoos covering him almost head to toe or the way his presence alone is menacing.

"Sure," he says in a gruff voice. He motions for us to enter a separate room, and he closes the door behind us. "What's wrong?" he asks, already assuming the worst.

"What does Luca like to eat?" I blurt out. My question has

Benito raising a dark eyebrow in confusion. "I mean, what's his favorite food? I would like to cook for him," I explain quickly.

"Ah," he says, nodding in understanding. "Well, don't tell him I told you this, but his favorite is his mother's recipe for spaghetti. I could call Greta, one of the old cooks that used to work for his father, and get the recipe. I'm sure she would remember how to make it. She could help you over the phone, talk you through it."

"Really? That would be wonderful," I tell him, smiling widely and so happy by his response that I could hug him. But I won't.

"Of course."

"Thanks, Benny!" I exclaim, blurting out the nickname without thinking.

He pauses for a moment and then a rare smile spreads across his face. "Benny? I like that," he says with a dark chuckle.

I can't help but smile as we leave the room and he leads the way into the kitchen, ordering the cooks to help me with cooking dinner tonight.

"We're going out later," Benito warns. Then, he quickly adds, "But I promise I'll try to get Luca back in time for dinner."

"That would be great. Thanks," I tell him.

Benito calls Greta on the house phone, and I listen as the older woman rambles on in Italian to the new cooks. They write down every word and assure us that they have all the ingredients already to make it.

I'm so excited to cook for Luca that I'm practically bursting. I know the way to a man's heart is through his stomach, or at least that's what my mama always said. And lord knows I need some kind of miracle to weasel my way into my husband's cold, dark heart.

CHAPTER 18

Luca

THE MUSIC AT the strip club filters through the speakers. Several of us, including Benito, a few other associates and Marco, are upstairs in the VIP section, overlooking the patrons down below. Most of the customers are drinking and throwing money at the women dancing on poles on the middle stages.

The club is big and popular. Marco makes a killing here, and I'm happy for that since I launder some of my money through his lucrative business.

"So, Luca, tell me, how is married life?" Marco asks me with a grin.

He's sitting across from me in the lounge in a matching leather chair. Marco is my age. We grew up together and have remained friends and business associates over the years. He was born into the mafioso, same way as I, and he thrives on the lifestyle and his family's money.

Marco runs every strip club in the city and surrounding areas. He loves the nightlife. I can only tolerate it in small doses, having gotten my fill back when I was just turning eighteen and we were hitting the clubs every single night even though we weren't exactly of proper age.

"Word of advice," I tell Marco as I light up a cigar, puffing on it and blowing the smoke up in the air. "Don't ever get married."

He chuckles heartily at my words, and everyone else in the room joins in on the laugh. We're surrounded by friends and business associates. Benito, my second-in-command, is by my side. I offered him a drink and a cigar, but he refused both. Benito always chooses to stay level-headed, and I suppose that's just one of the reasons why I trust him with my life.

Marco puts his forearms on his knees, leaning in towards me. "At least she's beautiful, no?"

I nod at his statement, hiding my true feelings towards his statement. I don't want people acknowledging my wife's beauty. I don't want people looking at her. Period. Just because I don't want her doesn't mean I want anyone else having her. And the thought of someone else touching her makes my blood pressure rise.

"Beautiful pussy in my bed every night? I wouldn't be complaining," Marco says before blowing out a puff of smoke from his cigar.

I stub mine out in the ashtray on the center glass table between us. "No complaints," I say with a grin even though I haven't fucked my wife. But I'm not willing to divulge my sexless marriage with my friends and colleagues. Let them think what they want to think.

Benito checks his watch for what must be the fifteenth time tonight. "Somewhere you need to be, Benito?" I ask him snidely.

"We missed dinner," he mutters.

I narrow my eyes at him. Since when the fuck does he care about missing dinner?

"Are you hungry? Let's order something from the restaurant," Marco offers.

Benito puts up his hand. "No need."

Marco shrugs and then turns his attention back to me. "I guess you won't be partaking in the girls tonight, Luca, since you're tied down now with a ball and chain."

I chuckle as I take a swig of whiskey. "I'd never turn down pussy," I tell him flat out.

"Well, if that's the case..." He motions to the girls dancing in the other room, and they instantly flock to him. He whispers in a tall blonde's ear, and she instantly struts over to me and perches on the arm of my chair.

"I know you like blondes the best," Marco says.

Before I met Verona, my preference was always blonde. But now...I think I might be developing a thing for brunettes. Shaking that crazy thought aside, I stare up at the sexy blonde as she trails her fingertips up and down my arm. The sleeves of my black button-up shirt are rolled up my forearms, and I can see her admiring my tattoos that run the length of my arms and down to my hands.

"How about you and me go have some fun in the VIP room, sugar?" the beautiful blonde asks.

Normally, I would take her up on her offer. But I instantly shake my head. "Not tonight, doll."

Someone makes the sound of a whip, and Marco asks, "Pussy whipped already, Luca?"

My eyes snap to meet his. He's challenging me. And I never back down from a challenge. "Of course not," I scoff. Standing, I tell the blonde, "Lead the way."

I hear a bunch of laughter and cackling behind me as the tall blonde leads me down the hallway to a private room.

She closes the door behind us, and I make my way over a leather couch. I finish off my whiskey and put the glass down on a nearby table as I watch her.

The music from the club filters through the speakers in the ceiling, and the blonde begins to move, dancing to the beat. She's sexy as fuck, but for some unexplainable reason, I'm bored with her already.

She comes closer to me, straddling my lap and grabbing my tie.

She grinds her lap against mine, but my dick doesn't even jump at the contact.

What the fuck is wrong with me?

My initial plan was to come here and get some kind of release from the painful blue balls I've had ever since Verona moved in. And now my dick suddenly decides to have a mind of its own?

I close my eyes as she kisses up and down my neck, and all I can think about is Verona. Her tight little body grinding against me, begging me to fuck her. How wet she got for me when I spanked her ass.

"Mmm, hello there," the blonde says as she grinds down on my hard cock.

My eyes snap open as I stare into the unfamiliar blue eyes. She climbs off my lap and begins stripping off her clothes. She wants to fuck, but I'm not in the mood, my dick quickly deflating.

She flashes me her pussy as she bends over the arm of the couch, baring herself to me. "I've been waiting for a night with the great Luca Vitale," she purrs. "The other girls said you fuck like a stallion. Left them sore for days from your big cock." She looks at me over her shoulder and bats her pretty blues. "They're gonna be so jealous when I tell them I fucked you first after your wedding."

Her words turn me right the fuck off. She wants bragging rights for getting me to cheat on my wife?

Standing, I tell her, "Get dressed. I'm not fucking you tonight."

My words seem to stun her, and it takes a few moments for her to understand them. But eventually, she crawls off the couch. I think she's reaching for her clothes, but instead she falls to her knees in front of me.

Before I can stop her, her hands are unbuckling my belt, unzipping my fly and reaching into my pants for my cock.

She pulls my flaccid cock out of my pants and stares at it while licking her lips. "Don't worry. I can get you hard, baby," she whispers before moving her mouth towards my cock.

Before her mouth can touch my cock, I quickly step back out of her range. She pouts and stares up at me with big, blue eyes.

I'm sure I could get her to beg for my cock. Hell, she would probably let me fuck every hole in her body without a condom. But for some fucked-up reason, I don't want her.

I tuck my dick back into my pants, zipper up and buckle my belt before pulling my wallet out of my pants pocket and throwing a few hundred-dollar bills down on the table. "For your trouble," I tell her before disappearing out of the room.

Marco and the boys are all talking and laughing when I join them.

Marco makes a show to check his big, expensive watch on his wrist. "Wow, was that a record, Luca?" he asks with a chuckle.

"What can I say? She was good," I lie. Benito gives me an indecipherable look before I tell him, "Time to go." I grab my suit jacket from the back of my chair and drape it over my arm. Then, to Marco, I say with a smirk, "Apparently, we're late for dinner."

Marco bursts into laughter. "Remind me never to get married, boys," he announces to the room.

Benito and I leave the club, and he drives me home. And I don't know if it's the alcohol or what the fuck is wrong with me, but I'm relieved to be going home...to my wife.

CHAPTER 19

Verona

I LOOK AT the clock and am not surprised that only a few minutes have passed since the last time I checked. I've been waiting for hours for Luca to get home. I made his favorite meal today, spaghetti, using his mother's recipe. I feel like I slaved away in that kitchen, cutting up tomatoes and making my own sauce. I mean, I even made the noodles by scratch! I spent all that time and effort… and Luca wasn't even home in time for dinner.

Before they left, Benny promised me he would try to get Luca home early, but that clearly didn't happen. Not that I can blame him for Luca's actions.

"The spaghetti was amazing, Verona," Dante says from the doorway. He must have just eaten some in the kitchen.

"Thank you, Dante."

"I'm sorry that asshole didn't show up to eat any," he says with a frown.

"It's okay. I should have made sure he didn't have plans first I guess," I say with a small shrug.

Dante opens his mouth to say something else, but the front door opens, and Luca and Benito walk in. Dante walks back into the kitchen, leaving me alone in the large dining room.

"What smells so good?" Luca asks when he enters the room.

I stand up slowly, and all the anger I had from earlier suddenly collects and pours out into my attitude. "I made you dinner."

"I'm surprised you didn't burn the house down," he says with a dark chuckle.

I narrow my eyes and stare at him. "I worked all day on making your favorite meal," I tell him.

His dark eyebrows rise in surprise. "You did?"

"Yes. Where were you?" I ask.

"What are you playing at?" he asks with a grin. "Are you trying to be the nagging wife in this play?"

"This isn't a play, Luca. This is real life!"

"Oh, and a real marriage, is it?" he scoffs.

His words are slurring, and I know that he drank a lot. But that doesn't excuse his behavior towards me.

"We're stuck in this together whether we like it or not," I explain. "The least we can do is try to make it work."

"Try to make it work," he says, laughing as if I told a funny joke. He walks closer to me, and then that's when I see it.

"What…what is that?" I ask him. On the collar of his white dress shirt is a red smudge.

He looks down and then back at me with those piercing, gray eyes. "What is what?"

"On your collar. Is that…is that lipstick?" I exclaim. The guilty look on his face tells me everything I need to know. "You were with someone else tonight?"

He shrugs nonchalantly. "And so what if I was."

"You cheated on me?" The question comes out in a whisper, because I'm so afraid of his answer.

He stares me down, his eyes dangerous, his brows heavy. "You think you can play wife and that I'll just be faithful to you like a real husband?" He takes a few more steps towards me. "We were forced to get married, Verona. Hell, I don't even *like* you!"

Tears fill my eyes as I lower them down to the floor. I can't even look at him right now. I'm so angry and hurt!

"I hate you," I whisper vehemently before brushing past him and running up to my room. I lock the door behind me and collapse onto the bed, crying. I thought I could change things between us. I thought I could make this marriage work.

But I was wrong. So very wrong.

CHAPTER 20

Luca

I HATE YOU.
 I can still hear Verona's words ringing inside of my head the next morning when I wake up hungover and full of regrets. I drank too much at the club. I almost slept with a stripper and cheated on my wife. Even though my marriage is anything but conventional, cheating on Verona would have been a mistake. It would have been *wrong*.

I don't know how to make things more civil between us, so I figure I'll just give her time to get over it. Time heals all wounds, or so they say.

It's after lunch by the time I crawl out of bed and get a shower. When I see Benito downstairs in the kitchen, I tell him, "I'm going to eat. And then we're going to train."

His eyes narrow. "You think you're in any condition to train today?" he asks.

"You think a hangover could stop me from kicking your ass?"

He moves his head from side to side, cracking his neck. "Bring it on, boss."

Fuck. Maybe I shouldn't have provoked the beast, but a part of me doesn't even care if I lose to Benito. Maybe I deserve to have my ass kicked for how I've been acting. It's just that being around Verona drives me crazy. I want to hate her. I truly do. Lord knows I hate her father and the rest of her family. But she makes it so damn hard. And that pisses me off to no end. Why does she have to be so...*nice*?

"She really made me my mother's spaghetti recipe last night?" I ask Benito.

He nods in response. "I promised her I would get you home in time for dinner, but that didn't exactly work out."

"You could have told me."

He shrugs. "Would it have made a difference?"

"No, probably not," I respond. In all honesty, if he would have told me he was trying to do a favor for Verona, I most likely would have stayed out even longer just to spite both of them. I'm fucked up like that. I don't like knowing that the two of them are conspiring behind my back about me. It's bad enough that I've heard her calling him *Benny*.

I open the fridge and grab the container of orange juice and a couple of leftover breakfast sandwiches. I'm going to need my strength if I'm going to be working out with my men today. They have been trained by the very best. Trained to maim, kill, do whatever is necessary until they reach their target and end goal.

"We'll start after I'm done eating," I inform Benito. "Tell the men to get ready. It's training day."

⁓

LESS THAN AN HOUR INTO TRAINING, I'm already bleeding from multiple places and barely able to breathe. I bend over with my hands on my knees, trying desperately to catch my breath.

The men I hired are almost all ex-military. They're used to training for long hours and barely breaking a sweat. It takes a lot out of me to keep up with them, but it's worth it. Training with them makes me a better fighter. And when you live in my world, you always have to be ready to fight.

"Told you that you were too hungover for this shit," Benito comments with a big grin.

"Shut the fuck up and come at me again. I dare you," I egg him on.

We're both shirtless and wrestling on the ground like our lives depend on it when someone calls, "Boss, phone call!"

Standing, I square up with Benito and shake my finger at him. "We'll continue this later, my friend." Picking up my discarded shirt from the ground, I wipe blood from my mouth. Then, I walk over to one of my guards and grab the cell phone from his hand. Putting it to my ear, I ask, "Hello?"

"Luca, how is married life treating you?" my father asks on the other end.

"About as good as can be expected considering I married a Moretti," I respond.

He chuckles at my answer. "Well, I called because I would like you and Verona to come to my house for dinner tomorrow night."

"Sounds good," I tell him. It will give me an excuse to force Verona to talk to me, because I know she'll be giving me the cold shoulder until then.

"See you around seven?"

"See you then." I end the call. Glancing around the property, I search the windows until I find Verona's room. The curtains move ever so slightly, and I can't help but smile. She's been watching us train. I wonder if she's touching her sweet, little cunt, thinking about me?

"More?" Benito calls from across the yard.

"Oh yes. Much more," I say with a grin. If Verona wants to watch, then I'll give her one hell of a show.

CHAPTER 21

Verona

WE'RE ON OUR way to Luca's father's house for dinner. I haven't spoken to Luca since the night when I found out he cheated on me. Or at least I *think* he cheated on me anyway. He never did come out and admit it, but he was definitely with a girl that night. The evidence of their encounter was clearly written in lipstick on the collar of his shirt.

I've been holed up in my room for a couple of days. Thankfully, Dante was bringing me my meals, otherwise I would have probably starved. Not once did Luca come to apologize or check on me. Not that I expected him to. That's simply not Luca.

Yesterday, I spent the day watching my husband train with his men outside of my bedroom window. He was bruised and cut and covered in blood...and it was the hottest thing I've ever seen in my life. Watching him use his fists to fight his way out of situations where one, two or three men were ganging up on him made me hot and bothered to the point where I was practically drooling.

I memorized every detail about his body, and I can't seem to get the images out of my mind. Luca's body looks like it was carved out of stone. His shoulders are broad, tapering to a narrow waist, and I swear he has an eight-pack and not a six pack. And his tattoos...they look like inky works of art stamped on his arms and hands.

Luca is dangerous...and hot. There is no doubt about that. He can turn me on with a single look. But with just a few words, he can also turn me right back off. It's like a light switch when it comes to Luca. It's either off or on; there's no middle ground. We definitely have a love-hate relationship, with an emphasis more on the *hate*.

The car ride to his father's house is full of tension. We both remain completely silent the entire way. I could make an attempt at small talk, but I wouldn't even know where to begin.

By the time we reach our destination, I am so overwhelmed with anxiety that I open the door and rush out of the car before Benito can even get out of the driver's seat. I'm just so desperate for fresh air and to not be in close proximity to my husband a second longer.

Salvatore Vitale is waiting on the front porch of his giant mansion that makes our home seem like an apartment in comparison. As I walk up the steps, I realize how much Luca looks just like his father. They both share the same dark hair and light gray eyes, although Salvatore has a tint of silver in his locks. I'm sure if they were the same age, they could probably pass for twins instead of father and son.

"Welcome, Verona," his father says, stepping forward, leaning down and kissing both of my cheeks. "You look lovely." He towers over me just like Luca.

"Thank you, Mr. Vitale." It took me over an hour to decide on what to wear tonight, but I just went with a little black dress and heels. You can never go wrong with an LBD.

"Please, call me Salvatore," he suggests. Then, his eyes go to his son, and I can feel that growing friction again, except it's not directed at me this time. "Son."

"Father."

A shiver runs through me, but it's not from the chill in the air. I can tell that this father and son relationship is strained, to say the least. I'm not sure why, and I'm sure Luca would never tell me the truth even if I asked.

We walk into the grand foyer, and my eyes take in every amazing detail. This house looks like it belongs in a magazine or on TV. It's so immaculate and extravagant. It's hard to believe that a little boy once lived here. I wonder if Luca was ever able to do anything out of line, like leave his toys strewn about, like all little boys do?

Salvatore leads us into the dining room. It reminds me of a grand ballroom instead of a place to simply eat. The three of us sit at one end of a long dining table that could accommodate forty guests. Salvatore sits at the head of the table, of course, and then Luca sits to his father's right while I sit to his left, straight across from Luca.

Drinks are served promptly, and I opt for wine and water, same as Luca, while Salvatore requests a whiskey on the rocks.

Once the servers have left the room, Salvatore asks Luca, "So, how do you like the new house?"

"It's fine," he says in response.

His father grunts. "Well, for the seventeen million I paid for it, I would hope it's more than just *fine*," he says sarcastically as he nurses the dark liquor in a rocks glass.

I didn't realize Salvatore Vitale bought us the mansion since Luca had never mentioned it. "The house is lovely. Thank you so much," I tell him with a forced smile.

"Finally, someone with proper manners," Salvatore mutters. "And you're welcome for your wedding present. It was the least I could do. I couldn't have you staying in Luca's bachelor pad in Manhattan now, could I? That's no place for a family."

I sneak a peek at Luca, who looks extremely uncomfortable. "Honestly, I would have been happy anywhere," I confess. Luca looks up and meets my eyes, and I can see his eyes narrow in confusion. He thinks I'm playing games with him, but I'm really not. I'm just trying to ease the thick tension in the room somehow.

"Ahh, so you're easy to please. Luca is a lucky man. That's so rare to come by anymore. Women are all about material things nowadays," Salvatore rambles on.

I wonder if he knows from experience and if he's been sleeping his way through New York and New Jersey ever since his wife died? I have a feeling based on his confession that he has. Maybe Luca has too over the years. But I don't want to think about the women that came before me.

Salvatore takes a swig of his liquor, finishing off the glass before putting it down. "My very good friend is hosting a party at his home Friday night. I would like for both of you to attend."

I smile at the invitation. A party sounds like fun and something a real couple would do. "That sounds wonderful," I say.

Luca shoots me a glare before turning his attention to his father. "I suppose we can go. Send me the details."

"Of course."

One of the staff enters the dining room to announce that dinner will be served momentarily. He goes around the table, refilling our glasses with wine before leaving.

"I had the chef prepare filet mignon. I hope you're not a vegetarian, Verona. Perhaps I should have checked with my son beforehand."

"That sounds great, and no, I'm not a vegetarian."

Salvatore seems pleased by my answer. "Easy to please. Eats something other than salads. Luca, I think you hit the jackpot with this one."

Luca stays quiet as he picks up his glass of wine and takes a long swig. When he sets the glass down, he ominously comments with, "Only time will tell."

"You have time," Salvatore remarks.

I pick up my own wine glass and take a drink just as Salvatore adds, "But not too much time. I do want grandbabies soon."

The wine I was beginning to swallow suddenly goes down the wrong pipe, and I begin to choke and cough.

"Are you all right, dear?" his father asks me.

I nod vehemently as I try to collect myself and silence my coughing. The thought of having kids with Luca seems so far off into the distance that I can't even see the light at the end of that particular tunnel.

Thankfully, the staff chooses that moment to enter the room with our meals, and we don't have to further that discussion.

"Filet mignon, balsamic roasted Brussel sprouts with bacon," one of the men says as he sets the plate down in front of me. "Enjoy."

"Thank you," I tell him. If it tastes as good as it smells and looks, then I'm in for a treat.

The three of us dig in, eating in silence other than the occasional comment from Salvatore about how good the meal is.

When we're finished and I can't possibly eat another bite, Salvatore asks me, "How did you like it, Verona?"

"It was delicious."

This pleases him but seems to piss off Luca. I just can't win with my husband it seems.

"She doesn't care for the food at home," Luca says quickly.

I stare at him. That's not at all true, but I don't even have time to correct him before Salvatore says, "Well, that's because you don't have a professional chef hired. You can't expect your new bride to eat peanut butter and jelly sandwiches every day, can you?"

Luca frowns at his father's words.

"Hire on Greta. She doesn't have much to do here since I don't entertain much. And to be honest, I eat out more than I eat here. I'm sure she would be happy to cook for you again, just like when you were younger."

"I'll consider it," Luca answers.

Greta is the one that helped me with Luca's mother's recipe for spaghetti. Just the thought of how that dinner was ruined puts me in a sour mood all over again, but I try to keep my emotions at bay since we're in his father's company. I can dwell on stuff later when I'm alone in my room.

Dessert is brought out next. A slice of tiramisu. I haven't had this dessert since I was a little girl. And even though I was feeling full, I eat every bite of it. It's so good, I just can't bear the thought of any of it going in the trash.

After dessert, we spend some time touring the house. Salvatore gushes about his expensive acquisitions, but what I notice more than anything is how cold and sterile the house feels. There are no family photos anywhere, and there are no signs that a young Luca even lived here.

I don't know the details behind Luca's mother's death. I only know that she died because my father mentioned it to me once when I returned from my great aunt's house for my grandfather's funeral. I don't know exactly how she died or when, but it doesn't really matter. Luca grew up without his mother; something I can definitely relate to.

I can't help but wonder what this house was like when his mother was still alive. Did she bring a warmth into this house? Did she give her son the love that he needed and deserved?

I know what it's like growing up without a mom and having a father who thinks you're a burden. My father never let go of the memory of my mother; however, and that's evident in how many photos and paintings of her that he has scattered around the house in her honor.

Salvatore Vitale is living in a home that seems to have forgotten his past love and former life. But maybe that's how he wants it. Maybe the memory of her is too painful for him. Deep down, though, I don't know if that's the case. He seems too cold of a man to hold on to sentimental things and something as trivial as memories or family photographs.

"I'm very pleased with how this evening turned out," Salvatore tells Luca at the front door when he walks us out. "I was going to wait to tell you this until tomorrow, but I'll tell you now. I'm going to give you a few more territories to run."

Luca seems pleased by this revelation, but he schools his features almost immediately. "Thank you," he murmurs.

Turning to me, Salvatore takes my hand in his and places a kiss on top. "It was a pleasure finally meeting you, Verona."

"Thank you. I feel the same way," I tell him.

"See you both Friday night at the party," he says before retreating back inside.

I don't know what I expected in meeting with Luca's father, but I think it gave me some insight into why Luca is the way he is, and I'm thankful for that.

Luca leads me down the steps and into the driveway to the awaiting car. I get in first, and Luca closes the door before climbing into the other side of the backseat.

The tension is back again ten-fold, and it feels like Luca is a coiled snake, waiting to strike at any moment. I know that if he wants to fight, then we'll fight, and I'll give him all the anger and fury that he wants and deserves.

CHAPTER 22

Luca

"MY FATHER CERTAINLY liked you," I tell Verona on the way back home. The whole night pissed me the fuck off. It's almost as if my father just completely forgot that the Morettis are our enemies. The way they were schmoozing together all night made me fucking sick.

"Is that a bad thing?" Verona asks from the other side of the car.

I sink my teeth into my lower lip to keep from blurting out that yes, it is a very bad thing. I wanted my father to give my wife the same treatment that I have been giving her. Treat her like the nemesis that she so clearly is.

"What is your problem?" she asks angrily.

The question has me swiveling in my seat to look upon the beauty across the seat. Sure, she looks pretty on the outside. But I'm sure her insides are as rotten and black as her father's. Morettis are scum. Every single one of them.

"My problem," I say with a smirk. "My problem is that my own father can't see you for what you really are."

"And what is that exactly?"

"A Moretti," I sneer.

She frowns as she glances out the window. "Well, at least Morettis aren't known for cheating on their wives."

Something inside of me snaps just then. Faster than I thought I could move, I'm up and out of my seat. My hand wraps around her neck, pinning her against the back of the leather seat.

I can feel her pulse beating angrily under my thumb as she gasps for air. "First of all, I didn't cheat on you," I hiss at her. I don't know why I feel the need to tell her the truth, but I don't want her tarnishing the Vitale name, even if it's in her own damn mind.

"You didn't?" she croaks out with wide eyes.

"I wanted to," I confess. "But I couldn't go through with it." I squeeze her throat a little harder, allowing my anger to take over. "And Morettis are known for one thing and one thing only."

She waits for my answer, gasping for air like a little fish out of water. I realize I want her to suffer, to fight for air just a little longer.

"They're fucking cold-blooded murderers," I tell her before releasing her and returning to my seat.

Verona coughs and chokes beside me as she desperately sucks air into her depleted lungs. I didn't hurt her...even though I wanted to. I only scared her. And maybe that's enough. For now.

CHAPTER 23

Verona

IT'S BEEN DAYS since Luca and I had our fight in the car. His confession that he did not, in fact, cheat on me made me feel slightly better. But then his other revelation has stayed with me like a dark cloud. I still can't get his words out of my mind.

Luca said that Morettis are cold-blooded murderers. I mean, perhaps my father has killed in the past, but Luca can't tell me that his father hasn't done the same. That's what happens in the mafioso — murder, mayhem, drugs, violence, war. They're all interconnected and expected.

Even though we've been avoiding each other all week, we still have a party to attend tonight. It takes me hours to get ready, but most of that time is spent on picking out a dress. Some of the dresses that Luca picked out for me are very risqué, things that I would never wear. But a part of me wants him to want me. I'm tired of my husband ignoring me and acting like I don't exist. I need to get his attention, and this is the only way I know how.

I take a long, hot shower, drying and styling my hair and doing my makeup until it's perfect. When I slip into the dress, it fits me like a glove. And after I slip into the matching high heels, I stare at my reflection in the mirror.

I don't even recognize myself. The dark red dress is short with a revealing neckline, and I'm almost tempted to change. But I decide to hold my head up high and rock this dress. I think I look hot in it, and I can't wait to see what Luca thinks. Maybe it will have him begging for my forgiveness. Oh, a girl can only dream.

I leave the room, my hands shaking as I descend the staircase. The party tonight could be a defining moment in Luca and my relationship. I can feel it deep down inside my bones.

Every click of my heels hitting a step causes a reverberation through me. What will Luca think of my dress? Will he like it? Will he be upset, angry? I'm scared to see what his reaction will be, but a part of me is also thrilled beyond reason.

Dante stands at the bottom of the staircase, waiting patiently. His back is turned towards me, but when he hears me approach, he turns. And his reaction is...unexpected.

At first, his eyes widen, and then they drift up and down, openly perusing me from head to toe, and I can see the longing in his dark eyes as they meet mine.

"Verona," he says, his voice gruff. "Are you sure you want to wear that tonight?"

I stop at the bottom landing and do a little spin for him. "What's wrong with it?"

He swallows hard. "Nothing. I just..." His voice trails off as he suddenly clears his throat and stares at anything in the room except for me.

I can't help but smile. If Dante is giving me this kind of reaction, I can't wait to see how Luca reacts.

"Is Luca ready to leave?"

"He already left in a separate car."

I frown. He didn't even wait for me? Well, that gives me even more reason to leave the house dressed like this. It will be a punishment for him for forgetting his wife.

I thought for sure he wouldn't even let me go to the party dressed like this. But now...well, now he has no choice. I have decided for him. I just hope he's ready.

CHAPTER 24

Luca

THE PARTY IS inherently boring, and I can't wait to be done for the night. I don't understand the point of masquerade balls. They're so fucking cliché. Everyone had to don a mask the moment they entered the mansion. But, hey, it gives me a chance to mingle through the crowd with a mask covering my true feelings and intents. That is a bonus.

Megatron by Laylow is coursing across the speakers scattered throughout the place, filling the room with a thunderous beat that feels like it's inside my veins as I make my way through the crowd.

I check my phone as I walk. Dante said that they would be arriving momentarily. I don't know why I didn't wait for Verona to get ready, but I just didn't feel like it. She's been ignoring me lately, and it's been driving me fucking crazy. So, maybe I decided to give her a taste of her own medicine. And not bringing her with me to an event is like a slap in the face.

All the couples around me are enjoying conversations together; and for a moment, I kind of wish I had Verona by my side. But then I throw that fucking thought out the window, because I can't allow myself to feel like that. We'll never be a *real* couple no matter how hard she tries to get under my skin.

I know she hates me because of our arranged marriage. And I don't know if she's purposely getting on my nerves or if it's just because she's trying so damn hard to actually make this work between us.

The music reaches its peak as a woman in a very short, very revealing red dress steps into the main entrance. Several men near me turn to look at her, commenting under their breath even with their wives within earshot.

The woman is beautiful, stunning. She has long, dark hair cascading down her bare, slender shoulders in waves. The dress looks like it was painted on, so short I can almost see her panties...or maybe no panties — I suddenly want to know which — as she descends the stairs to the main ballroom.

For some reason, I can't seem to force my eyes away from this woman. There's something so familiar about her. Like I've seen her in my dreams before or some strange, sappy shit like that.

I'm captivated by her, mesmerized by the way she moves. The top half of her face is hidden under an intricate red and black mask embellished with jewels and feathers. And I can't stop staring at her full lips encased in a blood red lipstick.

Her petite body moves like it was made for the bedroom as she passes by onlookers, just as equally enchanted by her as I am.

She has legs for days, and I take in every inch down to the red high heels adorning her feet.

Her head turns from side to side as if she's looking for someone. And the closer she gets to me, the harder my heart begins to beat. My cock twitches against the zipper of my tailored suit pants as she approaches.

Fuck, whoever she's here with tonight is a lucky man.

Tearing my eyes away from her, I check my phone again for the millionth time tonight. There is a text I missed from Dante telling me that they've arrived. I check the time. Three minutes ago.

Glancing up at the entrance, I look for my wife, but she's nowhere to be found. I curse under my breath just as a feminine voice says my name from beside me. I look down at the mystery woman standing next to me. "Yes?" I ask her, wondering if she's lost.

"What? You don't recognize your own wife?" she says with a grin.

It takes a few moments for my brain to process what I'm witnessing right now. The hot, petite brunette that I was just lusting after moments before is...Verona.

"Verona," I spit out through clenched teeth. "What the hell are you wearing?" I hiss at her.

"A dress," she says simply as if there's not a care in the world. As if not every man in this fucking place isn't staring at her and longing for her.

"You couldn't have worn something less revealing?" I'm seething at this point, ready to drag her out of this party by her fucking hair.

"You left without me. So, it's not like I could have asked you if it was something you'd approve of," she says harshly.

Ah, so she's upset that I didn't wait for her. And this is my punishment? Well, two can play at this game. "I definitely don't approve of my wife looking like a common whore," I tell her with conviction in my voice.

My words visibly affect her, and I can see the tears gathering in her eyes behind her mask. I can't bear to see her cry, so I walk away from her like she means nothing to me. I make my way to the back of the room, pulling out my phone and shooting Dante a text that he is never allowed to let her leave the house in this kind of attire ever again.

I've been so preoccupied with hating Verona that I didn't even know I could be attracted to her...until I saw her in a different light.

Now I can't stop thinking about those red-painted lips wrapped around my cock.

"Fuck," I mutter under my breath as I subtly adjust my cock in my pants. It clearly has a mind of its own. And in the middle of a crowded room is not where I want to be getting a boner like some teenage boy lusting after his first crush.

Holding my phone in my hand, I pretend to be immersed in some kind of urgent matter; but in all reality, my eyes can't stop staring at my wife. I watch closely as she runs off towards the women's restroom.

My cock throbs, painfully aching for her.

I realize I'm fucked in this moment. I never thought I would say this, but I'm attracted to my wife.

CHAPTER 25

Verona

AFTER HEARING LUCA'S hateful words, I run into the nearest bathroom and tear off my mask, staring at my reflection in the mirror.

Tears fill my eyes, but I refuse to let them fall. I won't let him win.

An old woman steps up beside me and washes her hands. She glances at me once and then twice and frowns. "Some guy make you upset, sweetheart?" she asks.

"Yeah," I admit.

"Well, if I was your age and looked like that, I'd be out on that dance floor dancing with every eligible man." She stares at me with her beautiful, blue eyes and winks before she says, "Make him pay for hurting you."

"Make him pay," I say, nodding in agreement. Gathering my mask, I replace it and turn to leave the bathroom. My eyes search the room, finding Luca leaning against a wall in the far corner of the room, away from everyone else.

He's not even looking for me. *He doesn't even care.*

Grabbing a champagne flute from one of the waiters, I down it in a couple swallows. I have another and then another before I feel like I have enough liquid courage for what I'm about to do next.

Making sure there's a clear view from him to me, I approach a younger guy standing in a group of men twice his age. "Would you like to dance?" I ask him.

His eyes roam my figure, and he nods his head vehemently. "Uh, yeah!" he says urgently.

We make our way to the dance floor in the middle of the room. The beat of the music is hard and fast, and I begin to move, swaying my hips while keeping a safe distance from the young man I just met.

He steps from side to side, clearly not knowing what to do. "Uh, what's your name?" he asks me over the music.

I'm about to tell him my name when an older gentleman steps up and says, "Run along and play, Junior." Then, feasting his eyes on me, he says, "Let's dance."

Well, I can't say no to that. At least this guy knows what he wants...and obviously knows what he's doing.

The man is tall and handsome with hair and eyes as black as night. He turns me around in his arms, pressing my bare back against his front as he grinds his hips against mine to the beat. His lips are near my ear as he asks, "Do you have any idea that you're the sexiest woman here tonight?" When I shake my head, he continues. "What does it feel like to have over a hundred men fantasizing about taking you home?"

I consider his words before I answer. "Powerful," I tell him honestly.

"Yes, powerful," he agrees. He turns me in his arms again so that we're facing each other. He's so tall that I have to look up to see his face. And it reminds me of the height difference between Luca and me. And that, of course, makes me think about Luca...my husband.

"I noticed you as soon as you walked in the door. I knew I had to talk to you. But I never thought I'd get a chance to dance with you. My name is Constantine Carbone."

I begin to tell him my name, but his fingertips suddenly graze along my bare back as he pulls me closer. Goosebumps cover my skin, but not the good kind. He's getting too close, too aggressive.

I try to pull back, but he holds me even tighter.

He leans into me and whispers into my ear all the naughty things he wants to do to me once he gets me home.

"Let her go, Carbone," says a commanding voice behind me. Shivers erupt inside of me, racing up my spine.

"What business is it of yours?" my dancing partner asks.

"She's my wife," Luca says through clenched teeth. He tears off his mask, and I can instantly see the look of recognition fill the other man's eyes.

"I'm sorry, Vitale. I didn't know she belonged to you."

"Well, now you know," he says before grabbing my arm and pulling me away from the man, away from the party and towards the front door.

I stumble a few times thanks to the few glasses of champagne I had and to the high heels, but Luca is quick to pick me up when I nearly fall and keep us moving.

Luca doesn't say a word as he leads me from the house and straight to a dark, sleek car parked outside. He swings open the door and practically throws me inside. I splay out on the backseat, waiting for his terror as he climbs in beside me.

He slams the door shut and tells Dante in the front seat to drive us home before he pushes a button for the partition between us and Dante to close. Once it's shut, he turns to me.

He's calm. Way too calm. And it's scaring me.

"Luca," I whisper. I'm about to apologize when he suddenly grabs me and pulls me closer. His mouth is crashing down on mine before I can even comprehend what's happening.

He doesn't ask if this is okay. He doesn't even ask if I want him.

He just takes. And I am so incredibly turned on that I feel like I could catch on fire.

This kiss is so powerful that I can feel little tremors erupting all throughout my body. I've never been kissed before, but I didn't think my first time would be like this. This kiss is raw, rough, and possessive. He kisses me with bruising force, like the world is coming to an end and we only have a few moments left to live.

Luca's tongue prods at my lips until I open my mouth for him, letting him in. Our tongues entwine in a desperate need for each other.

He pulls back, and I struggle to catch my breath. "You drive me crazy," he admits before his mouth is on mine again.

I'm boneless in his arms, a weak mess, and he takes the opportunity to conquer me. I'm trembling as his hands explore my body. He roughly grabs my breasts through my dress, kneading them until my nipples are hard peaks.

Then, his hands go lower...lower until they're lifting up my dress. He breaks the kiss to stare down at my thighs, and I can hear him sigh in relief as he whispers, "A thong."

I stare at him, confused. Did he think I wasn't wearing any underwear?

"If you hadn't been wearing panties, I think I would have had no choice but to punish you." He stares at me with his gray eyes glistening in the pale moonlight streaming through the dark windows of the car. "I might still punish you for dressing like this, for enticing all the men at the party...and for enticing *me*," he says, a dark threat permeating through his words.

So, he's upset with me because I turned him on? I don't even have time to comprehend that information before he says, "Get on your knees, ass facing me."

I swallow hard at his request, hesitating a second too long, because next thing I know, he's pushing me onto the seat and forcing me on my knees.

"Spread your legs," he instructs, his voice deep and full of lust.

My breathing is labored as I do as he says. This is a new side of Luca I have never seen before. He wants me. I can feel his desperate need.

And I can't help it, but I want him too.

I spread my thighs for him until my knees are as far apart as they can go on the backseat. I'm not prepared for the first smack to my right cheek, and I jump and squeal in surprise. One of his hands presses on my lower back, holding me in place as the other takes a turn slapping each cheek in succession until my skin feels hot and sore.

"So beautiful," he murmurs before he smacks me two more times, eliciting a moan out of my throat.

I don't know why, but the pain is turning me on.

His big hand kneads the tender flesh, getting dangerously close to my clit, and I'm begging silently in my mind for him to touch me there.

When his fingertip drags up and down my slit over my thong, I think I'm going to spontaneously combust. "You're so wet for me. Did that turn you on, dirty girl?" He moves the thong to the side, and I can feel his warm breath breathing onto my wetness before it turns cold, causing me to shiver.

"Please!" I cry out before I can stop myself. No man has ever done this to me before; and even though I'm nervous, I'm more turned on, and the lust is drowning out all of my reasonable thoughts.

"Tell me what you want," he instructs, wanting me to beg for it.

I sink my teeth into my lower lip. I don't want to beg. I want to tell him to go straight to hell. But my desire is too great for him at the moment, and I find myself whispering, "I want your mouth on me."

"What? I can't hear you?" he teases.

"Please put your mouth on me!" I cry out, shame burning my face.

His fingertip traces my slit until I feel him pushing on my most intimate area. "Have you ever been fucked here?" he asks, pressing on my tight hole.

I squirm under his ministrations. "No!" I want to tell him I've never been fucked *anywhere*, but I hold my tongue, because I'm so afraid he won't want to continue and give me the release I need right now. "Please, Luca," I plead.

"Fuck, I love hearing you beg," he groans. His finger moves down, swiping over my clit, and I jerk forward, feeling like I just got struck by lightning.

His hand moves from my lower back to around my hip, holding me in place. "You're really responsive," he comments in almost a whisper. "I like that," he adds with a dark chuckle that has my core clenching.

I remember the girls at the boarding school talking about their sexual encounters, and I always thought they were bragging or making stuff up. But when I feel the first swipe of Luca's tongue on my clit, I realize they were telling the truth. It does feel good, just like heaven and beyond.

I groan out loud, fisting my hands under me as he continues to lick me. He eats me like a starving man, the wicked sounds filling the interior of the car and turning me on even further.

I feel his fingertip enter me, and I cry out.

"Your pussy is so tight," he groans. "Fuck, Verona, you're perfect."

He pushes his finger in and out while his tongue lashes over my clit, and I close my eyes at the sensation. It's too much. Too great. Too powerful. A garbled cry escapes my lips as I come, riding his face unabashed, drawing out the pleasure as I tremble and sob under him.

He licks me slowly while I come down from the high, shivers erupting through my body. My legs tremble until I can't hold myself up anymore, and I end up collapsing onto the seat beside him.

I can hear his belt buckle before his zipper goes down. And when I sit up in the seat, I see Luca sitting there with his cock in his hand. My eyes widen at the sight. I've never watched a guy touch himself, and Luca is so comfortable doing it in front of me.

His cock is impossibly thick and long, and I swallow hard at the sight of it. I've seen porn before, of course, but most of the guys were never this size.

"I've been thinking about those red lips wrapped around my cock all night," he tells me darkly.

I lick over said lips and look up at him beneath my lashes. He wants my mouth on him, but I've never done that before. What if I don't do it right? What if he doesn't like it?

"Verona, please," he groans as he strokes his cock. "I need you."

Those words send a shiver up and down my spine, and all of my hesitations go right out the window. I need to make him feel as good as he just made me feel. He gave me pleasure, and I want to return the favor.

I move closer to him and lean down, mesmerized by his hand stroking up and down. He smells like cedarwood and expensive cologne, and my mouth waters as I stick out my tongue and swipe it around his head like a lollipop.

"Fuck," he hisses through clenched teeth.

I think that means he likes it, so I do it again and again until he's begging for me to put him into my mouth. I open wide, barely able to fit him inside as I swirl my tongue and swallow as much of him as I can.

I remember the girls at the boarding school saying to not use any teeth because guys hate that, so I wrap my lips around my teeth before going up and down on his shaft.

"Yes, just like that," he says, encouraging me. "Suck my cock, dirty girl."

I move my mouth over him as his hand intertwines in my hair. I expect him to push my head down and control the rhythm, but instead he simply wraps my long hair around his fist and lets me control the speed.

"I'm going to cum in that dirty mouth, Verona," he warns.

I can feel his cock twitch just before he erupts in my mouth, filling it to the brim. I have no choice but to swallow it all down as I continue to suck him. He groans loudly, the deep timbre of his voice filling the car. My clit throbs in response to his deep growls and moans.

"That's my good girl," he says as he shudders one last time from the pleasure.

Pulling his dick from my mouth, he looks down at me with a look of adoration. He smiles at me, and I realize this is a side of Luca that I've never seen before. Just like before with the jealousy, this is a whole other side of the enigmatic cube that makes up his personality.

He tucks his cock into his pants and zips them up.

"Are we almost home?" he asks out loud, and at first, I think he's asking me. But then I see the light for the intercom and realize I never saw him push it.

"Yes, sir," Dante responds gruffly through the speaker.

"Did you enjoy the show?" Luca asks him.

Dante doesn't respond, and I stare at Luca in shock. He must have pushed the button at some point when he was eating me out... and he made Dante listen to the whole thing.

Luca turns off the intercom and smiles smugly at me as the car comes to a stop.

"Why would you do that?" I ask, shame burning my face and chest.

"I've seen the way Dante looks at you. Sometimes people need to be reminded of their place and where they stand."

"You...you're an asshole!" I yell at him.

Luca continues to smile, unaffected by my response.

The door opens, and Dante is standing there, staring at me with an undecipherable look. I can barely meet his eyes as I whisper, "I'm sorry," before running straight for the house.

I don't stop running until I'm safely locked inside my room.

I thought I had seen a different side of Luca tonight, but now I know that it was all just smoke and mirrors. He's still a bastard. I just wish I had known what he was up to before I let him touch me.

CHAPTER 26

Luca

VERONA'S EFFORTS AT ignoring me have reached a new high. As I sit alone at the dinner table, the housekeeper informs me that my wife refuses to dine with me tonight.

Last night has been on my mind all day. I can still taste her sweetness on my tongue. And no matter how hard I try to forget her soft skin, I simply can't. I want her again. One taste wasn't enough. I'm fucking addicted.

"If she doesn't want to eat with me, then she won't eat at all," I inform the housekeeper. "Do you understand?"

"Yes, sir."

After she disappears from the room, I stare down at the rest of my steak, having suddenly lost my appetite.

What I did last night was cruel. But I can't deny that it made me feel better. Call it jealousy or what you will, but Dante needed to be put in his fucking place. I've seen the way he stares at my wife, like he could take her at any moment into his arms and comfort her like she's his. She is not his.

She is mine.

My hand curls into a fist, and I pound it hard against the top of the long wooden table. She can ignore me all she wants, but it's not going to change things. I won't cave. I was born into hatred for her and her family. And even though we were friends when we were kids, that doesn't mean shit now in the real world while we're adults. Even though she's my wife, that doesn't mean I have to like her or, god forbid, *love* her.

Even though my feelings haven't changed for her, last night something did change. I have a craving for her that I can't stop. A need for her to be under me, calling out my name as I pound my cock into her tight pussy. I want her to know who owns her body, and I want to reinforce it again and again and again.

My cock twitches in my pants. And when I press my palm down over it, I groan out loud. I'm so fucking horny I can't even think straight. Just thinking about her red lips wrapped around my cock drives me insane.

Frustrated, I pour myself another scotch and drink it down in one swallow. And then I pour another and another until I start to feel numb.

I've been known to down bottles of expensive scotch in one night. I would like to say I'm drowning my demons, but unfortunately, they know how to swim.

CHAPTER 27

Verona

MY STOMACH GROWLS with such intensity that it almost makes me dizzy. I'm so hungry. I skipped breakfast, lunch and dinner today just so I wouldn't have to face Luca, and now I'm paying the price.

For some reason, I thought maybe he would come up after dinner to apologize and offer me some food. But now I know I was way too naïve to think that would happen. It's nearly ten o'clock at night, and I haven't eaten a single thing since yesterday evening.

Fuming, I wrap a sheer flowered kimono around my midnight blue nightdress and venture out of my room. I tiptoe down the quiet hallway and make my way downstairs towards the kitchen. I'm crossing the dining room when I see movement coming from the table and stop dead in my tracks.

My eyes meet his from across the room. I can tell just by looking at him that he's drunk, but the almost empty bottle of scotch is a dead giveaway.

"What are you doing?" he asks, his words slurring.

At first, my mind draws a blank. I'm so taken aback by his relaxed state. His suit jacket is slung over the back of his chair, and his button-up shirt is hanging open, revealing a muscular chest that could easily be on the cover of a fitness magazine.

"Let me guess," he says, drawing out every word. "You're hungry."

"Yes," I whisper.

"Should have come down for dinner," he says with a shrug.

"You can't starve me," I say forcibly.

"I could if I wanted to. I could do anything I wanted to do to you actually," he confesses. "It's not like you don't deserve it."

His words have me taking a step back. "I don't deserve any of this!" I tell him vehemently. I'm tired of his constant animosity towards me. "I never did anything to you, Luca."

He closes his eyes when I say his name. "You are one of *them*."

"One of them?" I ask, not understanding.

"A Moretti," he sneers as if the name leaves a bad taste in his mouth.

I don't know what happens next, but I think I honestly have just reached my breaking point with him. "Fuck you, Luca," I hiss.

His eyes open and narrow as he stares at me. "What did you just say to me?"

"Fuck you!" I yell.

Before I can even blink, he is up and out of his chair and coming straight for me. Squealing in terror, I turn to run, but he's too fast. He hauls me up in his arms and over to the table, bending me over the edge and pushing my face into the wood. He grasps my arms behind my back and holds them in place with one of his large hands while his other hand grabs the nape of my neck.

"Say it again," he hisses at me through clenched teeth. "I dare you."

And so I do. "Fuck you!"

The next thing I hear is a ripping sound as my kimono is torn from my body, the lacy, delicate material falling into shreds around me.

His hand reaches for the hem of my nightdress, and I cry out, "Don't you dare!"

He hesitates and then says, "What will you do, Verona, if I touch you? Will you cry out my name and beg for release just like last night?"

My face flames with embarrassment.

"Maybe you want me to spank you and make you wet again," he whispers into my ear, the scent of expensive scotch sweeping over my face.

"Please. Stop," I beg.

He squeezes my arms before releasing me, scoffing in disgust. He starts walking away from me out of the room when I call after him, "I don't know what you think my family did to you, but we didn't do anything!"

He stops and turns, and the look in his eyes scares the hell out of me. In a few long strides, he closes the distance between us, wrapping his hand around my neck. He slams me up against the wall and leans in until he's only an inch away from my face. "Someone in your family killed my mother. I was only twelve years old when she was murdered in cold blood in our fucking kitchen," he says, his voice dangerously low.

"W-wh-what?" I sputter.

"Do you know what that does to a boy, seeing his mother die right in front of his own fucking eyes, in his fucking arms?"

"Your mother was murdered?" I whisper.

"I bet your dear old dad didn't tell you that one, did he? No, you were too spoiled, always sheltered and kept out of the loop on all of that shit."

"How do you know it was my family that did it?" I dare to ask.

"Because they always killed their enemies in the same way. By slashing their throat three times. The same number of daggers in the Moretti family crest."

Tears fill my eyes as I realize he's telling the truth. It all makes sense now. The reason why our families went from acquaintances to sworn enemies almost overnight. I knew his mom died, but I never knew the why or how behind it all.

I swallow hard against his hand wrapped around my throat. He squeezes, and I instinctively bring my hands up, grabbing his wrist.

"But I guess our grandfathers thought this marriage would bring some kind of peace even though I could never truly love anyone that bears the name Moretti."

My brain is working on overtime, trying to process all of the information. I guess I was kept in the dark, because my father never told me any of this. I had no idea that the Vitales blamed my family for the death of Luca's mother. No wonder their hatred runs so deep for us.

"Go get something to eat. Starvation isn't a cruel enough death." He releases me then, leaving me stunned into silence.

He walks out of the room, and I'm left alone. I glance at the kitchen, but I couldn't possibly eat anything now. My stomach cramps in protest, but I've completely lost my appetite. In fact, I feel as if I could throw up. The fact that Luca witnessed his mother's death makes me sick. He was so young and innocent. It explains why he grew up into the cold, callous man that he is now. Her murder changed him.

Now that I know the truth behind his hatred for me, it makes me fear for my safety here, for the safety of my father. With me in Luca's home, right next to the enemy, it makes us all vulnerable.

I decide right then and there that I will go visit my father in the morning and get to the bottom of all of this. If my father really is to blame for the death of Luca's mother, then that will change everything.

CHAPTER 28

Luca

I WAKE THE next morning with a pounding headache. I drank way too much last night, and now I must suffer the consequences.

I climb out of bed, every movement making the headache worse. I pop some painkillers and hop into the shower. The hot steam seems to help a bit. And by the time I'm dressed, I'm feeling a little better.

I walk downstairs and pause in the dining room. Memories of last night bombard me, and I curse out loud. I told Verona too much. I showed my cards. I told her my true feelings behind my hatred towards her and her family. And the look on her face told me exactly what I already knew — she didn't have a clue.

Of course her father didn't tell her that he was responsible for murdering my mother. I mean, why would he? I don't think that man has ever accepted responsibility for any of the bad shit he's done his entire life.

He's killed indiscriminately, but I bet Verona has no idea who her dear old dad truly is or what he's capable of. At least I know who my father is. I've witnessed firsthand the type of destruction he can bring to an entire family. I've always wondered why he didn't take out the Morettis when he had the chance, though. If it were up to me, they would have been eradicated from this earth a long time ago.

I know we never caught the actual person who slit my mother's throat. I've always envisioned it was Antonio Moretti himself, but that big, lump of shit couldn't have run fast enough out of the house that morning without tripping over his two fat feet.

No, it was definitely someone who was hired by the Moretti family. But why my mother? I never understood the answer to that question. It would have made more sense to try to take a hit out on my father. He was Antonio's rival, his sworn enemy. Why kill someone who was innocent?

Trying to clear my head, I walk into the kitchen.

Benito is drinking a cup of coffee while the staff mills about, cleaning up after breakfast.

One of the housekeepers walks into the room. "Breakfast, sir?"

Ignoring her, I ask Benito, "Where's Verona?" I wouldn't be surprised if she ran away after last night. She knows my true feelings towards her now. And even though we're bound by this contract, I don't doubt that she's terrified of me and what I might do to her.

"She went to see her father," Benito informs me.

"Fuck!" I yell, startling the young woman beside me. "Who drove her?" I demand.

"I believe it was Dante."

Dante. Of course. He's been a thorn in my side ever since I can remember. And now he's pushing my buttons when it comes to my wife. He's taking the role of her bodyguard to a whole other level. And if he thinks he can best me, then he has another thing coming. I guess putting him in his place the other night didn't change anything.

I'll just have to take it a step further to make sure he understands.

"Breakfast, sir?" the housekeeper asks again, her blonde bangs hanging in her eyes.

"Yes," I tell her. I might as well eat and get some of my strength back. I'll deal with Dante and Verona later.

CHAPTER 29

Verona

MY HIGH HEELS click against the polished hardwood floor as I make my way to my father's study. I know that's where he'll be. I have a lot of questions that I need answers to, and I'm not leaving until every single one is answered.

"Verona," my father says in surprise when I barge into the room.

I remember sneaking into his study as a child. The dark, antique furniture used to intrigue me, and I would sit for hours staring at the intricately carved patterns and reading through his old, dusty book collections.

This room would always bring me a sense of peace, because no one else was allowed in here. I wasn't even allowed, but my father allowed it when he wasn't conducting business.

I give Dante a silent nod before closing the door, effectively shutting him out. I trust Dante, and I'm thankful that he agreed to drive me here today, but I want this conversation to be between my father and me. I don't want any third-party opinions creeping in.

"Did something happen?" my father questions.

"I want you to tell me how Gianna Vitale died."

"You know how she died," he says, waving a hand, dismissing me.

"No, I don't. I figured it was a car accident or something sudden, but you never told me the truth. No one has told me the truth about what happened."

Papa stands and goes to one of the large, floor-to-ceiling windows that overlooks the property. After a long time, he finally says, "Gianna Vitale was murdered in her home."

"By who? Was it you?" I ask, desperation flooding my voice.

He turns to look at me. "Don't tell me you came here to accuse your own father of murder."

"I need to know who killed her."

"No one knows. Her killer was never caught. I heard it was sudden, a thief in the middle of the night."

"Did you know Luca watched her die?"

Papa grimaces at that information. "No, I didn't know." He ponders that information for a moment. "No wonder he became such a bitter, troubled boy."

"Did you know that the Vitales blame you for her death?"

"Yes, of course I do. That is what started the war between our families, after all. But I told them I didn't know anything of it, and I don't. I never did, and I never will. The case ran cold even with police." He walks over to his desk and sits down again. "I would never put out a hit on an innocent woman. Even if we had our troubles with the Vitales, Gianna was innocent."

"Luca said her throat was slashed three times."

My father doesn't seem stunned by that revelation. "Someone wanted to frame us; make the Vitales believe it was us," he says adamantly.

"Is that why you sent me away? Did you think they would try to take out their revenge on me?"

"Yes." He removes a cigar from a small box on the corner of his desk, snips off the end and lights it up, puffing his cheeks until the cherry forms on the end of it. A plume of smoke escapes his lips as he looks up at me. "I wanted to keep you safe. And that was the only way I knew how. I had to get you away from this place, all of this." He sighs and takes another puff from the cigar. "Everything calmed down when they couldn't prove that I ordered the hit or find the man who did it. But obviously Luca Vitale still harbors some ill will towards our family."

I want to tell my father that it's more than ill will. It's pure, undiluted hatred. But I keep my mouth shut. I'm not here to run away from home...even if Luca's mansion doesn't feel like home to me. Besides, I can't leave even if I wanted to thanks to the contract binding us to be married and living together.

"Grandfather thought the contract would fix everything for good?"

Papa nods. "The two patriarchs schemed behind all of our backs. They wanted harmony amongst the families once and for all." He sits down at his desk and rests the cigar on a nearby ashtray. "Valerius Vitale and my father were childhood friends. They obviously were sick of all the fighting, and this was the only thing they could do that would prevent any future war between the families. It was their dying wish to bring peace to all of us."

"I don't know if there will ever be peace," I mutter under my breath.

He shrugs one shoulder. "Perhaps not." Then he asks, "What else do you want to know?"

"Do you have any suspicions of who would have wanted to kill Gianna Vitale?" I ask.

He shakes his head. "No one knows. Otherwise, that person would already be dead."

That's true. If the Vitales knew who murdered Gianna, the man would already be six feet under.

"What else do you need from me, Verona?" Papa offers.

"Can we...can we spend the day together?" I ask him, and my question clearly surprises him. I need a break from Luca, and I haven't spent real quality time with my father in years. All this talk about Luca's dead mother makes me think about my mother.

I've already lost one parent. My father is the only family I have left, and I would be devastated if I lost him too. I know it's inevitable, but I can make up for lost time, starting today.

"Of course. For you, anything."

I smile at him. "Thank you, Papa."

"You know, the same ice cream shop we used to take you to when you were a little girl is still down the street. Would you like to go?"

"I would love that."

I know Luca won't be pleased about me being gone all day since I didn't exactly tell him I was leaving. But for all I know, he doesn't even know I left. And I'm guessing even if he does, that he definitely doesn't care.

CHAPTER 30

Luca

I CAN'T CONCENTRATE. Verona has been gone all day long, and it's been bugging the fuck out of me. Dante answered only one of my texts saying that she was at her father's house, and that was hours ago. All other texts have been ignored. And even though he's being paid by the Moretti family, I am going to reprimand that prick the moment I get my hands on him.

He drove my wife out of here without my permission. I don't give a fuck who he works for. He lives under my fucking roof. He eats my food. He shits in my toilets. He will listen to whatever the fuck I say. And if he doesn't like it, he will be out on his ass. I don't give a fuck how much Verona wants him as her bodyguard.

I demand order and control in my life. If I don't have those two things, then my world feels like it's spiraling into utter chaos. And the sooner Verona learns that, the better.

Eight o'clock rolls around, and I'm on my fifth glass of scotch when

I see the black BMW pull into the garage on the security footage. I watch impatiently on my laptop while Verona exits the car after Dante opens the door for her. Then, I track her movements through the garage and the house. She walks up the stairs to her bedroom without even so much as a glance into any of the rooms to look for me.

I'm seething, my hands clenched in anger as I stalk out of my office and go to find Dante.

He's in the kitchen, rooting around in the refrigerator when I approach him. "You took my wife without my permission?" I throw the accusation out there calmly even though I'm anything but calm on the inside.

"I didn't know it was against *the rules*," he says sarcastically, exaggerating the last two words and pissing me off even further.

"Let me make it clear for you. What my wife does or doesn't do is *my* business, not yours. From now on, you'll clear everything with me first, or you'll be out of a job."

"You can't fire me," he says, pulling a few things out of the fridge to make something to eat. "I don't work for you."

I shoot him an angry glare. "You don't work for me, but I can still kick your fucking ass out of my goddamn house."

"Verona wouldn't like that very much," he says, flashing me a cocky grin.

Dante is tall, but I'm taller and bigger than him. I doubt he's had the type of training I have had in my lifetime. It might be a struggle at first, but I know I could overtake him. I would like nothing more in this moment than to beat him into a bloody pulp. "I don't give a fuck what she likes or doesn't like. And the same goes for you. Run shit by me, or you're out of here. Got it?"

"Sure thing, *boss*," he says, and it takes every ounce of strength in me to not walk over to him and knock that smile off of his face along with a few teeth out of his goddamn mouth.

"And if the other night wasn't an indication of whose dick she wants, then I don't know what will wake you the fuck up," I hiss at him. That statement stuns him into silence, and now I'm the one smiling before I turn and leave the room.

I walk straight to my wife's bedroom. I startle her when I slam open the door. Her petite body is wrapped in a towel, her long hair dripping wet as she emerges from the adjacent bathroom.

I'm beyond the point of calm now. I'm fucking furious. "Where the fuck were you all day?" I roar. I want to hear the words from her mouth in case Dante was bullshitting me.

"I went to see my father. Is there a problem?" she asks calmly, seemingly not affected by my anger.

"Dante is not to take you anywhere without my permission," I demand.

Now this gets a rise out of her. She goes from calm to angry in two-point-five seconds. And I can't help but notice how cute she looks when she's pissed. "I have to ask for your permission to leave the house to see my father?" she exclaims indignantly. "Luca, that is absurd!"

"It's not absurd. It's smart. You know what kind of world we live in, Verona. You're not safe out there," I warn.

"I had Dante with me the whole time!" she counters, her voice raising to new levels.

And I don't know why, but it pisses me off that she relies on her bodyguard to keep her safe and not her own husband. Although, I guess I haven't given her many reasons to trust me. Hell, I've given her every reason *not* to trust me.

Trying to calm myself down, I pace the floor of her room. "Why did you go to see your father?" I ask even though I think I already know the answer to that question.

"To find out information about your mother."

I stop pacing and turn to look at her. "And?" I prompt.

"He denied any wrongdoing. He had no part in your mother's death."

"And you believe him?" I scoff.

"Of course I believe him! I was there. I looked into his eyes. He wasn't lying to me. He was telling the truth!"

"He would never tell you the truth," I say with a shake of my head. I take several steps forward until I'm standing directly before her. "You really think he'd admit something like that to his own daughter?"

"He didn't do it. Someone wanted it to look like he ordered the hit," she says vehemently, and I can hear the conviction in her voice. She believes him so wholeheartedly. She has no idea how wrong she is.

"He had my mother murdered to throw my father off of his game. They were fighting over territories. Your father ended up winning in the end. My father was crippled after my mother died. And that's exactly what your father wanted. That was his goal, and he achieved it triumphantly."

Tears fill her eyes as she stares up at me. "You're too blinded by your hatred to believe anything other than what you want to believe. There's no evidence that my father had any involvement. You can't prove anything."

"I'll prove it someday," I promise her. "And when you realize what a dirty bastard your father truly is, you'll —."

My words end abruptly when Verona suddenly slaps me in the face.

"You're the bastard!" she screams at me.

She raises her hand to hit me again, but I snatch her wrist. And then I capture the other wrist when she tries it again. "You really shouldn't have done that," I sneer. Pushing her roughly, I toss her backwards onto the bed.

She sprawls onto the mattress, and her towel opens slightly, revealing a silky thigh and part of her shaved pussy. My mouth instantly waters at the sight.

"Don't," Verona warns, but I can hear the uncertainty in her tone.

"Don't what?" I ask, climbing onto the bed and hovering over her. "Don't make you come with my mouth on your pussy again?"

"Stop," she whispers, her breath coming out in short, quick pants.

I trail my tongue from her ear, down her neck and down to between her breasts. She shudders under me, and my cock pushes painfully against my zipper.

"Please," she begs, and I stop to look at her.

"Please stop...or please continue?" I ask her, my voice deep and full of animalistic hunger.

Her honey-colored eyes are glittering in the moonlight streaming through the sheer curtains, and she has an unreadable expression on her face. Hell, I don't think even she knows what she wants at this point.

And so, when she doesn't verbally answer me, I reluctantly pull away from her. I've never forced a woman to do anything she doesn't want to do, and I'm not about to start with her.

"Goodnight, Verona," I tell her before I leave her room, slamming the door behind me.

CHAPTER 31

Verona

DANTE FOLLOWS CLOSELY behind me as I walk around the mall from store to store. Luca gave me his black credit card and told me to get whatever I needed that he didn't already buy. I don't get him. One minute he's a monster; the next he's trying to do something nice. It's like he can't make up his mind on whether he wants to hate me or not. Although, today, I swear he just wanted me out of the house for a while. We've barely spoken to each other for the past week or so since the night I slapped him in the face.

And while I admit it felt good to slap him, I regret doing it. Luca obviously harbors a lot of ill will towards my father, but I would too if I thought someone killed my mother. He has every reason in the world to hate the person who murdered his mother, but he's putting his anger on the wrong person, because my father didn't do it. I know deep down within my very soul that my father is innocent in all of this. If only I could prove it to him somehow.

"If I were you, I would max the credit card out on shit you don't even need just to spite him," Dante says, breaking me out of my thoughts. "We could even throw some of the stuff in the dumpsters behind the mall," he suggests, and I can hear the contempt in his voice. His hatred towards Luca is evident, but he tries his best to hide it from everyone but me.

"You know I wouldn't do that even if I wanted to," I tell him. I'm not like that. I know how hard people work for their money, and I know what it's like to live without the finer things in life. And even though Luca doesn't exactly do anything aboveboard, I don't want to waste his money. Besides, I'm not into spending blood money either.

I don't know much about Luca's business other than the few things I've heard the men in the house mention. Dante assures me Luca is the worst man on the planet, and maybe he is. Maybe I did marry a monster. He certainly acts like that sometimes.

But it isn't as if I had a choice in all of this. And it's not like we can just get divorced. I'm locked into this contract, this marriage, whether I like it or not. All I can do is try to make our relationship better over time, if that's even possible.

Sometimes it just feels like Luca can't stand the sight of me. I'm really at a loss for what I can do to make my time with him more tolerable. I try to stay out of his way, but out of sight, out of mind doesn't really work with him because he's so controlling and demanding.

He doesn't want to see me, and yet he wants to keep tabs on me all the time and know where I am at all hours of the day. It's so confusing.

Speaking of the devil, Dante's phone begins to ring, and he's quick to answer. "We're still at the mall," he says with an eye roll.

I can't hear the other side of the conversation, but I know it's Luca on the other end, asking for another update. He's called three times already, and we've only been gone for a couple of hours.

Dante hangs up the phone and shakes his head. "Controlling son of a bitch, isn't he?"

"I wish I could run away," I blurt out. I don't think I was even meaning to say it out loud, but it's too late to take it back now.

Dante's eyes meet mine, and in all seriousness, he tells me, "Then let's do it."

I shake my head. "He would find us."

"I would make sure he never did," he says so calmly and assuredly that it scares me.

While the idea of escaping my husband is both thrilling and exciting, I know it wouldn't end well. And if Dante helped me run away, I'm sure he would have to face the consequences. And if anything happened to my best friend, my *only* friend, I don't know what I would do.

"I'm just venting," I tell him, hoping that he believes me.

"You can always talk to me about anything, V," Dante assures me.

"I know. You're my best friend," I tell him with a smile. I point over to a store that sells household goods and gifts, and I say, "Let's go in there."

"Whatever you say," he says, following behind me.

CHAPTER 32

Luca

DANTE AND VERONA return from their shopping trip late in the evening. I wouldn't be surprised if she maxed out my credit card today. In fact, I'm anxious to see exactly how much she spent and at what stores. I know I already bought her enough clothes to last a lifetime, but I guess it wasn't enough for the *princess*. She needed more, more clothes, more material things to make her happy.

I shake my head as I watch them on the surveillance video getting out of the car. I expect them to start unloading shopping bag after shopping bag, but I'm blown away when Verona only appears with one bag before they walk to the garage door that connects to the house.

Confused, I click out of the surveillance video and look up the credit card charges on that particular card. Only one charge is on it... for forty dollars.

"Forty dollars?" I ask out loud. What the fuck?

I refresh the page, thinking I'm missing other charges, but nothing appears. Maybe the rest of the transactions didn't go through yet, but I know that's simply not the case. She spent all day shopping and only spent forty dollars of my money. And I can't help but wonder what the fuck she bought for herself.

There's a timid knock on my office door, and I hit a button to unlock it. Verona opens the door and stands in the doorway, looking shy and innocent. The monster in me rears its ugly head, wanting to pounce on her and force answers out of her. I want to know why she was gone for so long today if she only spent forty dollars on a single thing.

The bag is in her hand. I don't recognize the logo, but there are a lot of stores in the mall that I've never been in before.

"Are you busy?" she asks softly.

"No," I snap, causing her to wince at my tone. My frustration is getting the better of me, and so I try to calm down a little before telling her, "Come in."

She walks forward until she reaches my desk, and then she places the bag in front of me. "Here," she says.

I cock a brow at her. "What is this?"

"It's a gift."

"A gift?" I ask, confused. "A gift for who?" I demand.

"For you," she says with a grin.

Oh, so I'm amusing her. That's just great. I stare down at the bag, a frown on my face. "What is it?"

"You have to open it to find out," she says, her grin widening.

This whole situation is hilarious to her, but I'm finding it hard to see the humor in it all. She spent forty dollars...on me? That just doesn't make sense. She had a card with an unspeakable line of credit on it, and she used it on a purchase for me. What the fuck game is she playing at?

"I told you to buy yourself something," I tell her, my voice laced with anger.

She lifts her chin a little in defiance. "I didn't see anything I liked," she says, but I don't believe her. There are a lot of high-end stores in that mall and surrounding areas. I don't believe that she couldn't find at least one thing that she wanted or needed. Most women would have bought one of everything in the mall and not even blinked an eye.

"Open it," she prompts, shifting her weight from one foot to the next. She's nervous. Maybe she's afraid I won't like what she bought me?

"Fine," I scoff, grabbing the bag. I pull out the box inside and toss the bag aside. I read the front of the box out loud, "Zen Garden."

A bright smile is on her face as she nods enthusiastically. "It's supposed to be a stress reliever."

"You bought me...a Zen Garden." I shake my head, not even knowing what to say.

A frown mars her pretty face. "I'm sorry. I thought —."

"You thought what, Verona? You thought I would like to rake sand all day while I have more important things to do with my life?"

Tears form in her honey-colored eyes. "You could have just said thank you. That's what normal people do!" she shouts before turning and storming out of my office.

Pissed off, I stare down at the box. I scoop it up, ready to throw it in the trash, but I stop myself at the last second. Verona bought this for me. She wanted me to have this. She thought I would like it, I suppose. I think maybe deep down I just hate the fact that she thinks she has me all figured out when I can't even seem to figure her out one bit.

I always prided myself on the ability to read people. First impressions are important, and most of the time my life depends on me being able to sense what a person's true intentions are within the first few seconds of meeting them.

But when it comes to Verona, I just can't make sense of it all. And believe me, I have tried.

There's a missing piece of the puzzle when it comes to her. And just when I think I have the last piece I need, I realize it doesn't fit and that I have to start the whole thing all over again. It's infuriating, to say the least.

I want to understand her. I want to know what makes her tick. And ultimately, I want to use it against her.

I've always known my biggest foes greatest weaknesses and then used that knowledge in the best most possible way against them.

Could it be that I've been wrong about Verona this whole time?

No, I tell myself. *Impossible*. I'm never wrong about anyone.

But in the back of my mind I can't help but think that there's always a first time for everything.

CHAPTER 33

Luca

THE NEXT DAY, Benito walks into my office and stops dead in his tracks. "What in the hell is that?" he asks.

"A Zen Garden," I muse. The gift is in the center of my desk. Hell, I even moved my laptop to the side so that I could have more room for it.

"Where the hell did you get it?"

"Verona bought it for me." I never thought in a million years a Zen Garden would make me fucking happy or content, and yet here we are. I have been working on this thing for over two hours now. I started with unpacking the box. Included were several different styles of rakes and miniature Japanese ceramic figurines, along with rocks, moss, and cherry blossom trees.

I raked different patterns in the sand while I was on a phone call with one of my IT guys, and it helped to keep me calm when I learned that Constantine was planning on taking over some new territory on the west side of the city to help with his human trafficking ring. My IT guy was so surprised at my subdued reaction that he actually asked me if I was having a stroke since I had been quiet for so long.

After I was done raking, I set up the miniatures and arranged the trees, rocks and moss.

Benito walks up to my desk and studies the garden. "That's actually kind of...nice," he says. He picks up a rake and starts raking through the perfect pattern I had already created, messing it up.

I frown at him and snatch the rake from his hand. "I'll get you one for Christmas," I snap at him.

"So, Verona bought you this on her shopping trip yesterday?" he says, his lips tilting up in a grin.

"Yes. And that's the only thing she bought." I checked the credit card statement again this morning, and no other charges could be found to my dismay. I so wanted to be right about her, and once again she threw me for a fucking loop.

"Maybe she isn't the spoiled princess you thought she was," he suggests.

"I'm never wrong about people," I tell him.

He nods in agreement. "This is true. But you're never wrong about your *enemies*. Verona isn't your enemy."

"Yes, she is," I say pointedly.

"She may be the daughter of your enemy, but she did nothing wrong. She's innocent in all of this, Luca," Benito says. "Just like your mother was innocent."

His words infuriate me. "Whose side are you on anyway?" I snap.

"Yours. Always yours. I'm just trying to open your eyes to new possibilities."

"Verona isn't special. She isn't unique. I just have to figure out why she's trying to play me for a fool."

"Maybe she isn't trying to play you at all," Benito suggests.

"Just get the fuck out," I tell him. I'm done listening to him for the day.

"You just want me to leave so you can get back to work on your Zen Garden," he says with a chuckle.

"Leave!" I yell.

I can hear his big ass laughing the whole way down the hallway after he walks out of my office.

CHAPTER 34

Luca

WE ARE ALL gathered in the dining room for a family-style dinner...even though I would call us anything but family. Maybe a mixture of misfits — Dante, Benito, Verona and me.

Greta comes bustling through the door, a pleased look on her face when she sees everyone already seated. She had insisted on this type of dinner after "all of her hard work in the kitchen", as she put it earlier.

And even though I'd rather dine with a live, venomous python than be in the same room as Dante having a family meal, I'm willing to put my hatred for him aside for Greta's sake. Just this once anyway.

Greta started working for me a few days ago, and I can already tell she's extremely happy about having to cook for people again. She orders the servers around in Italian, and soon we all have in front of us a heaping serving of lasagna on our plates that just came out of the oven, homemade garlic bread and a caprese salad on the side with fresh mozzarella cheese.

"Everything looks delicious, Greta. *Grazie*," I tell her, which earns me a beaming smile that she wears the whole way back to the kitchen.

Verona, who is seated to my right, hums in approval as she takes a bite of her salad.

"Do you like it?" I can't help but ask.

"Yes, very much," she says before forking another piece of lettuce into her mouth.

Leave it to Greta to finally get approval from the princess. I don't think anything has been good enough for her since she arrived here.

Benito speaks up from my left. "So, Verona, what did you do after high school? College?"

I know he's just making small talk, but it irritates me. I don't want to hear about her posh lifestyle. I never had a chance to go to college, since running the family business always falls on the eldest son's shoulders. And with me being the only child, everything was placed on mine.

Verona takes her time wiping her mouth with one of the linen napkins and taking a sip of water before she answers him.

This should be good, I can't help but think. She probably went to one of the most expensive colleges in the country. The best daddy's money could buy. I wonder what kind of degree she got. Probably one that she would never use. Or maybe she was *undecided* the whole time, just riding out the college life for a while and living it up on daddy's dime.

"After boarding school, I went to live with a great aunt upstate," she says, completely blowing my theory out of the water.

"Boarding school?" I blurt out without thinking.

She gives me a small nod. "Not long after my mother died, my father sent me away to an all-girls boarding school in Utah."

"So this private school," I start, but she doesn't let me finish.

"Actually it was a boarding school for troubled girls, so it was kind of rough at times." And then she quietly adds, "I was bullied quite a lot."

Dante looks over at her with a sad, understanding smile, and I frown. Once again, Dante knows more than me, and it pisses me off to no end.

"And you were there for how long?" I question, curiosity seeping through my pores.

"Until I turned eighteen." She picks up her fork and tries the lasagna. She chews slowly, closes her eyes and then rolls them to the heavens above. "Greta is an amazing cook. How did she not make you fat when you were a teenager?" she jokes, but I know it's simply an attempt to change the subject.

I want to laugh, but I'm still in shock at the revelations laid out before me this evening. "I ran five miles every night after dinner," I tell her in all seriousness. I leave out the part where that was part of my brutal regimen placed upon me by my father. Five miles first thing in the morning, another five miles at night, training in between. It was grueling and never-ending, but my father wanted to make sure I was ready for war.

"Ah," Verona whispers before returning to her meal.

I glance at Benito, who raises a brow at me. He's wondering what the fuck I'm getting on about, but I can't even explain it to myself. All this time I was...*wrong* about Verona. And I'm never wrong. Right from the start I pegged her as a spoiled, rich, little princess. Nothing was ever good enough for her. When, in fact, she isn't spoiled at all. Her father sent her away after her mother died. So for years, she suffered in a boarding school states away from the only family she had left. She was all alone. That explains the attachment to her mother's dress. Hell, it explains a lot actually.

And once again, I feel like we have more in common than I ever thought we could. After my mother died, I felt like I had no one. Hell, Greta was the only one who acted like she gave a shit, and she was hired help. My father definitely wasn't around to be a parent. He put all of his time and effort into the mob's dealings and trying to bring down the Morettis.

Verona asks, "Is everything all right?"

I realize I've been staring at her and not speaking. "Your great aunt," I say before clearing my throat. "She was rich?"

Verona narrows her eyes at my question. "Yes, she had money, I suppose. Not that I ever saw a dime of it. She could stretch a dollar farther than anyone with the amount of thrift shopping we did over the years I lived with her. I don't think she ever stepped foot inside a store that didn't have *dollar* or *resale* in the title."

"I don't think she ever paid full price for anything in her entire life," Dante pipes up.

The puzzle pieces slowly start to click into place in mind. The suitcase full of "rags", as I called them. They were her only possessions. Verona was never spoiled. No one ever treated her like a princess. No, she fought to survive, having been bullied most of her life and dealing with the death of her mother in secret.

When I think about the way I've continued to bully her... throwing her things away...treating her like shit, like she's less than me...

Suddenly, I've lost my appetite. I pull my phone out of my pocket and glance at it before I lie to everyone and tell them, "I need to take this." Then, I stand and walk quickly out of the room.

Tucking the phone back in my pocket, I pace the hallway, listening to Verona's melodic voice drifting out of the dining room. Greta has come back in, and Verona is praising her cooking.

Why didn't I see this sweet, innocent side of my wife before now?

Because you didn't want to see it.

I had made up my mind that she was a certain way, and I couldn't see the forest for the trees.

Just hearing her voice makes me feel even worse, so I retreat into my office and lock myself away.

It's a half an hour later when Benito comes in. "Something wrong?" he asks. "You didn't finish dinner. Who was on the phone?"

"No one was on the phone," I tell him with a sigh. "I faked the phone call to get the hell out of the room."

Benito is quiet for a while as he tries to figure out why I'm acting so bizarre.

"She's not spoiled," I say, which causes him to look even more confused. I shake my head and tell him, "I thought Verona was some rich, spoiled, little princess. Nothing was ever good enough for her. She never had to run a dishwasher or lift a hand in the kitchen; hence, why she covered mine in bubbles."

"Ah, you were wrong about her," Benito concludes. "And you're just now finding out about all of this. Why?"

"Because I had a predisposed idea of her in my head, and I was too fucking stubborn to let go of it," I confess. "Because I wanted to hate her," I add.

Benito nods. "So now you know the truth."

"And what the hell do I do with it?" I ask.

"Start over," he suggests.

"Start over?" I ask, confused.

"Yeah. It's not too late. You can make amends with your wife."

But is it too late? Verona has told me before that she hates me. With good reason. I know that now. But I don't know if I can just start over with her. How do I make amends?

"Buy her a gift," Benito suggests. "Women love new things, like jewelry."

I shake my head. "Verona isn't like most women." I smile at that realization. My wife isn't into pretty, shiny toys. No, she's into sentimental things. And I think I have the perfect idea. "Get out," I tell him abruptly.

Benito doesn't even question me. He simply walks out of my office, leaving me alone to my thoughts and the crazy plan swimming in my head.

CHAPTER 35

Verona

AFTER THE NIGHT that Luca suddenly left dinner, I didn't see him again for a couple of days. I have no idea who was on the other end of that phone call, but I hope it's nothing serious. And I hope it's not him plotting revenge against my father, you know, the usual Vitale thing to do.

It's late in the evening when Benito informs me dinner will be served outside tonight. Confused, I try to ask him questions, but he walks away before I can get any answers.

I can't help but get excited about eating outside, though. The property is massive, so hopefully we'll be in a place where we'll be able to see all the stars. I've missed staring up at the night sky, which was an almost nightly ritual for me before I married Luca.

After I shower and get dressed for dinner in a simple navy-blue dress and matching heels, I bump into Dante in the hallway on the way to his room. "Are you changing for dinner?" I ask him.

"I already ate," he says with a furrowed brow.

"Oh." I just assumed the four of us would be dining again, but no matter. It must just be Benito, Luca and me. I know Luca can't stand to be alone with me in the same room for very long, so he'll use Benito and whoever else as a buffer so that he can tolerate me during the meal.

"I'm going to bed early. Goodnight, V," Dante tells me before leaning in and kissing my cheek.

I'm taken aback by the gesture, but it makes me smile. "Goodnight," I call after him before I make my descent down the stairs.

Sure enough, Benito is waiting for me. "Shall we?" he asks, extending his arm like a gentleman.

"We shall," I say with a giggle.

Benito leads me outside the patio, and I hold his arm a little tighter than necessary as we walk past the swimming pool.

"Don't worry. I won't let you fall in," Benito reassures me in a whisper.

"I'm surprised Luca didn't want to dine in the water tonight as a cruel joke on me," I tell him with a huff.

Benito is quiet for several steps before he says, "Be patient with him, Verona. Everything will work out in the end. You'll see."

I'm about to ask him what he means by that; but then we round the corner, and I stop dead in my tracks.

The backyard has been transformed into some magical place with fairy lights, a small, white tent with a table and two chairs. I'm in awe as Benito pulls me forward, and it almost feels like I'm floating to the most serene place in the world.

There's even a blanket with pillows laid out in the grass, and I am practically bursting with excitement. "Benny, did you do all of this?" I ask him.

"No. He did," he says, gesturing to the tent.

And that's when Luca steps out, looking brutally handsome in a black tailored suit. He's sans tie, and the buttons at the top of his black button-up shirt are undone. He looks like he just stepped out of the cover of GQ magazine, and I can't help but admit that my husband looks *hot*.

Benito carefully drops my arm and walks away, leaving Luca and I alone. My hands fidget at my sides. I don't know why I'm so incredibly nervous all of a sudden.

Luca motions to the table and chairs. "Please. Sit," he says.

He pulls out a chair for me; and when I'm seated, he slides me in closer to the table. "Thank you," I whisper to him.

I watch his every move as he goes to the other side and takes a seat across from me. I look around the gauze tent, which is decorated with more fairy lights than I've ever seen in my entire life.

"Benny said you did this," I say, my eyes darting around before finally landing on Luca. "*When* did you do this?"

"Today." He glances around and grimaces before confessing, "Took a long time too."

"I bet." Even though I want to let my guard down around Luca, I know I can't. This could just be another ploy to get me to trust him. I think back to the party, in the back of the car...when he tricked me into saying all those things so that Dante could hear them. Nothing Luca ever does is out of the kindness of his heart, so what does this grand gesture mean for me? He must want something big in return.

Before I can question him, a few members of the kitchen staff come out with our entrees. When they lift the silver lids, I'm expecting some fancy Italian dish. But I'm shocked when I see...a cheeseburger and French fries?

I laugh out loud at the sight. "What..." I can't even finish my sentence. "I haven't had a burger in so long," I say, my mouth watering at the sight.

"I thought we could try something *different* tonight," he offers.

I don't even wait for him to start. Instead, I pick up that big, juicy burger and bite into it. It's cooked to perfection and topped with all of my favorite things — lettuce, pickles, tomato and the perfect combo of mayonnaise and ketchup.

After I'm done chewing my first bite, I ask him, "How did you know I would like this?"

"It was just a hunch. After you told me you didn't really grow up around here, I figured burger and fries would be your go-to meal."

I nod in agreement. Whenever I was feeling down about stuff, I would always go to the nearest burger joint and indulge. It was only ever a temporary fix; but while I was eating, I could just pretend that everything was...normal.

I watch in amusement as Luca rolls up his suit sleeves and grabs his burger. He takes a hearty bite, the juices running down his stubbled chin as he chews. He's quick to grab a napkin and wipe his face, and the smile he gives me when he sees me watching is breathtaking. He looks so boyish and carefree. I would never assume that the man sitting across from me is a dangerous mafia boss.

No, right now it feels like we're on a date. A *real* date. Just two people getting to know each other without a care in the world.

The fries are fresh cut, salty and oh so good. I shovel a couple in my mouth after dipping them in ketchup, of course. "I'm assuming Greta didn't cook this?" I ask.

Amusement crinkles the corners of his eyes when he shakes his head. "No, I had one of the other cooks prepare this. Greta was upset with me when I told her we didn't want her pasta carbonara tonight."

"Maybe she can make it for us tomorrow," I tell him with a shy grin.

"Sure," he agrees.

We eat our cheeseburgers and fries in silence for a while. I'm actually enjoying Luca's company tonight. He doesn't seem so...tense and overbearing. Usually he has this aura around him that's so unapproachable. But tonight, everything feels different. I still don't know what to make of it all, though. My guard is definitely still up, because I've been tricked before by my husband.

After we're done eating, the staff brings out a mint chocolate cake, my favorite. My eyes bounce up to meet Luca's. "How did you know?"

He shrugs with a smile.

"Dante told you, didn't he?" I ask.

Instantly, the smile on Luca's face turns into a frown. "No," he says, his eyes narrowing. "Actually you chose that cake the first time we had a meal together."

"Oh." I shrug off his reaction to me mentioning Dante's name and dig into the cake. I savor every bite, even licking the fork clean after I'm done. "That was delicious."

Luca barely touched his cake, but he doesn't seem put off by it. It's almost like he wants me to be happy tonight, for some odd reason. I just wish I could figure him out.

After the plates are cleared from the table, I'm sipping on a very expensive red wine when Luca picks up something from underneath the table and places it near me on the white tablecloth. I stare at the wrapped gift in confusion. "What's this for?" I ask, feeling skeptical already.

"I wanted to give you something," he says before clearing his throat. "I haven't exactly treated you fairly since you arrived here, and I'm hoping to make amends." His eyes shift to mine before he adds, "Starting tonight."

The present is wrapped beautifully in white paper and teal ribbon. I carefully remove the ribbon and open the lid. My brows furrow when I inspect the contents of the box. It's some kind of photo album.

Curious, I pull out the album and open it to the first page. It's a beautiful black and white photograph of Luca and I standing at the altar in the church on the day we were married. Our eyes are locked in some kind of weird trance. I think it might have been the first moment I looked at him. The expression in our faces is a mixture of curiosity and amazement. The photographer captured it perfectly, and I'm taken aback by the raw magnetism we felt in that moment together without even realizing it.

"I didn't even notice the photographer," I admit to him in a soft tone. I was so disheveled and nervous that day that I wasn't able to focus on anything other than the fact that I needed to walk down that aisle and marry a total stranger.

I flip through the next few pages. There are more pictures of the wedding, people in attendance, and my father walking me down the aisle, which makes tears well up in my eyes. There are even candid photos of the back of my dress and veil and my bouquet.

"Wow," I gasp when I stare at all the photos in awe. "This is amazing," I tell Luca.

"You like it?"

I look up to meet his eyes, and I can see the trepidation in his expression. He really wants me to like this. "Did you...did you put this album together yourself?" I ask him.

"Yes," he says with a nod. "Do you like it?" he asks again.

"No, I don't like it." I can see his expression fall right before I tell him, "I absolutely love it."

His lips stretch into a grin, and I can't help but smile back. Flipping back to the beginning, I look at the photographs all over again, one by one. I'm so enamored by the album that I don't even realize Luca left the table until I hear him calling my name from somewhere nearby.

I glance over to where his voice came from, and I see that he's lying on the blanket in the grass that I spotted earlier. His suit jacket is now gone, and his black button-up shirt sleeves are rolled up, showcasing his muscular forearms and tattoos.

I gently set the photo album down on the table, and I slip out of my high heels before sinking my bare feet into the cool grass. I walk over to him and stare down at him, switching from foot to foot nervously.

Luca pats the blanket beside him with a warm smile on his face. I only hesitate a second longer before I sink down to my knees and lie beside him on the blanket.

"Give me one sec," he tells me before pushing a button on a remote. The fairy lights suddenly turn off, and then we're surrounded by darkness. "Now...look up," he whispers from beside me.

And when I look up to the night sky, I gasp in awe at the millions of stars in the sky.

CHAPTER 36

Luca

"AND THAT'S URSA Minor right there, or the Little Dipper," Verona babbles away from beside me on the blanket.

I've been smiling for what feels like an hour or more since she started excitedly pointing out every constellation in the sky. I had a strong feeling that stars would be her thing, because I knew what kind of books she was reading in our library. When I went in late one night, she was asleep and curled up with book about constellations, the universe, and aliens, of all things.

My wife is a space nut. And I kind of like it.

"Show me more," I tell her. I could listen to her talk about stars all night long.

She points to another constellation. "That's Perseus, the hero. He rescued Andromeda, the princess. And she is right there," she says, pointing to a nearby cluster of stars.

"So they are together forever," I say, turning my head to look at her.

"Yeah," she says with a smile.

"You know a lot about stars," I remark.

She's quiet for several seconds before she finally speaks. "Well, when I was at boarding school, I would sneak out at night and go lie in the grass behind the buildings. I always thought that maybe my mom was up there somewhere, looking back down at me." Her eyes get glassy as she stares up at the sky. "I missed her so much. It was the only way I could feel close to her."

I hate that she had to go through so much alone at such a young age. I was a little older when my mother died, but it was still rough. At least I had people, like Greta, making an effort at trying to get me out of my depressed funk. Verona had no one. She relied on the stars to make her feel better. No wonder she's so obsessed with stars and the universe. She wanted to believe in something, feel something.

It's scary how much we have in common.

My hand reaches for hers. Her skin is cool, a much lower temperature than mine, and it feels so fragile and delicate in mine. I intertwine our fingers, and I love how soft her skin is against mine.

"Luca?" she whispers.

"Yeah," I whisper back.

"Why are you doing this?"

Her question catches me off-guard. "What do you mean?"

"The dinner, this, all of this. What's the catch?"

I release her hand and sit up slowly, staring down at her. "Why does there have to be a catch?" I ask, my eyes narrowing.

"Because there always is with you," she says, sitting up.

She doesn't trust me. She thinks I'm doing this with ill intentions. And that pisses me off. Reaching for the remote, I turn the fairy lights back on and stand. "I just wanted to have a nice evening with you, Verona. Is that so hard to ask for?"

Fuming, I storm into the house. I worked so damn hard to make amends with her, and she just ruined it all with a few words.

By the time I'm in my bedroom, I'm regretting even doing anything nice for her. Fuck, I shouldn't have listened to Benito.

Start over, he had said.

Start over?

Maybe we can't start over. We had such a rough fucking start to this marriage. Maybe there is no saving it. And I don't know why the fuck I thought I could try.

CHAPTER 37

Verona

WHEN LUCA TURNED on the fairy lights, I could see the hurt in his eyes before he stormed off towards the house. I sit there for a long time, thinking over every single detail of what happened tonight. Luca has always been like a snake curled up in the corner of the room, just waiting to strike. I was waiting for the strike. But I guess this time it was never actually coming.

He did this...all of this...for *me*. Like maybe he truly wanted to make amends. I don't know why now, all of a sudden, but does that really matter? He was *trying*. And that's better than I can say for myself.

I grab the photo album from the table and my heels I discarded in the grass and rush into the house. I drop my things down near the door and make my way upstairs. I see light under his bedroom door on the way to mine, so I stop and knock gently.

The door opens, and my breath catches in the back of my throat.

My eyes slowly peruse him. Luca changed out of his suit, and now he's only wearing a pair of light gray sweatpants, which are hanging dangerously low on his hips, showcasing a perfect V. His broad, muscled chest and abs look like they were carved out of stone, belonging to some Greek god, and his arms are covered in sleeve tattoos going clear down to his fingers. The ink is black and white and violently beautiful, just like him.

My brain stutters for a few seconds before I finally blurt out, "I'm sorry!"

He takes a step towards me, leans down and whispers into my ear, "Like I told you before, Verona, if you come to my room in the middle of the night, it better be because you either want to sit on my face or get on your knees." When he pulls back, I see a glint of amusement in his gray eyes. "So which is it?"

I take a step back from him.

He cocks a brow before taking a step towards me. "If you run, I'll just chase you, Verona."

My heartbeat picks up speed at his words. And suddenly, I want him to chase me. I want to feel like the prey to this predator. Turning, I run down the hall to my bedroom and burst through the door with Luca right on my heels.

I squeal in surprise when he tackles me onto the bed. I twist in his hold until I'm on my back looking up at him and he's straddling my hips. One of his large hands has my wrists pinned to the bed above my head. I struggle, but it's no use.

Leaning down, he licks the side of my neck. When he stops at my ear, he whispers, "I like when you fight me, honey."

I practically melt when he uses the term of endearment with me. He's never called me anything like that before.

"Honey?" I question.

"Mmhmm. Honey, like the color of your eyes. Sweet, like your scent that drives me fucking crazy."

His lips trail kisses from my ear to my mouth, and then he's devouring me. His tongue presses against my lips, demanding entry, and I let him. His tongue sweeps inside, tangling with mine. And by the time he pulls away, I'm a quivering mess.

"Take off your dress, honey," he tells me, sitting back on his heels.

I climb off the bed and pull the dress up and over my head, throwing it to the floor. Shyly, I try to cover my matching navy-blue bra and thong with my hands, but Luca shakes his head.

"I want to see you. All of you."

I swallow hard, my nerves getting the best of me. Slowly, I unhook my bra, and soon it joins my dress on the floor. My hands are shaking as I remove my thong. I've never been naked in front of a man before, and I never knew how nervous it would make me.

"Fuck, you're beautiful," Luca whispers. He pulls down the waistband of his sweatpants, and his cock bobs free. My eyes widen at the sight of it as he begins to stroke it. "See how hard you make me, honey?"

I can't look away as he fists his cock, stroking the length over and over again with his large hand.

"Get on the bed. I want to taste every inch of you," he says before tucking his cock back into his sweats.

I lie down on the mattress. And when I try to cover myself again, Luca frowns. "Keep your hands above you. Hold on to the headboard," he instructs.

My breathing is unsteady as I do as he says. I grip onto the metal frame, holding on for dear life. I've been waiting for this moment for a long time. I never knew who my first would be, but I never in a million years thought it would be Luca Vitale. And I can't help the fact that I'm scared out of my mind. What if he isn't gentle? What if he hurts me?

Squeezing my eyes shut, effectively blocking out the world, I give in to the rest of my senses to guide me through this.

Luca leans over me, trailing his lips, mouth and tongue from my neck, down my jawline, to my chest and then my breasts. The heat radiating from his body is only fueling the fire stirring deep inside of me.

He kisses the side of my right breast gently, trailing his lips over my heated skin. Then, I feel his mouth on my nipple before he bites. *Hard.*

I cry out in surprise, and then I hear his soft chuckle.

He gives the same treatment to my other nipple until they're both aching and hard to the point of being almost painful. His lips move to my mouth while he kneads my breasts softly, running his calloused thumbs over my sensitive, pebbled nipples.

I groan into his mouth as he devours me, shoving his tongue inside and tasting me. And, oh, yes, I want more of him. So much more.

Luca pulls away, and my eyes snap open to watch him moving down between my legs. He gently parts my thighs and places a trail of kisses from my knee to my inner thigh. I'm shaking with anticipation when he leans down and places a kiss on my mound.

"You have the prettiest little cunt," he says, his filthy words setting me on fire. I wriggle under him, unable to control myself. I want his mouth on me again. I want to feel that undiluted pleasure that only he can give me.

His fingertip strokes the outside of my lips, teasing me. "Tell me what you want, honey. I want to hear the words coming from your naughty mouth."

"Please," I beg.

"Tell me," he demands, teasing me relentlessly. His fingers are so close to where I need them to be. *So close.* "Tell me what you want."

"Touch me, lick me, fuck me," I cry out, my words running together.

He chuckles darkly. "In that order?" His fingertip grazes my clit, and the sensation makes me groan out loud. "I think that can be arranged."

He spreads my lips and touches me so gently and softly that he's driving me insane. I'm practically climbing the wall with madness when I cry out, "Luca, please, I need your mouth on me!"

His fingers disappear, and they are instantly replaced with his tongue. I bite my lip to hold back a scream as he devours me between my legs. Oh god, it feels so good. I grip the bars of the metal headboard until my arms ache as I hold on for dear life.

"Fuck, you taste sweet like honey too," he remarks, drawing my attention to him. His tongue darts out of his mouth to lick his lower lip before he uses that devilish weapon on me again.

I'm a trembling mess as he sweeps his tongue over my clit again and again. My head shakes back and forth from the insane amount of pleasure building in my body.

"I want you to come for me, Verona," Luca says from between my thighs.

My frantic cries escalate as he begins working his tongue over my clit again. Unable to hold back any longer, I suddenly shatter around his mouth, crying out his name.

I go limp on the bed, my hands releasing the metal bedframe and falling beside me. My limbs feel like they're made of Jell-O, and I don't think I could move even if I wanted to.

I watch as Luca leaves the bed. He bends down to strip off his sweatpants and then stands up. My breath catches in my throat at the sight of his thick and long cock hanging between his muscular thighs.

Luca strokes himself once, twice, as he climbs onto the bed between my legs. Planting a hand beside my head, he leans down. "I touched you," he says, planting a kiss to my left breast. "I licked you," he tells me, moving to my right breast to place another kiss. "And there's only one thing left for us to do, honey."

He stares at me, waiting for me to say it. "Fuck," I say, the curse sounding foreign coming from my mouth.

"Yeah," he agrees with a smirk.

My body is vibrating with anticipation and lust under him as he positions himself between my thighs. He lines up his cock and then enters me in one, long stroke. I cry out when he tears through my virginity, the pain and pleasure both incredible at the same time.

Luca suddenly stills above me, and the only sound in the room is my rapid breathing. I swear I can hear our heartbeats it's so quiet.

Reluctantly, I look up at him, and he's staring at me with an unreadable look on his face. "You're a virgin," he whispers. When I nod, he curses under his breath. "You should have told me," he hisses.

"I'm...I'm sorry," I answer nervously.

"What have you done with your previous boyfriends?" he demands.

"I-I-I never had a boyfriend. You were my first kiss. You've been my first...everything," I admit, my face burning with embarrassment.

His brows dip in confusion as he slowly absorbs my words. And then his mouth is suddenly crashing down on mine, taking me roughly, possessively as his hips start to move. I cry out, and he swallows down my moans as his huge cock gently rocks in and out of me.

Suddenly, he pulls back, his gray eyes dark from his blown pupils. "You're mine," he tells me vehemently.

"I'm yours," I whisper in agreement.

"Only mine." His thumb traces over my bottom lip, and he watches the movement before his eyes meet mine again. "Tell me."

"Only yours."

And then his lips are back on mine, his tongue shoving its way past my lips, claiming me and completely devouring me. His hips piston frantically as he picks up the pace, and my nails dig into his shoulders as the pleasure starts to build up inside of me, driving me crazy with desire. He feels impossibly thick inside me, and I groan as he stretches me.

"Luca!" I cry out as I detonate around him, my inner walls spasming and clenching him so hard that it causes him to curse.

He kisses my lips, my face, my neck, my chest as I come apart beneath him, the torturous rhythm of his hips causing an endless wave of pleasure to wrack my body.

"Verona," he whispers in awe as he stares down at me. He fucks me slowly and deeply, chasing his release. He slams into me one final time before he quickly pulls out. His gray eyes flutter shut as he gives in to his own pleasure, his warm seed spilling out over my stomach and pussy.

Rolling onto the bed beside me, he collapses against the mattress. "Holy fuck," he hisses. "That was..." His voice trails off, unable to find the right words for what just happened between us.

"Yeah," I agree with a giggle. I knew sex with Luca would be good, but I didn't expect the pleasure to be that mind-blowing. My limbs feel heavy, like I wouldn't be able to move even if I wanted to. I feel like I ran a marathon, and I don't know why, but I feel deliriously happy in that moment.

My happiness is short-lived, however, when I feel Luca's weight shift in the bed as he gets up and walks away. Tears fill my eyes as I realize he's not going to stay the night in my bed. I mean...why would he? I don't know why I expected to be cuddled after sex. That's not who Luca is.

Suddenly, I feel something warm and wet between my legs as the bed dips beside me, and I gasp before I realize it's Luca.

"Let me clean you up," he whispers soothingly to me.

I watch as he gently rubs a warm washcloth between my legs and over my stomach. "Thank you," I murmur.

After he's done, he takes the washcloth to the bathroom, turns off the light and comes back to bed, surprising me when he crawls in and pulls me to his chest.

I close my eyes, listening to his heartbeat as it lulls me into a deep sleep.

I don't get much sleep that night; however, because several times Luca wakes me up by entering me or licking my pussy until I'm coming so hard I see stars.

It feels like a dream, but I swear I hear him tell me, "I'll never get enough of you," before I finally pass out from complete and utter exhaustion.

CHAPTER 38

Luca

THE NEXT MORNING, I wake up with Verona curled up in my arms. I've never slept with a woman in the same bed before, so at first I'm confused and disoriented by her warmth enveloping me. I stare down at the top of her head and study her beautiful face and the way her long, dark lashes are fanned out over her cheeks.

God, she's beautiful, I think to myself.

Something changed between the two of us last night. To know that I'm her first for everything, that she trusted me enough to give up her virginity makes me feel...I don't know...protective of her. And it's more than just a possessive feeling like I don't want anyone else to play with my toy. No, I want to protect her in a way that makes me want to kill anyone for looking at her the wrong way.

Sure, I still view her father as my enemy. But just like Benito told me the other night, Verona is innocent, just like my mother was. I need to stop taking my anger out on people who don't deserve it. And Verona definitely doesn't deserve that.

I pull her closer to me and kiss the top of her head. She doesn't even stir. No, she's fucking exhausted. And she has good reason to be. I couldn't get enough of her last night. I would wake up with my cock aching for her or my tongue watering for a taste of her. I devoured her pussy too many times to count. And the way I was able to just wring orgasm after orgasm out of her made me feel like a powerful sorcerer. She came for me on my command. Only me.

I pull her impossibly closer, my cock longing to be inside of her again even though I had her several times last night. I know I need to give her a break today. I have no doubt that she'll be sore when she wakes up.

But as soon as she's ready, I'll have her again and again and again. Last night wasn't enough to quench my thirst. I'm practically starving for her.

Reluctantly, I roll her over to the other side of the bed and slowly crawl out. I stare around the bedroom. It's opulent; there's no doubt about that. But it's time for a change. Knowing that she's in here all alone every night is no longer an option for me. I need her close. Having her in my arms last night and waking up with her in them this morning was an indescribable feeling, and I need to experience it more than once.

I dress quickly and fish my cell phone out of my pocket, texting Benito some instructions. And then, after looking longingly back at Verona one last time, I return to my room for a much-needed shower. Even though I would love to, I can't stay in bed with her all day long, ravishing her. She needs a break from me even though I know I won't be able to give her much of one.

CHAPTER 39

Verona

I WAKE UP the next morning...or afternoon? The sun streaming through the windows makes me think that it's way too late for morning. Panicking, I sit up and glance at the clock on the nightstand. It's nearly two in the afternoon. I slept in. *Really* slept in. But after last night, I was so exhausted that I'm sure I could have slept even longer.

Swinging my legs over the bed, I stand up and instantly feel the soreness between my legs. I have a pressing urge to pee, and I go to the bathroom to take care of my business.

After I'm done, I wash my hands and stare at myself in the mirror. My hair is all messed up and out of place, my lips are swollen, and I look like I was thoroughly fucked. A smile lifts the corners of my mouth as I remember that I truly was. Luca couldn't keep his hands to himself last night, and I know that he spent the entire night with me.

He left at some point this morning, though. Not that I can blame him. I slept most of the day away, and Luca has a business to run.

I walk out of the bathroom and go to the closet to look for an outfit for the day before I take my shower. But when I turn on the light, I realize all my clothes are gone. The only thing left hanging is a robe. Shocked, I grab the robe and wrap it around my naked body.

Walking back into the bedroom, I realize the clothes I had on last night are gone. Running into the bathroom, I glance into the shower. Not surprisingly, everything is gone from in there as well.

Cinching the tie around me tighter, I try to wrack my brain as to what is going on. Is Luca throwing me out? All of my stuff is gone, so that can be the only explanation. He screwed me, and now he's gotten his fill of me. I'm no longer useful to him.

Fuming, I stalk out of the room and head downstairs. I pass Dante on the way, and his eyes look me up and down before his dark brows furrow.

He stops me in a hallway. "What's wrong? What did he do to you?" he asks quickly.

"I need to talk to Luca. Where is he?" I ask hurriedly.

He motions over his shoulder towards the kitchen. "He just finished lunch."

I walk in the direction of the kitchen with Dante on my heels. I burst through the swinging door and see Luca smiling, talking to one of the head chefs. He looks like he's in a good mood. Probably because he got laid and the fact that he's probably moving in a new girl soon enough to take my place.

I storm into the room, and Luca turns, his smile fading as he stares at me in confusion. "Verona," he says before his eyes dart to Dante behind me.

"You took my things!" I stop an inch in front of Luca, hating the fact that I have to look up at him to meet his gaze. "Are you throwing me out? It wasn't bad enough you had to fuck me between my legs. You have to fuck me by kicking me out of your house too?" I practically scream.

The entire room is silent as Luca stares down at me. A smirk pulls at the corner of his mouth, and I want to smack it right off of him. "I moved your stuff into my room, Verona," he says calmly. "And just so everyone knows," he says, glancing around the crowded room, "Verona is not going anywhere." He makes it a point to look in the direction of Dante behind me before his eyes return to mine. "Now, if everyone will please leave the room, I think my wife and I have a misunderstanding we need to correct."

It doesn't take long for the staff, cooks and Dante to clear the room.

"I didn't know you'd wake up so...hostile," Luca says with a grin. He steps forward, forcing me backwards until my back hits the wall. Then, he's caging me in with his arms. "Can you still feel me inside of you?"

I nod in response as my core clenches.

He leans down to my ear and whispers, "Are you sore?"

"Yes," I whisper with a shudder.

"That's a shame," he says softly before placing a kiss on my neck below my ear. "I'll give you some time to recover, but I can't wait long, Verona. I need to be inside of you again. Soon," he threatens before taking a step back away from me.

His phone rings, and he's quick to pull it from his pocket. When he glances at the screen, he tells me, "I need to take this. Why don't you go to my...*our* room and get ready?" he asks, correcting himself. "I want to take you somewhere nice for dinner tonight."

Then he walks away from me while he takes the call, leaving me breathless. Damn him. I wanted to be mad at him, but he turned my world upside down once again. He moved my stuff into his room. No. *Our room*. That's what he had said. Our room.

I'm practically on cloud nine when I leave the kitchen. I'm barely halfway across the dining room when someone grabs my arm and hauls me backwards.

Dante's piercing dark glare is on me as he stares me down. His hand is around my arm in a bruising grip as he asks, "You fucked him?"

"Dante, what are you doing?"

"Answer me!" he demands, gripping me tighter and no doubt leaving finger-shaped bruises on my skin.

"He is my husband, Dante," I explain quickly, grimacing from the pain. I can see the possessiveness in his eyes and exactly what Luca has been warning me about. Dante likes me for more than a friend, but I've never returned his feelings, and I definitely won't now that I'm married. "Let me go. You're hurting me!" I hiss.

My words seem to have an effect on him, because he finally releases me. "You're really taking this lie of a marriage too far, V," he says.

"It's not a lie." Not anymore. But I don't add that last thought. Maybe it felt like a farce at first, because Luca and I are so different, and he treated me so badly at first. But last night something changed between us. I don't feel inferior to him anymore. I feel like I'm his equal. He wants me as much as I want him, and I think we could honestly make this marriage work even if we were forced into it at the beginning. "I just want to be happy," I confess to Dante, who sneers at my words.

"It's only a matter of time before he breaks your heart. Don't come crying to me when he does," he says before walking out of the room.

His words stay with me for a long time after that. Will Luca break my heart? I mean, it's highly likely. But we are legally bound by marriage. It's not like he can divorce me or walk away. We're stuck in this union together. And if last night is any indication as to the kind of life we could have together, then I'm willing to take a chance...even if it means getting hurt in the end.

CHAPTER 40

Verona

"YOU'RE BEING QUIET," Luca says from across the table.

I look up at him, meeting his silver gaze. "I'm sorry," I tell him sincerely. After Dante's confrontation and his refusal to accompany us to dinner, feigning illness instead, I've been distracted. But Dante isn't part of the equation at this moment, and I know I need to focus on my husband.

"Penny for your thoughts?" Luca offers.

I want to tell him about Dante and what he said and did, but I don't. For some reason, just like when we were kids, I want to protect Dante. I don't want him to get in trouble. And I have a feeling that if Luca knew Dante put his hands on me and left bruises, which took me twenty minutes to cover up with makeup, he would be upset. Well, more than upset. Hell, Luca would probably burn the world to the ground with his fury.

"It's nothing," I tell him with a wave of my hand, dismissing the idea. I glance around the empty Italian restaurant. "So, how did you get us reservations like this?"

"I know the owner, and he owed me a favor," he says with a grin.

"So, he cleared out his entire restaurant on a busy Saturday night for you. Wow, must have been one heck of a favor."

"It was," Luca says seriously, and I can't help but wonder what the circumstances are. But I know he probably wouldn't tell me, so I don't press. "Are you enjoying the food?" he asks as he takes a bite of his carbonara.

"Immensely," I admit. The caprese salad was delicious and so is the main course I opted for — chicken parmesan. "I haven't had this since I was a kid."

"Your mom used to make it?" he asks.

I give him a nod and instantly miss her. When she died, it was like a part of me died with her. And I don't think that hole in my heart has ever healed. "She was a great cook. My father used to complain about how much weight he gained when he ate her cooking," I say with a laugh.

Luca stares at me with a thoughtful look on his face. "You miss her."

"So much."

"I miss my mother too," he says, and I'm surprised by his vulnerable admission.

I reach across the table and take his hand in mine, squeezing it gently for support. He gazes at me for several long seconds before squeezing back. I can't help but wonder if he still blames my family for his loss, but I don't want to bring it up and spoil our evening together. It's been an amazing night with Luca, and I honestly feel like I'm on a real date with my husband.

The waiter chooses that moment to reappear. "Dessert, *signore?*" he asks.

Luca's heated gaze lands on me when he says, "I know what I want for dessert." Then he adds, "But it's not on the menu." To the waiter, he says, "Leave us. We're done for this evening."

"Yes, of course, *signore*," the man says before disappearing from the room.

I swallow hard as Luca stands up from the table, dropping his napkin down on his discarded food. He extends a hand to me, and I take it, my hand shaking from anticipation.

Suddenly, he turns me around in his arms and bends me over the table. The wine glasses spill from the sudden movement, the dark red liquid soaking into the white linen tablecloth.

Nervously, I glance around the room and at the windows. The shades are pulled down, but someone could still walk in at any moment. "Luca!" I whisper in panic.

But he's not listening. Instead, he drops to his knees behind me, and I feel the air brushing my backside as he lifts up the skirt of my black dress. His hands slide up and down my legs as I try to steady them in my high heels.

"*Perfetta*," he whispers before placing a kiss on the back of each of my thighs. His fingers hook into my thong and pull it down my legs gently. "Lift your foot," he instructs, and I do, as he removes my thong. "Now spread your legs," he tells me, his voice deep and gruff with desire.

I spread my legs a little, but then I hear him *tsking* at me.

"Wider, Verona," he says. "Yes, that's my naughty girl," he says when he's finally satisfied.

I expect him to lick me then, but he surprises me when he stands up. I start to move, but he places a hand on my shoulder. "Stay right there," he whispers. "Fuck, you look gorgeous bent over the table like that." He circles around me, and I can hear a groan escape his lips. "I should tell the waiter to come back in here so he can witness your beautiful pussy and ass on display." I open my mouth to protest, but then he quickly says, "But I don't want another man to see what's mine."

His possessiveness sends a shiver through me. My legs are trembling in anticipation when I feel the heat of his body again. He drops to his knees once more, and he doesn't waste time before licking me from my clit to my tight, little hole. I gasp at the feeling. It feels so wrong, but, god, it feels good.

"I'm going to claim this too," he says before pressing his thumb against my hole. "Soon," he threatens.

His thumb keeps the pressure on my tight puckered hole as his tongue finds my clit, licking me into oblivion. His tongue, mouth and lips feel so good against me that I turn into a boneless mess, gripping the linen tablecloth beneath me in a death grip. "Luca!" I cry out.

His thumb penetrates me, making the sensations tenfold, and I suck in a strangled breath. "Oh god, oh god!" I cry out.

"God can't help you now," he growls from behind me before his mouth returns to my clit.

Incoherent words tumble out of my mouth as the pleasure builds up inside of me until I finally reach the peak and drop over the edge. I shatter into a million pieces on his tongue as he fucks my tight hole with his thumb, dragging the pleasure out of me with every movement.

A loud moan rips from my throat as the pleasurable waves keep crashing through my body. "Please!" I beg, and I don't even know what I'm asking for at this point.

But he makes the decision for me, pulling out his thumb and licking my clit slowly once...twice...three times before he finally stops.

My fingers grip the tablecloth, afraid to let go because my legs feel like jelly, and I don't think they could support my weight right now.

"That was the best dessert I've ever had," I hear Luca say from behind me. He wipes his mouth with his napkin and then gently pulls down my dress. He doesn't put my thong back on me, so I have no idea where that went.

"Are you ready to leave?" he asks calmly like nothing even happened, like he didn't just completely wreck me in the middle of the restaurant.

"I...I don't think...I can walk," I say between staggered breaths.

I see several hundred-dollar bills flutter to the table before he lifts me up and into his arms. My head rests against his chest as we leave the restaurant.

Benito is waiting at the car, and he flashes us a rare, shy smile as he opens the back door. "Dinner was good?" he asks.

"It was good. But the dessert was fucking delicious," Luca says, making me blush.

Once we're in the backseat, Luca pulls me to him, and I fall asleep in his lap on the ride home. My last coherent thought is that this man, my husband, is going to be the death of me.

CHAPTER 41

Verona

IT'S THE MIDDLE of the night when I wake up in bed. Alone. Wrapping a kimono around me, I make my way downstairs. A soft light is shining under the door of Luca's office, so I knock gently. A moment later, the lock disengages, and I enter.

Luca is sitting at his desk, his attention focused on the laptop in front of him. He glances up at me. "Couldn't sleep?" he asks with a warm smile.

"No." I stay at the door, waiting.

"Come here," he says, pushing his chair back a few inches from his desk. When I approach, he pats his leg, and I take a seat on his lap. He snuggles me close to him, placing a gentle kiss on the top of my head.

I really love how affectionate Luca has become. It's almost like he can't get close enough to me sometimes, and I feel the same exact way. It's like I want to crawl inside of him to just be closer.

"What are you doing?" I ask. On the screen is a video that looks like it was taken from a powerful camera high above a huge warehouse with a lot of shipping containers near a boating dock.

"Watching aerial footage from our drones."

"What's in the shipping containers?" My curiosity pulls me closer, examining every frame of the footage.

"People," he says.

My world comes crashing to a sudden halt. "Like...human trafficking?" I can't stop myself from asking.

"Yes," he answers, confirming my worst fear.

I'm up and out of his lap in a split second, my hackles rising. "You are buying and selling people?" I accuse him, my voice rising to a fever pitch.

"Whoa, calm down, tiger," he says, putting his arms up in a placating gesture. "Put the claws away and listen to me for a second." He pauses the video and turns to me to give me his full attention. "I'm trying to put a stop to it. It's happening in this city at an alarming rate, and I'm not going to allow it."

His words instantly make me feel better. I knew Luca wasn't a *good* man, per se, but I'm glad to know he's trying to help instead of exacerbating this growing problem.

"The man you danced with at the costume ball," he starts.

"Yeah?"

"His name is Constantine Carbone. He's the one running the human trafficking in the city."

A shudder rolls through me. I danced with the devil himself, and I didn't even know it. If I had known what that man was doing and what he was capable of, I would have never let him touch me with those evil hands.

"I've been trying to trade him territories where he can sell drugs instead and make one hell of a profit, but he's not budging. He found his niche, and he's running with it, making money hand over fist."

"Is it just women he sells?" I ask.

"Women, men." Luca hesitates before adding, "Children."

I close my eyes and swallow hard past the lump forming in my throat. When I open them again, I look at Luca and tell him vehemently, "You have to stop him, Luca. You can't let him do this."

"I'm trying everything in my power to put an end to this. I promise you I will stop him as soon as I can," he vows.

I nod, taking comfort in his words. Climbing back into his lap, I let him hold me for several minutes while I try to process all the information he just dumped on me. Then, I ask him, "What are you looking for in the footage?"

"Any signs of people coming and going. If anyone is taking food and water to any of the shipping containers."

"Let's watch it and see if we can figure anything out."

"You don't want to go back to bed?" he offers.

"No. I want to help."

He kisses my temple and clicks the keypad to start the video again. "That's my girl."

CHAPTER 42

Verona

WHEN LUCA TOLD me to dress up and that we were going out in the city tonight, I have to admit I was a bit nervous. I took my time getting ready, picking out the perfect dress for a night out on the town.

Looking at my reflection in the mirror, I turn around several times, making sure I look perfect. The floor-length silver sequin dress fits me perfectly. The front is modest with a scalloped V-neck. But that is where the modesty stops with this dress. Slipping into a matching pair of silver high heels, the slit up the side all the way to my hip reveals my entire leg and thigh. And the back is scandalous as well, dipping almost too low and revealing almost too much.

I decide to wear a matching shawl over it until we get to our destination. I have no idea if we'll be indoors or outdoors, so I don't want to get cold.

My makeup is smoky and dark with a pale pink lip, and I decided to wear my hair down in loose waves. Smiling at my reflection, I think Luca will approve of my decisions tonight. Part of me wonders if we'll even make it to where we're going.

My core clenches just thinking about how many times he was inside of me today. Too many to count. It's like he can't keep his hands off of me. Not that I'm complaining. I want him just as much, maybe even more at times. Even though our marriage was out of convenience, we're certainly acting like real newlyweds.

I walk out of our bedroom and downstairs, carefully navigating the stairs in my sky-high heels. Luca emerges from his office and stops in his tracks when his eyes meet mine.

I watch him openly peruse my body from head to toe and back again. His tongue slips out to skate over his bottom lip, and I can't help but be mesmerized by the action.

He's dressed impeccably in a three-piece tailored suit that fits him perfectly. It's all black, and he looks dark and dangerous. He fixes an expensive watch on his wrist as he walks over to me; and when he reaches my side, I'm met with a kiss to my cheek.

"You look lovely," he whispers in my ear before gently biting my earlobe. "Fuck, I wish we didn't have to go to this thing. I want to stay home, send the staff away and fuck you in every room of this house tonight."

His dirty words have my thighs squeezing together. "Do we have to go?" I ask, blinking up at him.

The corners of his mouth tilt up in a smile. "My naughty girl. You tempt me so." Cupping my face in his hands, he kisses me so passionately that my knees threaten to buckle. And just as soon as the kiss began, it ends, leaving me wanting more. "I promised a friend I would attend," he says begrudgingly. Luca grabs my hand and leads me to the front door. "Let's go. The sooner we get there, the sooner we can leave, and the sooner I can be inside of you tonight."

His filthy promise has me buzzing as we climb into the car driven by Benito. On the way, Luca's hand strokes my bare leg through the slit in my dress. My entire body is buzzing and on fire by the time we arrive.

I'm surprised to see we've parked in front of an art gallery. There are people lining the sidewalks, taking pictures, and waiting for the show.

Benito opens the door for us, and Luca climbs out first. Then, he turns back to me, extends his hand and gives me a devastatingly beautiful smile. I take his hand and let him help me out of the backseat of the car.

I decide to leave my shawl behind, and the moment Luca sees the back of my dress, he hisses beside me. "Fuck, honey, if I had known what the back of your dress looked like, you wouldn't have made it out the front door," he whispers in my ear before leading me into the huge building with floor-to-ceiling windows and glass doors.

Two men swing open the glass doors, allowing us entrance into the gallery. There are only a handful of people including us in the main room. A man dressed in a bedazzled pink and white tie-dye suit comes rushing over the moment he spots Luca. They speak in rapid Italian to each other, and the man air kisses both of Luca's cheeks before grabbing his hand and shaking it. "Thank you for coming to my show." Then the man sets his gaze on me from behind his matching pink and white glasses. "And this must be the wife I've heard so much about."

So Luca has been talking about me. I sneak a glance at my husband and can't help but smile at how uncomfortable he is at being exposed by his friend. I turn my attention back to the artist. "I'm Verona."

"Verona Vitale," the man gushes. "Ah, it sounds like a supervillain name. I love it!" he exclaims with a chuckle. "I'm Leonardo Lombardi, but you can call me Leo." He sweeps his hand around the large room before adding, "Please take a look around before the rest of the people waiting are allowed in. VIP status for a good friend of mine," he says with a wink to Luca. "I'll see you both soon," he tells us before walking over to greet another couple who just walked through the door.

Luca leads me over to the paintings hanging on the wall. They look grandiose and amazing against the plain white wall behind them. Luca holds my hand as we walk. He squeezes it gently and says, "Go ahead and ask. I know you have questions."

"Many," I admit with a grin. "Where did you meet someone so... interesting?" I can't help but ask. Luca seems to attract more of the dark and serious type, so it's nice to see him with such a bright light in his catalog of friends.

"He used to be a waiter at my favorite restaurant in the city. He was always so depressed, rarely smiled, but he was one hell of a server."

I can't see Leonardo Lombardi wearing a dull uniform, waiting on tables. No wonder he was depressed. He seems like he's larger than life now; happiness personified.

"One day I asked him what he wanted to do with his life besides wait tables. And he told me he wanted to be an artist." Luca walks to another painting and studies it intently. "I told him to show me his art, and he did." He smiles fondly at the memory. "Let's just say I was blown away."

I look over my shoulder at Leo as he walks around, greeting people with a huge smile on his face. "You helped him, didn't you?" I ask, turning my attention back to my husband.

"I gave him some contacts in the art world. Set him up with some funds. No big deal," he says, waving it off like it's nothing.

But it's not nothing. He changed this young man's life. And now look at him — hosting his own art show in a huge New York City gallery. Not many people can say they accomplished that in their lifetime.

I squeeze Luca's hand and beam up at him. "You're amazing. Do you know that?"

He simply shakes his head. "I just threw some money at something, and it worked out."

"No, it was so much more than that," I tell him firmly. I stop walking and so does he. When he looks down at me, I can't help the feelings that are pouring out of me. "You made his life better. Look at him now. Without you, he'd still be waiting tables and be miserable."

"Verona," Luca growls.

I know he doesn't like to be told he is a good man with a heart of gold underneath all of that hard, rough exterior, but I don't care. First with the human trafficking ring he's trying to stop and now with Leo... I just want him to know how much he means to me. "I love you, Luca Vitale," I tell him softly.

His gray eyes widen at my words. A myriad of emotions cross over his face — shock, confusion, and disbelief. He opens his mouth to say something to me, but then Leonardo suddenly announces in a microphone that the show is about to begin.

People from the street begin to flood into the art gallery through the front doors. Luca pulls me close and says, "I want you to pick out a piece that speaks to you."

Well, it's not exactly what I wanted to hear, but that's okay. I didn't really expect Luca to say the three words back to me. I mean, he might never tell me he loves me. And honestly, I think I'd be okay with that. I know Luca isn't ever going to be the overly affectionate type or the type of man to confess his feelings for me openly. Not willingly, anyway.

I push all those thoughts aside, though, because I'm more than excited to pick out a painting for our home. It feels like such a normal thing a couple would do, and every time we do anything *normal*, it's one step closer to feeling like this is a real marriage that can and will work.

We take our time looking at each painting. I'm starting to think I'll never find one that *speaks to me*...until I do.

The painting isn't overly done or extravagant like most of the others. This one is simple. A light gray background with shadows playing around the centerpiece — a gilded birdcage. The door is open. There is no bird in sight, indicating that the bird is free and living its best life somewhere, no longer trapped in its cage.

"This one," I announce to Luca.

He stops walking and stares at the painting for a long time. Then, he gives me a nod and says, "Yes, this is it." Squeezing my hand, he looks into my eyes when he tells me, "You're the bird in this painting, Verona. I never want you to feel trapped or alone again. I want you to always feel free."

"I feel that way with you," I tell him, squeezing his hand back.

He tilts his lips into a smile before he tells me, "I'll make the payment arrangements. Be right back." He places a chaste kiss on my cheek before leaving me alone with the painting.

The crowd of people has thinned out over the last hour or so, and I feel like I can finally breathe. I'm not used to being around a lot of people. When I lived in boarding school, there were a lot of girls there, but I mostly spent my time alone in my room, reading. And when I lived with my aunt...well, her idea of a fun time was sitting at home, knitting. We hardly ever ventured out unless it was to a thrift shop, and half the time I wasn't even allowed to buy anything.

Tears fill my eyes as I stare at the painting. I was the bird. I was caged. I wasn't free.

And Luca changed my life by marrying me. I feel safe with him. I feel like my little, closed-off world opened up into a much bigger and better universe that I never knew existed.

I step closer to the painting that Luca is currently in the process of purchasing and stare in amazement at each and every paint stroke that Leonardo put on the canvas. From far away, the painting looks like a picture. But up close, I can see all of his hard work, his heart and soul that he put into his work.

"Beautiful piece, isn't it?" asks a deep voice from beside me.

I turn to the stranger, ready to agree with him and maybe brag about how my husband is paying for it as we speak, but then I see a familiar face and freeze. "Constantine Carbone," I say out loud before I can stop myself.

"I see from the look in your eyes that Luca told you about me since our last meeting." He smirks darkly. "I guess my reputation really does precede me."

I go to move away from him, but he reaches out and grabs my arm. It's not a bruising grip, but it is firm, like I don't have a choice on whether to run from him or not.

Constantine Carbone is an attractive older man, but the fact that he traffics women and children makes him vile and ugly in my eyes. He's a cruel and abhorrent monster, and I don't want to be in his presence a moment longer than I have to.

"The last time we met you were begging for attention from anyone but your husband," he says, bringing me closer to him. "What changed?" He searches my eyes for answers as I stare up at him, my breathing labored and uneven. "Ah," he says as if he found the answers in my gaze. "You fell for him."

With his free hand, he tucks a strand of hair behind my ear, grazing my cheek, and I recoil in disgust from his touch. Those hands. So much blood and death on those hands.

He grins at my discomfort. "You know, Verona, if you were mine, I would treat you like a queen. We would travel the world together."

"And you would pay for it from the blood of the women and children that you sell?" I spit back at him.

He chuckles at my response. "Feisty." His eyes search mine before he adds, "I like when a woman puts up a fight. No wonder Vitale has kept you." Leaning down, he runs his tongue along my cheek, tasting my skin. "I bet you taste like heaven and suck cock like a little whore," he whispers into my ear. "If you wouldn't want to be mine, I bet I could get a pretty penny for a cunt like yours."

Grimacing, I pull away from him, hating that I can still feel his touch on my skin. "Stay away from me!" I warn him.

"Or what?" he asks with a smug grin.

"Or this," Luca's voice says from beside me. I can hear the gun cocking before I even see it. Luca pulls my back to his front and places a kiss on my temple before raising the gun to his foe. "You know better than to touch what isn't yours...*again*, Carbone," Luca hisses.

I glance around the room and watch several people's startled faces when they see the gun in my husband's hand. "Please, Luca. You're drawing attention."

"I don't give a fuck," he growls. His eyes never leave Constantine. "You've made a deadly mistake here tonight. One I won't soon forget or forgive."

"No, I don't suppose you will," Constantine says as a slow smile spreads across his face. He walks slowly around us, cool and collected as if he doesn't have a gun pointed right at him. "I'll just be on my way out." Looking at me one last time, he says, "See you again soon, Verona," and it sounds more like a threat and a promise than a goodbye.

I shudder at the way my name slips off of his evil tongue. Luca pulls me closer and tucks the gun away when we're finally alone. "I paid for the painting. Let's get the fuck out of here before I lose my goddamn mind," Luca tells me.

I nod in response, unable to speak.

On the way out the door, people are gawking at us, but I don't even care at this point. My entire body is shaking, and I feel sick. Just having Constantine's hands on me tonight and breathing the same air as him makes me nauseous. Not to mention the fact that he licked my face! He actually tasted me.

Constantine Carbone is an evil, vile man. I'm furious that he thought he had a right to touch me. Bile rises up in my throat, and I have to swallow hard to force it back down.

Benito is waiting outside of the car parked at the curb, and he opens the door with a questioning look on his face. I climb in the backseat without a word, and Luca is quick to follow me.

Once the door shuts, Luca lets out a slew of curses. He runs his fingers through his thick, dark hair, pulling at the ends angrily. Then, he turns to look at me with a look on his face that sends chills up my spine. "What did he say to you? What did he do? Tell me everything."

I start from the beginning, not leaving anything out. And by the time I'm done, Luca is eerily still and quiet.

After several seconds, he pushes the button for the intercom and tells Benito to pull over. Once the car comes to a stop, Luca whispers, "Get out."

I stare at my husband in confusion. "What? I didn't do anything wrong."

"Get out of the car, Verona," he says gruffly. "I won't tell you again."

Tears fill my eyes as I open the door. We're parked on the curb of a busy street, and I carefully climb out of the car when it's safe so that I don't become roadkill by the oncoming traffic. By the time I round the back of the car, Luca is already outside, pacing the sidewalk.

I've never seen him this angry before, and it's scaring me. "Luca," I say softly, my voice trembling. I'm shaking all over, fear and trepidation coursing through my veins.

He walks into a dark, narrow alleyway between two stores, and I reluctantly follow him. "I shouldn't have left your side tonight," he says so softly I almost don't hear him at first.

"Luca, please, let's go back to the car," I beg.

I turn to leave, to walk away, and then suddenly I feel his hand wrapping around my throat. In a quick movement, he pulls me backwards and twists me in his arms so that we're face to face. "You're mine, Verona," he growls before his mouth crashes down onto mine.

I don't know if it's his fierce possessiveness that's gotten to him or the fact that he could have lost me to that evil man tonight, but Luca is expressing himself the only way he knows how. And I let him.

He pushes me until my back is against a brick wall, and his grip suddenly tightens around my throat. I gasp into his mouth for air, and he takes the opportunity to devour me, shoving his tongue into my mouth and claiming me with such brutality it's almost frightening.

Just as I'm getting lightheaded from lack of oxygen, Luca releases my neck and bends down, reaching for the hem of my dress. He lifts it higher and higher until it's pooled around my waist, exposing me. He then forces the fabric into my hands, making me hold it.

"No panties. My naughty wife," he whispers in my ear as he drags his finger up and down my slit. It doesn't take long for me to get wet for him. It's just my body's natural response to his touch.

I watch in horror as he drops to his knees in front of me, no doubt ruining his expensive suit in the process. "Luca, please," I beg him. "Not here. Not like this."

Trembling, I glance to the end of the alley. Benito is standing guard with his back towards us, but there are people walking by. Anyone could look in and see us. Anyone could hear us, including Benito.

"Luca, no, wait!" I cry out. But then I feel his tongue running along my slit, and all my thoughts and fears instantly melt away. I close my eyes and rest my head back on the brick as he eats me like a starving man in the dirty alleyway.

All of this is filthy and wrong, but I don't care. I want it. I want him.

I moan loudly as Luca's talented mouth, lips and tongue go to work. My fingers squeeze the material of my dress until they go numb. "Oh, god, Luca, I'm gonna..." I don't even get the rest of the sentence out before I'm tumbling over the edge of pleasure. My body trembles as the orgasm wracks my body. Luca continues to lick me until I beg him to stop.

I feel high on the endorphins running through my body. I'm barely aware of Luca's presence until I hear his belt being undone and his zipper going down. He grabs my hips and hoists me up until my legs are wrapped around him. And then I feel the head of his cock at my entrance. I barely have time to take a breath before he's impaling me. I cry out from the shock of it. It hurts but feels good all at the same time. He begins to piston his hips, pulling and pushing his cock in and out of me the entire way so that I feel every inch of his length. And I no longer care about the people who might be watching or hearing us. All I can feel is Luca inside of me, his cock claiming me as his.

The brick wall is scraping against my bare back, and I know I'll have to deal with the consequences later, but I couldn't care less right now. "Yes! Luca!" I cry out.

With one hand gripping my left hip, his right hand goes back to my throat. He squeezes while staring into my eyes as if testing my response. My eyes widen as he tightens his hold on me, no doubt leaving finger-shaped bruises on my skin as he holds me in place and fucks me harder than he's ever fucked me before.

Maybe it's the lack of oxygen...or maybe it's because we're outside in public where anyone can see us and watch, but I don't think I've ever been so turned on before. All too soon I'm reaching the edge again before I can even comprehend it. I'm dizzy and almost to the point of passing out as I gasp out Luca's name and my pussy grips his cock in a death grip as I ride out the most explosive orgasm of my life. Starbursts explode behind my eyes as I let out a silent scream.

"Yes, Verona," he groans. "Come for me. Only me."

He slowly releases my throat, and I gasp for air. My lungs are desperate for oxygen, and it takes a while for the dizziness to subside. "Only you," I agree once I catch my breath.

Luca stares into my eyes as he confesses, "I would kill for you."

Okay, so it's not the three words that every girl wants to hear, but I know when it comes to Luca, that might be the closest thing to *I love you* that I will ever get. "I love you," I whisper.

With those words spoken, Luca lets out a guttural sound that sounds almost feral as his seed spills inside of me. He fucks me until he's completely exhausted and spent. And then he collapses against me, pinning me to the wall.

We stay like that for a few minutes, me wrapped around him,

until his cock softens. His lips kiss my neck softly, no doubt trying to soothe the bruises. Then he finally pulls out of me and helps me put my shaking legs down to the ground. I wobble in my high heels as he pulls out a handkerchief from his suit jacket pocket and cleans me up. He throws the used handkerchief in a nearby dumpster before looking at me.

It's almost like the spell he was under is broken, because I can see the moment he snaps back to reality. "Did I hurt you?" he asks as he gently pulls down the hem of my dress.

I shake my head.

"I need your words, honey," he tells me, lifting my chin to make my eyes meet his.

Everything that happened tonight comes rushing forward in the forefront of my mind, and I'm suddenly crying. Luca pulls me close and holds me, whispering apologies in my ear. But it's not the fact that he just fucked me in a dirty alleyway where people were probably watching us. No, it's the fact that Constantine Carbone had his hands on me. He wants me. He threatened to sell me, and the thought of him taking me is terrifying.

"What if Constantine comes for me?" I suddenly pull back and ask.

Luca stares into my eyes and tells me, "I will never let that happen. He will have to kill me first." He pulls me into his arms and holds me for a long time before finally saying, "Let's go home."

CHAPTER 43

Luca

BY THE TIME we get home, Verona is curled up on my lap in a deep sleep. I hate to wake her, but I don't want her sleeping out in the car all night in the cold. I don't know exactly when Verona snuck her way into my cold, dark heart, but she did.

I care for her. I never thought I would ever care about anyone. It scares me, but also soothes me in a way. Maybe I'm not a complete monster after all.

She told me she loved me. I close my eyes, still hearing her melodic voice say those words. Fuck, I will savor them forever. I don't know if I'll ever be able to say them back, but I know I have stronger feelings for her than I've ever had for any other human being in my entire life.

And the thought of anyone taking her from me has me seeing red. Just thinking about Constantine touching her or thinking he could ever claim any rights to her makes my pulse hammer in my veins like an angry war drum.

And maybe war is the answer when it comes to Constantine. I've gone to war for far lesser things. And now that Verona is the most important person in my life, I want everyone to know the lengths I will go through to protect her. I would die for her, come back to life and kill everyone all over again. My vengeance knows no bounds on this earth or in the afterlife.

"What's wrong?" Verona asks, her head still in my lap.

"I thought you were sleeping," I say with a smile.

"I could feel you tense up. Did something happen?"

"No. But we are home. I just didn't want to wake you."

She sits up and stares at me with her honey-colored eyes. She looks thoroughly fucked with messy hair and smeared makeup, but I don't think she's ever looked more beautiful. "Fuck, you're gorgeous," I tell her before placing a kiss on her lips. "Let's get you to bed."

"And where are you going to be?" she asks as we climb out of the car.

"Benito and I have some things to discuss," I say simply before glancing at my first in command. Benito gives me a nod, and I know he'll understand what must happen when it comes to Constantine once I explain to him everything that transpired tonight. I'm tired of dragging my feet when it comes to him. Since Constantine won't comply, I'm going to have to force his hand. It's now or never at this point. I want to burn his entire empire to the fucking ground, preferably with him in it.

Verona catches up to me before we reach the front door and grabs my hand, pulling me back to her. "Luca, please, don't do anything you'll regret."

I cock a brow at her. Has she been reading my mind?

"If you're upset about Constantine, let it go. He's dangerous. I don't want you even being in the same room as him, let alone going after him."

I put my palm on her cheek, and I love the fact that she sinks into my touch. "I've tried being lenient with him, and it obviously didn't work. He knows he crossed a line that should have never been crossed tonight. I want to put him down like the dog he is."

Verona pulls away from me, anger swarming in her eyes. "No."

"No?" I ask with a dark chuckle.

"I'm telling you no to getting revenge on him. You can still help the people he's taken, but from afar and by alerting the proper authorities, if need be." She touches the lapels on my suit before smoothing them down. "Besides, if you leave, who will be here to protect me? Constantine will come for me when he knows you're vulnerable and busy trying to take him down."

I can see the fear in her eyes when she talks about him, and it almost makes me back down. Almost. "Honey," I start, but she doesn't let me finish.

Suddenly, she wraps her arms around me. "I can't lose you, Luca. Please don't do this."

And just having her close to me makes the ice around my dark heart melt a little more. "Okay, honey. I won't." But I honestly don't know if I'm telling her the truth or lying. I guess only time will tell.

CHAPTER 44

Verona

I WAKE UP the next morning to the most soothing massage of my life. I groan in pleasure as fingers skate over my back, rubbing in some kind of sweet-smelling moisturizer.

"The sounds that come out of that dirty, little mouth turn me on, honey," Luca says from beside me.

I turn my head and stare up at my husband. He's wearing a black button-up shirt with the sleeves rolled up over his muscular forearms, and black slacks. His hair looks like it's still damp from a shower.

"What time is it?" I worry.

"A little before noon. You slept a long time. Something must have exhausted you last night," he says with a smug smile.

"I think *someone* exhausted me," I quip. It's those rare smiles of his that I live for. He looks so young and relaxed when he's like this.

His smile quickly fades as his fingertips graze over my neck. "Do these hurt?" he asks.

There must be bruises on my neck from when he held me tight against the wall last night while we fucked dirty and raw in the back of an alleyway. And just the thought of it has my thighs clenching under the sheet. "No," I tell him honestly. "I'm not made of glass, Luca. You can't break me," I assure him.

A cocky smirk replaces the frown, and I can't help but wonder if he's thinking about ways to possibly break me. I hope they all involve him inside of me, but I don't say my naughty thoughts out loud. Going from virgin to practically a nympho with Luca has been a rollercoaster ride. It's like I always want him. And when we're not having sex, I'm thinking about it. I suppose that's normal for all newlyweds...especially if one or both saved themselves for marriage, right?

"What are you thinking about?" he asks me, and I hate that he can read me so well that he knows when I'm deep in thought.

"I was wondering if our marriage is normal or not."

He cocks his head to the side and chuckles darkly. "It's anything but normal, honey. Trust me."

"Not the whole arranged marriage thing. I mean...all the sex."

His dark brows furl together. "Oh. *That*," he says with an amused grin. Pulling back the sheet, he smacks my ass, leaving a creamy handprint behind. "I think our normal can be whatever we want it to be."

"Have you ever been like this with another woman before?" After I ask the question, I instantly regret it and want to take it back, because what if he says yes? What if this is the norm for Luca?

"No," he says. "I never fucked the same woman more than once. Never wanted anyone enough to actually want to," he says with a shrug. Reaching over to the nightstand, he wipes off his hands on a towel. "Lift your hips, honey." When I lift them, he sticks a bolster pillow underneath my stomach, which causes my hips and ass to lift up in the air.

And then he grabs a bottle of oil. Squirting the liquid on my backside, he rubs his hands over the globes of my ass, massaging deeply.

I groan from the sensation. "That feels good," I murmur.

"Spread your legs for me, honey," he tells me huskily.

I do as he says, and he puts his knees between my thighs. His large hands massage the oil into my cheeks, and then I feel a fingertip gliding down the entire length of my slit. He plays with my clit, making me squirm underneath him.

"I love how wet you get for me," he says as his fingers trail up to my entrance, dipping in and grazing over my G spot, making me groan loudly. He gathers wetness on his fingers and then goes higher, tracing over the rim of my puckered hole. I immediately tense up, but Luca whispers, "Relax, honey. I won't hurt you."

I feel his thumb pressing against my tight hole, and I desperately try to relax. Luca told me before he wanted to claim my ass, and I've been dreading it. I'm expecting it to hurt, but when his thumb enters me, I don't feel much pain. It's just...strange.

He fingers my clit as his thumb pushes in and out of my back hole. I wriggle under him, nonsensical words coming out of my mouth as the pleasure quickly mounts.

"I don't want you to come until I'm inside of you," he warns.

He climbs off the bed, and I turn to watch him take off his clothes. His hard cock bobs up towards his stomach, and I swallow back a gasp. How will it ever fit inside of me back there?

He's between my legs again, and I feel the head of his cock notched at my back entrance. I whimper nervously. "It's okay, honey," he whispers soothingly to me as he smooths his other hand over my hip.

My fingers wrap around the sheets in a death grip as he pushes his cock into me. "Luca!" I cry out.

"Touch yourself for me, honey."

My right hand reluctantly releases the sheet, and I reach down between my legs until I find my clit. I rub the little bundle of nerves with my fingertip, and it feels so good mixed with the pain, but I'm still not totally relaxed.

"That's it," Luca hisses. "That's my naughty girl."

He pushes further into my ass, and I finger myself faster, needing the pleasure to mask the pain. "Please!" I cry out, but I honestly don't know if I want him to stop or continue.

"Breathe, honey. Relax. I'll make it feel good. I promise."

His voice calms me, and I'm able to relax enough that he can enter me the whole way. When I feel his trimmed pubic hair touching my ass cheeks, I know he's fully seated inside of me. I expect him to fuck me hard, but he doesn't. Luca takes his time, easing in and easing out, adding more oil when needed and stroking my back, murmuring praises as he fucks me nice and slow.

When he wanted to claim my ass, I never thought it would be like this. It feels good. More than good. My fingers stroke my clit as he fucks me, and it almost feels like an out of body experience.

I groan and move my body in rhythm with his cock, grinding down on my fingers.

"I'm so close, honey. Your ass feels so damn good around my cock. So tight," he grunts as he rocks in and out of me. "Come with me," he begs.

His words are my undoing. I detonate around him, my entire body on fire with pleasure. I almost scream, it feels so good.

"Fuck! Yes," Luca groans before pulling out of me. I feel rope after rope of his seed striping my backside as he comes.

Our harsh breathing fills the room. That was so intense and unexpected. I close my eyes and begin to relax again when I feel Luca rubbing his cum into my skin.

"What are you doing?" I question.

"Marking you," he says, his voice husky and raw.

That whole thing with Constantine really did a number on him, and I don't think I was ever really in danger at the art gallery. Still, Constantine could come for me if he wanted to, I suppose. But he'd be going up against Luca and his army of men. And I don't think Luca would ever let him win that war.

Smacking my ass playfully, Luca announces, "Let's take a shower."

He gets off the bed and helps me to stand. Then, he pulls me into his arms. I can feel something different in that hug, as he holds me, the hug lasting way longer than normal. It's almost like Luca senses something bad is going to happen to us, and it scares the hell out of me.

Maybe just the thought of losing me is making him fall for me. And that's probably scarier than anything else in his dark, twisted world.

CHAPTER 45

Luca

I'M SITTING IN my office the next morning when there is a knock on the door. I hit a button for the door to unlock and raise my voice to tell my employee on the other side to come in.

Aldo Allaband enters. He's tall and skinny with brown hair and brown eyes. His skin is pale because he spends most of his time indoors on a computer.

He pushes his glasses up the bridge of his nose as he takes a seat in one of the leather chairs in front of my desk. "You wanted to see me, sir?"

"Yes, Aldo. How did your training go?"

"Very well, sir. I excelled in all of the programming and hacking tests they gave me."

I smile. I already knew how well Aldo did, but I just wanted to hear it come out of his mouth. Aldo is one of the smartest, brightest young men I know, so I had all the faith in the world that he wouldn't disappoint me.

I first met Aldo when he was a college student majoring in electrical engineering and computer science at MIT, struggling with paying his tuition. His mom had just died in a car accident, and his father was never part of his life. Before his mother died, she had been working three jobs to support her son's dream of going to a good college.

When I learned of his situation, I presented him with a proposition. I wanted him to come work for me. But first, I wanted the college student to graduate and then go study with a team of underground anonymous hackers. The hackers are the best in the world, and I wanted Aldo to be part of the elite group.

I paid for the rest of Aldo's college tuition and all of his bills and expenses, past and present. Hell, I even paid for his mother's funeral since the kid was desperately trying to make payments on it with no end in sight.

I saw something in him when I first met him — ambition. I knew right then and there that he would be a great asset to our team. And now he's ready for whatever I throw his way just when I need him the most.

"Constantine Carbone," I say. And just speaking that name out loud has my blood pressure rising.

"Yes, sir." Aldo quickly grabs his smartphone out of his pocket and begins typing in a note.

"I want you to monitor his activities. I want to know what he's doing, where he is at all times. And if you can dig up any more dirt on him, do it."

Aldo nods as his thumbs type frantically on the phone.

"And I want you to move here to the compound full time. Tell Benito to get you whatever you need. We will supply whatever you ask for."

"Yes, sir," Aldo says.

"And one other thing."

"Sir?" he asks, looking up from his phone.

"I want to book a trip for me and my wife."

Aldo's brows raise over the top of his glasses. "A honeymoon, sir?"

"Yes, precisely," I agree. "But she doesn't like water, so it can't be anywhere tropical," I quickly add.

Aldo thinks for several seconds. "I can research some places and send my list of ideas to you, sir."

"That would be great," I tell him. "And I want somewhere private. I don't want to have to worry about her any more than I already do now. I want us to have…fun."

The concept is foreign on my tongue and in my mind. I don't think I've had fun since I was a child, but Verona does something to me that makes me want to feel relaxed and less weighed down by life and work when I'm around her. And, more importantly, I want her to have a good time. I love the way she smiles, and her laugh makes me feel like everything is right in the world just by hearing it.

"I'll get working on this right away, and I'll send you what I find." The young man stands and tucks away his phone. "I'll move my stuff in this afternoon. I don't have much to pack."

"Thank you, Aldo. You're dismissed."

"Thank you, sir."

I watch Aldo leave, and then I send a text to Benito about what just transpired so that he is in the loop. I want him to get whatever Aldo needs, because the boy is our greatest asset at the moment.

I promised Verona I wouldn't go after Constantine Carbone. But I don't see anything wrong with keeping tabs on him. That certainly wouldn't be breaking my promise.

And if Constantine is going to attack, I will know where and when. And if he thinks he's coming for my wife, well, he's got another thing coming. He'll soon find out who really rules this city.

CHAPTER 46

Verona

A FEW DAYS later, I wake up to Luca waving a gift in front of my face. Over the past couple of days he's seemed happier, having almost completely gotten over the whole Constantine fiasco that happened at the art gallery, and I'm glad for that.

"What is it?" I ask, sitting up in bed.

"Open it and find out," he says before setting the present down on the mattress in front of me.

The only gift I've ever received from Luca was our wedding photo album, and I don't think anything could top that. Still, I'm curious to see what he's done, so I carefully untie the silver ribbon from the white box and open it.

Inside is a small flip style cell phone. I carefully pull the phone out to study it.

"I had Aldo, my IT guy, modify it a bit. There is a tracker programmed into it that works independently whether the phone is on or off. The battery lasts for years instead of days. And my number is programmed into the speed dial. You can call me anytime by just pressing and holding the number one key down."

After I absorb all of that new information, I furrow my brows in confusion. "What's going on? Am I in danger?"

"No, of course not. This is just a precaution. Call it peace of mind for me, if you will." His fingertips graze my jaw, and he turns my head so that my eyes meet his. "I want you to keep this on you at all times, Verona. Can I count on you to do that?"

"Yes."

He smiles at my answer. "Okay, good." Then, he releases me and nods to the box. "There's more inside."

Turning my attention back to the gift, I lift a piece of tissue paper to reveal two plane tickets. I pick them up and read the destination — Aspen, Colorado.

"What's in Colorado?" I ask, confused.

"Our honeymoon," he says before placing a kiss on my temple and standing up. "Our plane leaves in a few hours. Pack only the essentials. We'll buy warmer clothes when we get there."

A smile forms on my lips as I realize Luca planned this trip for us. Just us. No bodyguards. No first or second or third in command. Only us.

I'm overcome with happiness, so much so that I jump off the bed and tackle my husband. I catch him off-guard, but he still manages to fall with me in his arms to the floor gracefully.

"I take it that you're happy?" he asks with a chuckle.

I lean down and place a kiss on his lips. "So happy," I agree.

"Good. That's all I want."

I give him another kiss before I quickly climb off of him and run to the closet. "I need to pack!" I say, my voice high-pitched and weird with excitement.

Luca simply shakes his head in amusement before he leaves the room.

After we land in Aspen, Colorado, we have a rental car waiting for us at the airport. It's a big Chevy Suburban with huge winter tires. I wonder out loud if it's overkill, but Luca informs me we'll need it for where we're going.

Excitement is dripping out of every pore in my body on the car ride to our destination, and I'm so nervous that I can barely sit still.

"I don't think I've ever seen you this anxious before," Luca remarks, reaching over to hold my hand. "Well, maybe on our wedding day."

"I thought I was going to pass out just from my nerves," I confess.

He gives my hand a light squeeze. "Well, I'm glad you didn't. Although I do recall you saying 'I do' in the form of a question like we were on an episode of *Jeopardy*."

I laugh hard at that. Our wedding day was so hectic and nerve-wracking. I didn't know which way was up or if I was coming or going. But I'm glad we got through it. And even though we had a rough start to our marriage, we got through all of that too. Honestly, I wouldn't want to be married to anyone else.

"I love that sound," he remarks.

"What sound?"

"Your laugh. I love making you laugh."

"Well, I love you making me laugh," I tell him with a grin.

The GPS announces that our destination is coming up, so I look out the window, searching for the place we're going to be staying at. All I can see is snow and trees, however.

Luca navigates the SUV up a plowed driveway to a gated entrance. He hits a button inside the car, and the gate opens a second later. Luca drives on through, and the driveway seems endless. But all the waiting is worth it when I see the house.

The two-story black and brown house looks inviting and straight out of a painting surrounded by all the tall pine trees and snowy mountains.

"I'll get our luggage later," Luca tells me when we get out of the SUV. "Let's explore the house first."

"Okay," I say, giddy with excitement.

Luca unlocks the front door, and we walk into the grand entrance. The floor plan is open with exposed wooden beams everywhere. The first floor consists of a formal living room, a dining room next to a huge, modern kitchen, a recreation room, a den with a huge flat screen tv on the wall hung over a fireplace, and the master bedroom with a ginormous walk-in shower in its spacious bathroom.

I glance up the spiral staircase wrapped around a huge tree trunk leading upstairs. "How many bedrooms are there?"

"Seven," he says before pulling me into his arms. He plants kisses along my neck and up to my ear before he whispers, "And I'd like to fuck you in every single one of them before we leave."

"Promise?" I ask, my voice thick with desire.

"Promise," he says before grabbing my ass and pulling me flush against him so that I can feel his arousal.

I don't know if there's ever a time when Luca doesn't want me. And, god, it feels so good to be wanted.

"Let's start with the master bedroom," I suggest.

"That sounds like a great idea," he says before hoisting me up over his shoulder and carrying me fireman-style down the hall towards the room.

"You're such a caveman!" I tell him.

"Only when it comes to you," he confesses.

CHAPTER 47

Verona

THE NEXT MORNING, we wake up in each other's arms. We crossed three of the seven bedrooms off our list last night, and we miraculously ended up back in the master bedroom, completely exhausted before we finally fell asleep.

The huge bed is positioned facing a wall of glass, and the view from the floor-to-ceiling windows is breathtaking. With the sun rays streaming between the tall pine trees and the glistening snowy mountains in the distance, it feels like we're in a movie.

Luca traces his fingertips up and down my arm as I listen to his heart beating. I could lie here all day and have no regrets. Just being with him makes me feel loved; makes me feel safe. Like nothing can hurt me in this world.

"Although I hate saying this, we can't stay in bed the entire time we're here," he says with a sigh.

I chuckle. "Oh, that wasn't your plan all along? To bring me somewhere secluded and ravage me?"

In a quick move, he's on top of me, straddling my hips and pinning my arms to the bed. I squeal in surprise as he leans down to plant kisses on my neck. "I would love to keep you here all day and ravage you, but I want to explore the town and have fun with you also."

I raise my hips off the bed, grinding against his morning wood. "We can have fun here too," I quip.

"God, I've created a monster." A deep chuckle vibrates through his chest and into mine. "My wife is a complete nympho."

"So is my husband," I say with a grin.

"Only for you," he says before kissing me.

The kiss soon grows heated, and I can feel the wetness pooling between my thighs. Pulling back from him, I look up and say, "If we don't get out of bed now, I don't think we'll ever leave it."

"True. Let's take a shower," he says suggestively while waggling his eyebrows.

I can't help but laugh at the funny gesture. It's nice to see Luca being so relaxed. He's never like this at home, and it's sad in a way. I think here he has less to worry about and can be himself with me. He doesn't have to be the demanding, controlling boss that he is when we're at home.

"Separate showers," I demand. I know if we take a shower together, it will only end up with him being inside of me. "Let's try... delayed gratification."

"Delayed gratification, Mrs. Vitale?" He flashes me a gorgeous panty-melting smile. "I don't know if I can wait until tonight to be inside of you." He grinds his hard bulge against my center, and I almost change my mind right then and there.

"I don't know if I can wait either," I agree with a groan.

But as soon as he climbs off the bed and I no longer have his warmth surrounding me, I instantly regret my earlier decision to wait. "Wait!" I call to him as he walks out of the room.

"Too late!" he calls back. "Go get a shower. I'll shower in one of the other bathrooms," he shouts from down the hall.

"Damn it," I say with a sigh as I stare up at the ceiling.

Slowly, my hand slides down my stomach and is almost at the apex of my thighs when I hear him yelling, "And no touching yourself until tonight!"

"Damn it!" I groan loudly.

CHAPTER 48

Verona

"I'VE NEVER SKIED before today," I say for the millionth time as I wobble on my skis on the snowy embankment, my legs making me suddenly look like a newborn baby giraffe on ice.

"That's okay," my personal instructor, Peter, says. "I want you to try putting your hands on your knees. It will help you to stop doing that windmill thing you have going on with your arms."

Feeling beyond embarrassed, I do as he tells me, and I'm pleasantly surprised that it seems to help.

"See?" Peter says, beaming up at me. "Much better."

"Thank you," I say with a sigh. I'm starting to think skiing just isn't in the cards for me, but I want to try my best since Luca planned this whole trip for us. We're still on the green slope for beginners, and I have barely made it down the first tiny track. Peter has eagerly been trying to show me the basics, but I've fallen what feels like a hundred times already, and I'm afraid my butt will be bruised for weeks after today. At least I haven't hit my head yet. I guess that's a plus.

I watch my instructor as he starts showing me a new maneuver, which I can already tell I will never master. Peter is young and handsome. He looks more like a surfer than a skier with his blond hair and sparkling blue eyes. But even though he's handsome, I only have eyes for one man.

Speaking of my husband, I glance over as he watches Peter and I from a short distance away. His goggles are on top of his head, and I can see his gray eyes boring a hole into my instructor. He wasn't keen on letting Peter teach me to begin with, and now I can practically see steam coming out of his ears.

I giggle, knowing that it's pissing Luca off. Is it wrong that I absolutely love it when my husband gets jealous? Just the way he acts like a possessive, feral animal turns me on. And I can't help it when my thighs automatically clench together.

"Knees apart," Peter tells me, and I almost laugh out loud. If he only knew what was going on inside of my head.

Losing my concentration, I spread my legs too far and begin to windmill my arms again, eventually falling for the hundredth and one time today. "Ouch," I say out loud while internally apologizing to my butt.

"You're getting better! You went way longer that time without falling," Peter encourages me as he reaches down to help me up. "So, where are you from?" Peter asks, making small talk, but I can see in his eyes that he's attracted to me. *If he only knew who I was married to*, I think to myself.

"Uh, I grew up in New York City," I start to answer, but then this time, unlike the previous times, Peter begins to brush snow from my ski suit. I mean, it is pretty much caked on at this point. His hands start on my outer thighs and work their way around to my backside, lingering maybe longer than necessary on my derriere.

Luca is out of his skis faster than I can blink and on his way over to us, hoofing it in his boots through the thick snow. "Okay, Peter, that's enough lessons for today," he snarls.

Peter looks at him and says in protest, "But we still have thirty minutes left that you already paid for."

"Consider it your tip," Luca says. "Go help one of your other clients. I've got this."

"Oh-kay," Peter drawls out before handing me his business card. Then, he gives me a wink before telling me, "Don't be afraid to call me if you want any more lessons, Verona."

Oh my god, this guy must have a death wish, I can't help but think to myself.

"*Mrs.* Vitale," Luca sternly corrects him.

"Oh, sorry. Mrs. Vitale," Peter repeats, blushing. He clearly couldn't see my wedding ring under the thick gloves on my hands, so it's not exactly his fault for trying.

I watch as the poor guy skis away from us towards the main lodge, no doubt wondering what the heck he did wrong.

"You could have been nicer to him," I say with a sigh.

"And he could have kept his hands off of you," Luca retorts.

"Be careful, Luca. Your green-eyed monster is showing," I tell him, grinning.

He pulls me into his arms, my back flush against the front of his hard body. I can feel the growing bulge of his cock pressing into my bruised behind, and I gasp. "I have another monster that I'd like to show you. It's been aching to be inside of you all day."

I laugh and wiggle my behind against his arousal. "Maybe I can see it later."

"Definitely," he promises. Turning me in his arms, he cups my face in his large palms and leans down for a kiss. "Fuck, it was driving me crazy to see his hands on you. I wanted to cut them off!" he proclaims, seething with anger.

"So violent," I say before placing a kiss on his lips. "I like it."

He smirks at me. "You would," he whispers before his mouth

crashes against mine, and his urgency takes my breath away. "Want to get out of here?" he asks when we finally come up for air.

"I thought you'd never ask."

⁓

On the drive back to the house, Luca is still seething about the instructor touching me. He has a death grip on the steering wheel, his knuckles white with his forearms tense and vibrating with anger. The tension is so thick in the SUV that I could cut it with a knife.

When we finally pull into the driveway, I decide to try to lighten the mood a bit. I climb out and immediately go to a pile of snow. Quickly, I make the biggest snowball I can manage before I sneak back to the SUV.

Luca rounds the corner, confusion lacing his features. "Verona, what are you —?"

I throw the snowball, effectively silencing him as it smacks him right in the face. Okay, so maybe I went for overkill, because now he's covered in snow from the top of his head, his face, his shoulders and part of his chest.

I cover my mouth to silence my gasp as I watch him slowly wipe the snow from his face. His gray eyes blink open, and I can see the anger in them.

"Run," he whispers.

"What?" I ask, thinking I misheard him.

"Run, Verona."

I don't even think twice before I take off running into the snow. I don't get far before Luca is on my heels, chasing me down like a lion would with his prey. My legs carry me as fast as they can, but Luca is faster.

He pushes me facedown into the snow and mounts me like a wild animal. I'm struggling to get my bearings when I feel cold air on my backside. Bent over a snowbank, I realize Luca just pulled down my pants, exposing me to the elements...and to him.

His fingertips press into the bruises on my skin, and I cry out in pain. "That hurts!"

"Well, it's about to hurt even more," he says darkly before bringing a hand down on my ass.

The combination of the bruises and the cold air makes the smack ten times worse, and I hiss out between clenched teeth.

He slaps my other cheek, and I cry out, "No more, no more! I'm sorry!"

"What was that? You're sorry?"

"Yes, yes, yes!"

I feel his fingertip run up and down the length of my slit. "Why, honey, you're wet for me."

I hang my head in shame. Admittedly, I've been wet for him all day. Just seeing his jealous side made me all hot and bothered earlier, and Luca is just plain hot when he's angry.

"This is going to be hard and fast, honey," Luca tells me. "Don't come."

"What?" I barely get the question out before I hear the sound of his zipper, and then his cock is pressing against my entrance. My wetness allows him to ease right in, and then he's fucking me like the beast that he is.

It feels so good, and I can feel my core starting to clench around his big cock, but then I feel Luca's hand coming down on my ass, and it jolts me out of the orgasm I was about to experience.

"This is your punishment, honey," Luca hisses. "This is for my pleasure. Not yours." He pumps his hips, enunciating every word as he says, "Don't...you...dare...come."

I try to move, but every time I do, I just sink down further into the snow. So, I'm forced to just lie there and take it, feeling every inch of his hard cock inside of me and desperately trying not to come.

"Fuck, yes!" Luca roars behind me as he finds his release, pulling out and marking me with stripes of cum on my bruised ass.

He takes a few seconds to come down from his high before he

helps me up and fixes my pants. My legs are shaking from the cold, and I'm so horny I could scream right now.

Luca chuckles, and that earns him a vicious glare from me, which only makes him laugh harder.

"Delayed gratification, Mrs. Vitale. I seem to recall you wanting that," he says with a smile before walking away from me.

I flip him off and sulk the whole way back to the house.

CHAPTER 49

Luca

KEEPING VERONA ON the edge all day has been quite entertaining, to say the least. And knowing that she's so horny and desperately craving my cock, and only my cock, makes me feel powerful, like I can conquer the world.

"Let's play some pool," I suggest while we're sitting on the couch watching TV. She's been trying to hump my bones all afternoon and evening, and I haven't given in to her yet.

"You want to play pool. Now?" she asks with a heavy sigh, and I can hear the disappointment in her voice.

I bite back a grin and tell her, "Yes, let's play."

I get up from the couch and extend my hand to her. When she reluctantly puts her hand in mine, I pull her up to a standing position and lead her over to the rec room.

A pool table sits in the middle of the room. There are various other games and electronics that we could play with, but I want to see Verona bent over this table as she strokes a long stick with her hands. Fuck, it's going to take all of my willpower to actually play the game and not put *my* long stick in her.

I pick up a pool cue and hand Verona one. The balls are already racked on the table, so I tell her, "Ladies first." I watch anxiously as she lines up a shot, breaking the cluster of balls and sending them scattering over the pool table. She manages to get one of the balls in a corner pocket.

"Stripes," she says.

I grin. "Then I'm solids."

She bends over the table, and my cock presses painfully against my zipper as I watch her swing her hips in an effort to get a good angle. I bite back a groan as I watch her stroke the pool cue between her fingertips before she releases it, smacking the tip against the number nine ball. She gets the shot in, and, fuck, color me impressed.

"I married a pool shark," I tell her, and she giggles.

"My great aunt had an old pool table in the basement. I used to play for hours since we rarely left the house."

I frown at that statement. Her great aunt was a real piece of work. I can't believe Verona's father would send his only daughter to live with someone like that. The woman barely took care of Verona. She didn't buy her things or spoil her the way she deserved. I'm just glad that I can make up for lost time and give her the life she used to probably only dream about.

I watch her hit four more shots in until she finally misses one. I take my time lining up my shots, smacking ball after ball in and ultimately winning the game.

"You win," she says.

"What's my prize?" I ask as I turn to her.

At this point, she's pouting, thinking I don't want her when, in reality, I've never wanted her or anyone else more in my entire life than in this moment.

"Whatever you want," she answers before her pink tongue darts out of her mouth to lick her lips.

"Whatever I want?" I pace around the floor, looking her up and down. She's still mad about earlier when I wouldn't let her come. I guess I should make it up to her, but I want to tease her a little more first. I love that she's so hot and wet for me.

"Get on the pool table, Verona," I tell her. She raises her brows in confusion. "Don't make me tell you again. Climb on the table, lie on your back and hang your head over the edge."

She carefully hoists herself up onto the table and does what I instructed. With her head hanging over the edge, her beautiful, long neck is exposed. I stroke her silky, smooth skin and feel her swallow hard under my hand.

"Do you want to suck my cock?" I ask her.

"Yes," she answers without hesitation.

I smile, satisfied. "Tell me."

"I want to suck your cock," she says softly.

"Mm, honey, I love hearing filthy words come out of your sexy mouth." I pull down my sweatpants over my hips and position myself in front of her. I watch in awe as her pink tongue darts out and licks around the crown. "Open wide for me, honey," I tell her. When she does as she's told, I feed my cock between her bee-stung lips and into her soft, wet mouth. My cock swells in her mouth as she tastes me, licks me and sucks me.

I watch my cock slide down her throat. She gags, but she doesn't fight me or try to make me stop. "Fuck, you're perfect for me," I praise her with a groan. Her hand reaches out to touch my thigh, and then she's kneading my heavy balls while she continues to suck me. I pump my hips slowly, making her take every last inch of me in her mouth and throat before pulling out again. I'm so fucking close, but I don't want to come just yet. Stepping back away out of her reach, I tell her, "Your turn."

I walk over to the oversized couch and lie down. "Your throne is awaiting, my queen," I tell her before I motion for her to join me.

Verona slowly gets undressed and walks over to me. "You want me to..."

"I want you to sit on my face, Verona. I want to taste that pussy before I ravage it with my cock."

She shudders at my words before climbing onto the couch and positioning her thighs on either side of my head. Grabbing her ass, I pull her down to my mouth. I don't start slow. No, I fucking devour her, relishing in the sounds of her whimpers and cries above me as she holds on to the back of the couch for dear life.

I lick, suck and bite gently, feasting on her like a desperate, starving man. She begins to squirm, trying to escape the intense pleasure, but I wrap my hands around her thighs and hold her to me, not caring if I even breathe at this point. I focus my efforts on her clit, driving her crazy with lust as she begins moaning loudly.

I know she's close, so I remove my hands from her thighs and move them around to stick a few fingers into her trembling pussy and press one finger inside of her tight, little puckered hole.

Verona cries out, "Yes, Luca!" And then she's almost screaming as she grinds down on my fingers and face, coming so hard. I can feel both of her holes gripping me so damn tight, and I can't wait to fill her with my cock and feel it all over again.

I keep licking her until she begs me to stop. When her legs eventually stop shaking, I tell her, "I want to watch you ride my cock, honey."

Moving down my body, she positions herself over my waiting cock, which is weeping in anticipation for her pussy. She slowly sinks down on my length until she's fully seated. And fuck, it feels like heaven.

"Your greedy little cunt has been craving my cock all day, hasn't it?"

"Yes!" she cries out.

Verona works her hips, grinding down on me. I grip her hips in a bruising hold as I lift mine to meet her on every downstroke, and it only intensifies the feeling.

Her hands go to her breasts, and she plays with her little rosy nipples, turning me on even more. I love watching her play with herself. "Touch your clit for me, honey."

Her hand moves from her breast, down her stomach and in between her legs. She grinds against me as she fingers herself, and I don't think I've ever seen a more erotic sight before in my life. I'm going to keep this image ingrained in my brain forever.

"Fuck," I hiss through clenched teeth. "Your body was made for sinning," I tell her.

"So was yours," she groans.

I grip her hips, driving her down my cock harder and harder and bringing us ever closer to the abyss we both crave.

Liquid pleasure floods through my veins as I throw my head back onto the couch and come harder than I think I've ever come before.

Verona continues to grind down on me, chasing her own orgasm until she shatters on my cock. She collapses on my chest, exhausted, and I continue to fuck her nice and slow by pistoning my hips in a relentless rhythm while she rides out wave after wave of pleasure on my cock.

When we're both fully spent, I relax my legs and hold her to me. Our chests rise and fall rapidly in a rhythm together until we're both able to catch our breath.

"Can you die from having too many orgasms?" she asks softly.

A loud chuckle erupts out of my chest. "I don't know, but it would be one hell of a way to go, wouldn't it?"

We lie on the couch for a long time after that, and eventually she falls asleep on top of me. I don't want to move her, but I don't want her to get cold in the middle of the night. So, as carefully as I can, I move her off to the side of the couch so that I can stand up. Then, I pick her up in my arms and carry her to the master bedroom.

I tuck my sleeping beauty into the bed, covering her up. And then I do something I've never done before in my life. I watch her sleep. I don't even realize I'm doing it until a chill starts to set in, and I realize I've been standing there for several minutes, just watching her.

And in that moment, it just kind of hits me all at once, like a ton of bricks.

I'm in love with Verona Vitale.

I love her more than anything on this fucking planet.

I would kill for her. I would live for her. But more importantly, if it came right down to it, I would die for her.

She is my entire world now. And I'll do whatever it takes to protect her.

CHAPTER 50

Verona

THE NEXT DAY, something is different about Luca. He isn't his normal, brooding, controlling self. He's more demure, quiet. It could just be that he's still tired from last night. I know I am. Those orgasms knocked me out. Literally. I don't even remember Luca carrying me to bed last night, but he must have, because I woke up this morning warm and snuggly inside the king-sized bed under a mountain of blankets.

After we both shower and get dressed in our warmest clothes later that morning, we take a trip into a nearby small touristy town. It's our last day in Colorado, and Luca suggested we stay away from the slopes and just do some sightseeing. I overwhelmingly agreed with that idea, because between skiing and riding him last night, my legs are officially out of commission. I need to recover, and some light walking sounds way better than trying to balance myself on skis all day...or on another kind of pole.

Luca parks the car and puts some change into the meter as we step up onto the sidewalk. The town looks like it's straight out of a Hallmark movie. The numerous store windows are decorated with Christmas lights and tiny trees and wreaths, and there are decorations hanging from every streetlamp and sign. It's only the beginning of November but seeing all the holiday décor really puts me in the mood for Christmas.

The first place we go to is a little coffee shop on the corner for some hot chocolate. The day is cold with a breeze, and the hot liquid is just what I need to stay warm. Back in New York, it doesn't get bitterly cold like this until December or January, so I'm not used to the sudden change in weather.

We walk hand in hand, enjoying the scenery and each other's company as we explore the town. "We need to buy something to remember this place," I announce as we enter yet another store.

"Like what?"

"I don't know yet, but I'll know when I see it," I assure him. We walk through the store, browsing separately for a while. There are a lot of touristy things to buy, but none of them catch my eye. Then, I walk past a wall of magnets. It reminds me of the magnets Mama used to put on our fridge at home. Whenever her and Papa went anywhere, she would buy a magnet as a little memento to remember the time and place. Since she was always in the kitchen cooking something or other, she looked at the magnets often. I was never allowed to play with them or move them. They were sacred to her.

And their tradition can now become ours.

Searching, I find the perfect one. It has the town name over a picture of the town and even has the snowy mountains in the background, which I have come to absolutely love.

I pull the magnet from the metal wall and find Luca. "How about this?" I ask him before placing the magnet in his hand.

He stares at the souvenir and smiles. "That's perfect."

I can't help but smile back. "We could collect magnets at every place we visit. Maybe someday our fridge will be full of places we've been to."

He looks up at me with a strange look on his face. And then his mouth is suddenly attacking mine in the middle of the store. His tongue demands entry against my lips, and I grant him access. His tongue sweeps over mine as he devours me.

Realizing where we are and that we probably have eyes on us, I put my hands between us and press lightly on his chest. When we finally come up for air, I tell him, "Jeez, if I had known you liked magnets so much, I would've bought a ton of them the other night."

A deep, hearty laugh comes from Luca, and it makes me smile. "It's not the magnets, Verona. It's you. I want to see the world with you." He pulls me close and whispers in my ear, "With you by my side, I don't think there's anything I can't do. I could conquer the universe with you beside me."

I blush at his words. It's hard to believe that not that long ago Luca hated the very sight of me. I would go so far as to say he loves me now, even though he hasn't said the words out loud yet. Actions speak louder than words, though. And if today is any indication of his true feelings for me, then I would say he's fallen for me just like I have for him.

After we pay for the magnet, we walk outside. It's starting to snow. Snowflakes cascade down around us, melting against our heated skin as the world blurs into the background. It feels like it's only us on the entire planet right now.

Luca pulls me to him so that we're only a few inches apart and stares down at me with a look on his face that I can't quite decipher. "You're so beautiful," he whispers to me.

I blink up at him with snowflakes sticking to my long lashes. "Thank you for bringing me here," I tell him. "The past few days have been some of the best in my life."

"I feel the same way," he says before placing a kiss to my forehead. "You're freezing. Let's go back to the house and get you warmed up."

"That sounds like a great idea," I agree.

～

Later that night, Luca doesn't fuck me hard and fast. No, he makes love to me. He caresses and kisses and licks every inch of my body and fills me with his cock so slowly that my orgasm is almost euphoric.

And after he reaches his release, Luca looks into my eyes and tells me, "Verona, I love you."

Tears fill my eyes and I bite my lip, desperately trying to hold back my emotions. I never thought I would hear those three words come from his mouth. And I'm not sure if I can even process them right now.

"Say something," he says, his eyes searching my face.

"I love you too," I tell him quickly. "So much. More than anything or anyone on this entire planet, Luca."

He groans at my words and places a sweet kiss on my lips. He rocks in and out of me, and I can feel him growing hard again.

"You're insatiable," I tell him with a giggle.

"Only for you," he confesses before kissing me until we're both needy and breathless.

We spend the rest of the night making love, and I can't think of a better way to end our honeymoon.

CHAPTER 51

Verona

THE MOMENT WE land in New York, I can sense a change in Luca. Gone is the carefree Luca I had grown to love while we were on our honeymoon. Now, he is back to being his brooding, serious self. But I understand why he has to be that way. You can't be perceived as weak in the world we live in. Weakness will get you killed.

When we get back to the house, Luca carries our luggage in. There is a large, wrapped package inside the door, and Luca remarks, "Our painting arrived."

"Where should we hang it?" I ask him.

"Wherever you want to," he tells me.

"Hmm, I'll think about it," I say before I walk into the kitchen to place the magnet that we bought yesterday on the fridge. It looks so foreign on the stainless-steel surface with nothing else around it, but it makes me smile and look forward to our future together. Maybe one day we'll have the entire fridge filled with mementos of our adventures together.

Warm arms wrap behind me, and I sink into his touch. But when I smell an unfamiliar cologne, I wrench away and spin around so fast it almost makes me dizzy.

"Dante," I gasp. "What are you doing?"

"I can't hug my friend?" he asks, trying to play the whole thing off as friendly when it clearly wasn't. "I missed you," he says with a warm smile.

Luca enters the kitchen and looks between Dante and me with a frown. "Leave us, Dante," he says with a severe tone.

Dante gives me one last longing look before he reluctantly leaves the kitchen.

"What's wrong?" Luca asks, coming to me and pulling me into his embrace.

It's scary how well he can read me now. "Nothing," I say, trying to downplay what just happened with Dante. I don't want to get him into trouble, and I definitely don't want to ruin Luca's good mood that he's been in for days now. "I was just putting our magnet on the fridge."

He peers over my head, and a big smile appears on his face. "We'll add more soon," he promises.

I look down at the floor when I tell Luca, "Maybe I can talk to my father about having Dante return to his house to work for him."

Luca puts his finger under my chin and forces me to meet his gaze. "Did something happen?"

"No, no, it's not that," I lie. Recently, Dante's actions have been weirding me out, but I don't want to alarm Luca. I know Dante would never hurt me. But I think his feelings for me are growing, even though I'm not reciprocating them in any way. Maybe it's because I'm married now, and the whole wanting what he can't have thing? I'm not sure. "Maybe you could hire someone else to protect me when Benito can't?" I suggest.

"I'll make some calls first thing tomorrow morning," he assures me. He seems happy about my decision. Leaning down, he kisses the top of my head. "Why don't you go get some rest? I know you were tired on the plane, but you refused to stop looking out the window."

"I am pretty tired," I say with a yawn.

"I'm going to catch up on things with Benito. I'll see you tonight for dinner," he says before placing a quick kiss on my lips.

"Sounds good," I agree. I walk out of the kitchen and almost run smackdab into Dante. Was he listening at the door? "What are you doing?" I ask him curtly.

"I'm going to get something for lunch," he says, but there's something off about his tone and demeanor.

I walk past him and to our bedroom. I'm even more convinced now that having Dante move out of the house is the best decision for Luca and me. Dante is proving to be like a third wheel when I'm trying to build a relationship with my new husband. Luca and I have come so far, and I'm not going to let anyone ruin our chances at real, forever love. Not even my best friend.

CHAPTER 52

Luca

BENITO ENTERS MY office a short time after I've settled down at my desk. The look on his face is serious and drawn, like he's been contemplating how to tell me bad news for a while.

"You received a delivery," he tells me.

I smile. "I know. I saw the painting by the door when we arrived home."

"No, not that. Something else came in the mail." He approaches and slides a manilla envelope across my desk. I stare at the envelope. It seems innocent enough. I turn it over and notice my name scrawled on the front in unfamiliar handwriting. "Who sent this?" I ask.

"We don't know. It appeared in the mailbox the other night."

I frown at that revelation. A hand-delivered letter can't contain anything good when you live in the kind of world that we do.

Opening the envelope, I dump the contents out on my desk. Photo after photo of Verona appears before my eyes. Some are far away, through a telephoto lens, like Verona and I in the airport just a few days ago. And others are close, far too close for my liking. Her at the mall, shopping. My fingertips grip the edges of the photos that are zoomed in of her ass and breasts, and I crinkle the edges as a fury erupts inside of me.

"And you have no idea who did this?" I ask him.

"No, boss."

"That's not what I want to hear. I want to know who sent these and why. What's their fucking game?" I demand, standing and pounding my fists against my desk.

"We were hoping that maybe you would have an inkling as to who might have done this. Give us a lead," Benito suggests.

I stare at the photos and look up at him. There's only one man who would do this. One man who has threatened Verona, touched her, tried to take her away from me. "Constantine Carbone," I say. "He threatened Verona the night of the art gallery. Told her he'd see her again soon." I glance down at the pictures. "He has to be the person behind all of this."

"We should have gone after him the moment he laid a finger on Verona."

"I know," I agree, nodding. "But I promised her I wouldn't go to war over it." I sit down at my desk and lock eyes with my most trusted friend. "Now I don't think we have a choice."

"I'll get the men prepared," Benito says before leaving my office.

I sit in the room alone, pissed off and over-thinking everything. I can't believe just an hour ago I was planning vacation trips in my head with Verona. I wanted to travel with her, leave this world behind us. But that's the thing with the mafioso, you can never leave. Not unless you're in a casket. I shouldn't have entertained such childish illusions. And thanks to letting my guard down, I have to come back home to this fucking mess.

My eyes dart to the pictures once again; and the longer I stare at them, the more furious I become.

Constantine fucked with the wrong man. If he wants a war, then that's exactly what he's going to get. Because I won't back down, and I won't fucking stop until he's dead.

CHAPTER 53

Verona

WHEN I WAKE up the next morning, Luca is nowhere to be seen. I vaguely remember a call in the middle of the night that took him away from me in a hurry, but he promised I had nothing to worry about.

I slowly sit up, and a wave of nausea hits me instantly. I barely make it to the bathroom in time before I'm retching in the toilet.

I groan as I flush and manage to pull myself to look at my reflection in the sink. A sheen of sweat covers my face, and I quickly rinse my mouth out with water before brushing my teeth and swigging some mouthwash.

It's a good thing Luca wasn't here when I woke up. He wouldn't have wanted to witness that mess, and he would have been worried.

I guess the jetlag really got to me...or maybe I have food poisoning. I'm trying to think of what I ate last night while I'm rummaging through the lower cabinet for a towel and washcloth when I spot a box of tampons. Furrowing my brow, I try to think of the last time I needed a tampon. It's been...weeks. A month? More than a month?

"Oh, no," I gasp as I try to count back how many days I actually haven't had a period. I can't even remember the last time. Luca and I have been fucking like bunnies for a while, and I can only recall one period.

"Oh, my god," I groan, wiping my sweaty face with my hand. Pregnancy isn't something that Luca and I have discussed. I mean, we knew the consequences from having sex...*so much sex*...without condoms, so I'm assuming he wanted children. But he's never mentioned it. What if he doesn't want children? That would be completely irresponsible of us not to use protection then.

I pace the bathroom, trying not to freak out. Then another thought hits me. What if he assumed I was on birth control? What if he thought we were protected the whole time and that's why he never wore a condom?

My inner thoughts are strangling me to the point that I'm having trouble breathing. I'm panicking and overanalyzing every single thing, but I can't help it. Luca is so hard to figure out at times; and when it comes to this, I have no idea how he's going to react.

Placing my palms down on the countertop, I steady myself. I can't allow myself to overreact to something that I'm not even certain of. First things first, I need someone to get me a pregnancy test. Once I take it, then I can decide the next step.

"Baby steps," I tell myself out loud, and then I cringe at the word *baby*. Oh god, this is going to change everything.

∼

It's later that morning when I encounter Benito in the hallway. He looks like he's in a rush and already has a destination in mind, but I quickly pull on his arm and beg him to follow me. He reluctantly does as I ask.

"I need your help," I tell him.

"What is it? Did something happen?" he's quick to ask, concern lacing his features.

I swallow hard. I'm trusting Benito with more than I've ever trusted anyone before. But I'm too afraid to ask Dante for this favor, because judging by his recent reactions to Luca and my relationship, he'll just flip out on me and wouldn't help me anyway.

I lean up on my tiptoes and whisper into the giant's ear, "I need you to get me a pregnancy test."

He pulls back, his eyes wide. "What?" he asks as if he misheard me.

"I need the test, Benny," I say vehemently. "And I want you to keep this between you and me. For now," I add quickly. "I'll tell Luca. I will. I just want to be the one who does it...when I'm ready," I tell him in a rush.

He groans and swipes a hand down his face. "Luca is not going to be happy that I'm leaving the house when we've been under attack since last night."

"We're under attack?" I ask, panic lacing my voice.

"We have it under control," he assures me. He glances at his watch. "There's a pharmacy not too far from here. I can be back here in less than fifteen minutes."

"Thank you, Benny!" I exclaim, wrapping my arms around him in a hug.

He stiffens against me, probably not used to such emotion or maybe even affection at all. He clears his throat until I back away from him. And then he's out the door, retrieving me something that might change my entire life.

CHAPTER 54

Luca

BEFORE I EVEN made the decision on when and how to attack Constantine, our entire computer server went under attack late last night. Someone cracked into our main computer and sent out a virus, infecting every computer connected to the network.

Aldo has been desperately fixing the problem, but he hasn't been able to give me a definite answer yet on who is behind all of this. My assumption is Constantine, of course, but it could be any number of enemies that I've accumulated over the years.

I'm biding my time when it comes to going after Constantine until I have hard, concrete proof. And then, once I do, I'm personally going to destroy his empire until there's nothing left but burning ashes on the charred fucking ground.

First the photos and now this. It all has to be connected. I just wish I knew who was behind it all and what their reasoning is behind it. If they want money, they can have it. But if they want something else...if they want *someone* else, then that's a whole other matter, and they'll have to go through me first to get to Verona.

My office has officially been taken over by my men. Aldo is in the corner, furiously typing away on his laptop, while he barks out instructions to the other IT guys on my team. There are computers, monitors, laptops, cords, wires and cables everywhere. It's a fucking mess, but we're working on borrowed time here.

I know this is the safest place on the property given that the walls were specially reinforced. Hell, even the glass in the windows is bulletproof. I spend most of my time here, so I needed to make sure it was secure.

We have a secret underground bunker on the property, and I'm sure we'll be going there shortly, but I feel safe here for right now. Besides, the reception in the bunker is spotty, at best, and we need as much communication as we can get right now.

Looking around the room, I ask, "Where the fuck is Benito?"

A second later, Benito rushes into my office. "Sorry, boss. Got hung up on something."

"We need everyone here," I tell him sternly. I don't need any of my men to go missing when we're under attack.

"Understood," Benito says with a nod.

"I managed to effectively wipe out the virus on our system," Aldo says, which elicits some cheers and whistles from the rest of my team. "I'm still trying to figure out how they cracked into the network to begin with. I'm tracing everything back now."

"Hurry, Aldo," I tell him with urgency. I need to know what the attacker's game is that they are obviously playing. Do they want to harm us by trying to steal information, or is it something much more sinister?

CHAPTER 55

Verona

TWO PINK LINES.
I stare down at the tests. Benito ended up buying me three just in case, and I'm glad that he did...although all of them read the same results.

I'm pregnant.

I have spent the entire morning and afternoon in our bedroom, pacing and freaking out. Luca hasn't appeared even once, and I don't know if that's a good thing or a bad thing. I want to tell him about the baby, *our baby*, but I have no idea what his reaction is going to be.

Wiping away the stray tears from my cheeks, I gather the tests and hide them in the counter under the sink. There's a time and place for everything, but Luca being stressed out and trying to combat a cyber-attack is definitely bad timing.

After a nice, hot shower, I go to the closet and put on some comfy clothes — a pair of black yoga pants and an oversized tie-dye hooded sweatshirt.

There's a small pocket on the yoga pants, and it's the perfect size for the cellphone Luca insists I have on me at all times. When I pull the sweatshirt down, it hides the pocket and the phone. Even though I usually feel silly having the phone on me, I feel safer having the phone with me today, especially since someone is trying to breach my husband's security.

I dry my hair, blowing it straight, and put on a little makeup — some mascara, blush and a pink glossy lipstick. I don't need much to enhance my natural features, but I want to look pretty since I've felt sick, bloated and gross for most of the day.

I slip on a pair of socks and sneakers and make my way downstairs. The house is eerily quiet.

"Verona," someone says my name, and I nearly jump out of my skin.

I turn to see Dante, and I instantly sigh in relief. "You scared me."

His eyes skate over my body, perusing me so openly that I suddenly feel shy. Dante never lets his true feelings show, but I know he's attracted to me. I don't know why I'm just noticing it now. Maybe it's because of everything Luca has been telling me...

"Where's Luca?" I ask, and that seems to break him out of his trance.

"They're all in his office trying to figure out who's behind the cyber-attack."

I turn to go in the direction of the office, but Dante grabs my arm, hauling me back to him. "You really shouldn't be here. It's not safe."

I stare up into his familiar, dark eyes. "I'm sure Luca can make that decision." Then, I shrug out of his hold and continue on my way to his office.

The door isn't locked. And when I walk into the room, Luca and his team, including Benny, are gathered around numerous computers and laptops. Luca looks up when I enter, and I can almost see the look of relief on his face.

He glances at the expensive watch on his wrist and frowns. "I'm sorry I've been gone all this time. Have you eaten?"

I nod even though it's a lie. My stomach has been in knots all day, and I was barely able to keep down a piece of toast earlier.

I walk over to him and stare at the laptop in front of him. The code running across the screen hurts my eyes, and I don't know how he's analyzing anything in that mess.

Luca pulls me into his lap and places a soft but chaste kiss to my lips. In my ear, he whispers, "I can't wait to be done with this, so I can take you to our bedroom and get lost for hours in your sweet, tight pussy."

I wriggle on his lap, instantly turned on even though we're in a room packed full of people. His teeth nip at my neck before his arm wraps around me possessively. My stomach does a flip knowing he's holding me...and our baby...even though he has no idea.

Suddenly, the lights in the room go out, and then there's a loud explosion coming from the other end of the property.

"Fuck," Luca hisses, holding me so tightly to him that it scares me.

Benito is the first to speak in the darkness. "Hector reported an explosion just went off near the guard tower on the western side of the property. One of the guards was hurt, but he's going to be okay." He flips on the light on his phone, as so do several others, illuminating the dark room.

"This has to be Constantine," Luca says, slamming his fist down on his desk and causing me to jump. "I should have killed that motherfucker when I had the chance!"

Constantine Carbone. The man I foolishly danced with at the ball, and the man Luca almost killed for touching me at the art gallery. Little did I know how deep their rivalry went. And now he's attacking our home, putting us in danger.

Is this all my fault? I can't help but wonder that question even as Luca squeezes me tighter to him as if he's afraid of letting go.

"Benito, I want you to take Verona to the safehouse." He gently pushes me off his lap as we both stand. "It's not safe for her here right now, and I can't concentrate on what needs to be done with her in danger."

"I'm not leaving," I say at the same time Benito says, "I'm staying."

Luca narrows his eyes at his first-in-command. "You will do what I say!" he demands.

"My place is here, with you," Benito answers, standing his ground. If Luca's first in command is anything, it's loyal. And his loyalty to his best friend knows no bounds.

"I'll take her," Dante says, having suddenly appeared in the room at some point.

Luca stares at him, and I can feel the apprehension rolling off of him in waves. I turn to Luca and say, "I don't want to leave. I want to stay here with you."

He closes his eyes and nods as if making an internal decision. "Dante will take you to the safehouse. He knows where it is." Then, he turns his attention to Dante. "Take one of the SUVs. Call us as soon as you arrive and if any problems arise along the way," Luca rambles off the instructions.

"No!" I exclaim, clinging to Luca. "Please, Luca! I'm safe here. With you!"

He shakes his head as he stares down at me. "You're safer where I'm not," he tells me. Leaning down, he places a kiss on my lips. "I will come get you the moment it's clear. We'll be together again soon," he says before kissing me again.

This kiss feels like the last, for some god-awful reason, and I cling to him for dear life, kissing him like our plane is going down.

Luca is the first to pull away before saying, "Now, go." Then, to Dante, he says, "You're responsible for her. Don't make me regret this decision," he threatens.

Dante gives him a nod before turning his attention to me. "Come on, Verona. We have to go quickly."

Tears fill my eyes as he rips me away from my husband. I stare back at Luca, trying not to cry and failing miserably before Dante drags me out of the room and towards the garage that houses all the vehicles.

Opening the back door to a black SUV, Dante impatiently waits for me to climb into the backseat before slamming the door and running to climb into the front seat. He revs the engine, hits a button for the garage door to open and peels out of the garage.

I fasten my seatbelt, my hands going protectively over my stomach. "Please, Dante, slow down! I don't want to die on the way to the safehouse!" I cry out.

"Sorry," he says.

We make it past the front gate, and he seems to slow down a little as we venture down the road. I turn in my seat and watch the dark house in the distance. And then that's when the darkness lights up with fireballs as explosion after explosion erupts within the house.

I scream at what I just witnessed and reach for my seatbelt, unfastening it quickly. I reach for the door handle and pull, but it's locked.

"Please! Dante, we have to go back!" I scream at him. I hit the unlock button, but it locks before I can reach the handle.

"We can't go back, Verona!" he yells. "We have to go to the safehouse, just like Luca wanted."

"What if Luca's hurt? He could be hurt! He could be..." No, I won't even let myself think like that. Luca can't be dead. *He is not dead.*

Tears stream down my cheeks as I desperately try for the handle again, but I know Dante is holding down the lock button.

"We're going to the safehouse, Verona, and that is final," he tells me, his voice devoid of emotion as he stares straight ahead.

I stare back at the fire engulfing the house as Dante speeds up, driving us away from it.

Sobs tear from me as I assume the worst. And what makes me cry the hardest is that I never got the chance to tell Luca that I'm pregnant with his child.

CHAPTER 56

Verona

I'M WRINGING MY hands in my lap as Dante drives us to... who the hell knows where. I don't even know where the safehouse is or how long it's going to take before we get there. It could be in another state, for all I know.

We ditched the SUV we were originally in because Dante said that's what Luca wanted him to do. And now we're in an old sedan that he hotwired in the parking lot of a gas station. Even though I didn't want to believe it was part of Luca's plan, I have no idea what he and Dante discussed. I mean, I didn't even know about the safehouse. And Dante hasn't ever given me a reason not to trust him, so why start now?

"How much longer?" I ask Dante, and I don't care if I sound like a whiny child on a long road trip. I need to know how soon we can stop so that he can try to reach out to Luca. I need to know he's okay.

"Not much longer," Dante says, and his voice sounds different, weird.

He's also acting weird; has been ever since we left the house and he refused to let me roam more than a few inches from him this entire time, even when he was hotwiring the car. I guess that's the biggest reason why I haven't told him about the cellphone I have safely tucked in the pocket of my yoga pants. The longer we're in this car, the more I feel like I can't fully believe or trust Dante. But deep down I know that's probably just absurd. Dante would never hurt me. I've known him almost my entire life.

And yet my hands keep sweating and my heart won't stop pounding in my chest every time I meet his eyes in the rearview mirror. Something has changed, and my fight or flight response is kicking into gear against my best friend. I need to find out why.

"Can you call Luca now?"

"He's dead, Verona," he says so assuredly that it sends a chill up my spine.

"You don't know that!" I protest vehemently.

"I know. And he is," he says through gritted teeth. Then he adds, "You don't have to worry about him anymore."

My eyes fill with tears, but I refuse to let them fall. I was right in not trusting Dante. He's changed ever since I married Luca. He's become more possessive and unpredictable.

Feeling desperate, I keep my eyes locked on the rearview mirror to make sure his eyes are on the road before I carefully retrieve the cell phone from my pocket. I flip it open, turn the volume the whole way down and press and hold the number one button. Once I see the call connecting, I quickly close it so that the light doesn't give me away and tuck it back into my pocket.

If Luca is alive...or Benny...or anyone, hopefully they'll get the call and be able to trace it.

"Dante, how much longer?" I ask.

"I already told you, Verona, not much longer," he says vaguely. "Fuck, you're just like your mother. So impatient."

I grow angry at his comment. How dare he talk about my dead mother like he knew her better than me. I'm surprised he even remembers her. He was only around her for a short period of time before she died.

"Don't talk about my mother like that!" I yell, my voice thick with overwhelming emotion.

A crazed laugh escapes his lips, and the car swerves on the road as he cackles loudly. "Your mother was a cunt," he spits out. "Always asking me to do things for her, like I was her goddamn servant. So entitled."

I shake my head at him. My mother was never like that. My mother was the sweetest person on the planet. "You're lying," I tell him.

"She deserved to die. Just like Luca's mother." His hands tighten on the steering wheel, his knuckles turning white. "Once I killed your mother, I knew that his was next. It just took a little longer to get to her."

The breath leaves my lungs in one gasp as I try to process his words. "W-what did you just say?" I stammer, not believing him.

"Your father took my mother away from me. Killed her right in front of me. Along with my father, but hey, he was a bastard that deserved to die anyway. But my mother...no, my mother didn't deserve that horrible fate." He moves his head from side to side, cracking his neck. "I wasn't able to have a mother, so you didn't deserve to have one either." He continues on with, "Your mother wanted pudding that day. Always asking for shit," he hisses angrily. "So, after the cook was done making it, I crushed up a bottle of sleeping pills I found in her medicine cabinet and mixed them in." A sadistic smile tugs at his lips. "She stumbled around and around, knocking into things, before I led her outside to the pool. Just a small push was all it took until she fell in."

"You monster!" I scream at him. Unbuckling my seatbelt, I reach into the front seat and start pounding him with my small fists.

He easily deflects my hits and swerves the car off the road, slamming to a stop. I fly into the seat in front of me, the wind knocked from my lungs. I gasp for air to return to my lungs as he looks back at me with a hateful look in his eyes.

"You weren't supposed to be the one to find her. I wanted your dad to discover her body floating in the pool." He shrugs nonchalantly. "I wanted him to feel the same pain I felt when I lost my mother."

When I'm finally able to suck in a full breath, I hiss at him, "We saved you! We took you in."

"Saved me?" he scoffs. "Your father ruined my life!"

The car is filled with silence for a long time. And then I have to ask, "But why Luca's mother? What did she ever do to you?"

"The Morettis along with the Vitales made the decision to kill my family after my father betrayed them. They were all in business together, you see. So, after they murdered my mother and father, I wanted the families to go to war, destroy each other. There was only one way to ensure that would happen." He hesitates, staring off into the distance as if remembering something. "I snuck into the house early one morning and killed Luca's mother. I killed her the same way the Morettis had killed so many before her, three slashes to the throat, so that the Vitales would assume it was them. And the Vitales believed it. They went to war with your father, trying to overtake everything he owned. The war went on for years, and both families just tore each other apart at every fucking chance they got." He shakes his head and sneers. "And then this little wedding fucked everything up. I wanted more blood to be shed. I wanted them to wipe each other out of existence. I wanted to watch your father's empire crumble to the ground."

I silently sob in the backseat. There are no words for Dante's betrayal, the hurt he caused both of our families. I feel ashamed that I ever had feelings for this monster. All the times he consoled me after my mother's death, when he was responsible for it the entire time, makes me physically ill.

Dante climbs out of the car and looks around, checking his phone. "We're here."

"Where?" I ask.

"Right where we're supposed to be," he says vaguely before opening the back door and dragging me out by my hair. I scream and kick, fighting for my life in the darkness surrounding us.

I'm vaguely aware of the phone slipping out of my pocket and landing on the road beneath me as I fight him.

Dante drags me down the road for what feels like a mile before we come to a stop. In the darkness, I can see the moonlight cascading off the dark water. And as he continues dragging me towards it, panic begins to set in. "No, no, no!" I beg, thinking he's going to drown me in that water.

Dante throws me to the ground and towers over me. "Time to get in the boat, sweetheart," he sneers.

"No! I won't! I can't!" I cry out, hysterical.

"Well, since you won't do it the easy way, we'll have to do it the hard way," he tells me right before something hard smacks me in the head and the world around me goes black.

CHAPTER 57

Luca

MY EARS ARE still ringing from the deafening explosion that just happened, and it takes me several long minutes to gather my composure and take in my surroundings.

The house around us is burning and smoke fills up my lungs as I take a deep breath. Coughing, I struggle to crawl out from under the rubble of what used to be my desk and fail miserably. I'm stuck under here. Blood trickles down my forehead and into my eyes as I call out for my men.

Some of them answer. I guess some is better than none.

Someone grabs me, pulling me out from under the charred desk. *Benito.*

"Gather what we can, and let's get the fuck out of here," I instruct him. A huge hole in the side of the mansion is our exit point as we carry out as much equipment as we can.

"Mr. Vitale," my head IT guy, Aldo, says when he emerges. He looks worse for wear; his dark hair disheveled, his face blackened with soot and his glasses askew on his young face.

"Yes," I answer quickly, wanting to know what he knows.

"I was able to trace the signal that triggered the explosions. It didn't come from Constantine or any outside source. It came from inside our own network. It took a little while to trace the source, but I know it was from a phone on or near the property that generated the explosions."

"Fuck!" I hiss, looking around at my group of men. I know none of them are responsible, but then who? Who the fuck would want to hurt us? Who the fuck would try to *kill* us?

Realization suddenly dawns on me, and I demand, "Where's Verona?"

"You sent her away with Dante," Benito says slowly, no doubt thinking I hit my head too damn hard and forgot.

"Track the SUV. I want to know exactly where they are."

"It's going to take a few minutes to get the servers back online," Aldo instructs as he sits down on the grass with a laptop.

"Hurry the fuck up!" I tell him through clenched teeth. My gut is telling me Dante is somehow behind this and that Verona is in trouble. And the fact that I handed my most prized possession, *my queen*, over to that bastard makes my chest ache like someone is thrusting a thousand knives into the dark cavity.

"We need to move everyone to the underground bunker on the other side of the property," Benito says hurriedly. "I doubt if Dante knew about it. He might be ready to set off more bombs in the main house, and we can't risk losing anyone else."

I nod in agreement. "Yes, let's move to the bunker." Normally, I don't worry about my own life; but if I'm dead, who the hell is going to save Verona? I need to stay alive...for her.

∽

AFTER WE'RE all safe in the bunker and our generators are up and running, along with the backup servers, Aldo, informs me that the tracker on the SUV stopped at a small gas station outside of the city.

I go to him and look at the map. "That's not in the direction of the safehouse. He's not taking her there. He's taking her somewhere else." I stare at the time that has passed since the SUV stopped. Twenty-five minutes. Dante didn't simply stop to fuel up. He ditched the car, knowing we would be tracking him. "Get the surveillance footage from the store. They abandoned the SUV. We need to know where they went."

"Right away, sir," Aldo tells me.

Benito walks into the bunker with one of our staff that has a nursing background. She looks around the place warily as she's escorted straight to me. "You have some wounds that need to be addressed," Benito says.

I wipe at the blood still streaming down my face. "Head wounds always bleed hard and fast," I say, shrugging him off.

"You can't help Verona if you're passed out cold," he informs me, making me rethink my decision.

"Fine," I say with a huff. Then, I look at the young brunette, who is practically shaking with fear. "Quickly," I instruct her.

"Yes, sir," she says with a nod before reaching into her medical bag for what she needs.

As she's cleaning the wound and stitching me up and I'm trying not to curse and move from the pain, Aldo tells me he has the footage. "They left in a small four-door sedan."

"Trace the license plate. See if we can get a hit on any of the cameras in the area," I say. "Fuck!" I yell at the girl when she pierces my skin at a particularly sensitive area around my temple.

"I'm sorry, sir," she says.

I close my eyes and curse under my breath. "It's all right. Keep going. Hurry," I tell her.

Three more sutures are in when my phone in my pocket begins to ring. I'm quick to answer it without even glancing at the caller ID.

I hear nothing at first, but then voices begin to speak, having their own private conversation.

Furrowing my brows, I pull the phone back and stare at the caller ID.

Verona's name on the screen has my heart skipping a beat. I call for Aldo and tell him to connect the phone to a laptop to trace the call and to put the call on speaker so that we can hear the conversation.

Hearing Verona's sweet, melodic voice has an instant calming effect. But then when I hear Dante's much deeper, crueler voice, the anger builds right back up inside of me. My hands clench at my sides as I listen to him tell her that he killed her mother.

Verona's sobs fill the room, and it's almost too much to bear.

"I'm done, sir," the little nurse tells me, and I wave her away.

Benito escorts her out of the bunker before returning to my side, listening intently to the call.

When Dante begins to talk about killing my mother, my anger reaches a fever pitch. "That son of a bitch!" I roar.

I let the enemy into my home. The man that I've hunted for so long was right under my nose this entire time. He will suffer for his crimes. I will make him pay ten-fold. I will paint this entire fucking city with his blood.

I hear Verona and Dante struggling, and the phone falls, her screams fading off into the distance. "I will burn this entire world to the fucking ground until my wife is back in my arms," I tell everyone in the room, making it crystal clear of my intentions. "How long until you get their exact location?" I ask Aldo.

He looks up from his laptop and pushes his glasses up higher on his nose. "Almost got it, sir."

I turn to Benito. "Let's get the vehicles ready. Aldo can alert us on the way where we need to go. We can head to the gas station first, and hopefully have the information we need by the time we get there."

Benito nods in agreement, but he seems hesitant about something. Coming closer, he says lowly, "I need to tell you something private, boss."

"What is it?" The look on his face is something I've never seen before. Emotion. Benito is always so stoic, it's hard to remember that he's an actual person and not a fucking robot. And, shit, I don't think my heart can take any more devastating news.

"Your wife requested a pregnancy test this morning. She wanted discretion, and I gave that to her. But I thought you should know."

Pregnancy test? Verona is pregnant?

My legs suddenly give out, and I stumble into a nearby chair.

"I didn't see the test results," Benito informs me.

But I already know the result. I can feel it down in my dark fucking soul. Verona is pregnant. She hasn't had her period in a while, and I would know since I haven't been able to stop myself from being inside of her every waking moment.

She's pregnant with our baby. And Dante has them.

Clenching my fists, I rise and look at Benito. "We need to go. Now!" I demand.

He motions to several men in the room, and all of us run out of the bunker and to the SUVs in the garage so fast that it's a blur. All I can focus on is my wife and getting to her as quickly as possible.

Horrible thoughts barrage me as we fly out of the driveway and down the road. Verona didn't want to leave, and I made her go. I forced her to leave with Dante, the very man who killed both of our mothers.

If anything happens to Verona or the baby, I'll never be able to forgive myself.

CHAPTER 58

Verona

I COME TO gradually. My head is throbbing painfully, and it's difficult to even open my eyes. My throat is dry as I try to speak and fail miserably.

"Shh," Dante whispers from beside me. "You're all right, V. I had to knock you out, but we're here now."

Where is here?

I force my eyes to open as wide as they will go. The old cabin is open and decorated sparsely. A few kerosene lamps are scattered throughout the place, illuminating the old wood and rickety furniture.

I look down and realize I'm tied to a chair in the middle of the living room. I instantly struggle against my bonds, but Dante hushes me.

"You'll only hurt yourself, V," he instructs. "Don't waste your energy. I tied you up pretty tight. You're not getting out any time soon." Then he adds, "Even if you do...we're surrounded by water. And last I checked, you don't swim."

Despite his words, I continue to struggle until I'm too tired to do so. Then, I simply slump into the chair and begin to think about what happened just before I was knocked out. I made a phone call to Luca. Hopefully he was able to trace it and can find me before it's too late.

If he's alive, a little voice in the back of my head says.

Tears fill my eyes as I think about my life without Luca. Even though we had a horrible beginning to our marriage, I grew to love him with all of my heart and soul. He's the father of the baby growing inside of me, and I have no doubt that he would love his little boy or little girl more fiercely than anyone in this world.

"Are you thirsty?" Dante asks me. He's in the kitchen now, several feet away from me.

I shake my head. I'm not thirsty or hungry. I just want to be freed and able to return home. "Let me go, Dante. Please," I beg him, my voice raw.

He turns towards me with an angry look on his face. "This is our chance to be together now, V, and I'm not going to let anyone or anything ruin it."

I hang my head. Luca was right all along. Dante was obsessing over me, and I just couldn't see it. I should have listened to him. I should have told my father I didn't need Dante to watch over me. Luca was protecting me, keeping me safe. And, of course, once I'm away from my husband, I'm in more danger than I've ever been in my entire life.

I hear Dante approaching, and I look up just as he lifts a bottle of water to my lips. I turn my head, but he grabs the back of my neck, forcing me to drink. I sputter and try to swallow, coughing when he finally releases me.

"I can't have you getting dehydrated," he explains.

My hands curl into fists against the wooden arms as I glare at him. "Oh, you care about me now?" I practically scream. "You killed my mother! You obviously don't give a shit about me!"

"On the contrary, V," he says, sitting down in a chair across from me. "I love you. I've never loved another human being in my life... other than my own mother. But she was taken away from me by your asshole father." He leans over to me, and I flinch away from his touch. Frowning, he drops his hand. "I want to be with you. I won't get another chance like this. With Luca dead —."

"He's not dead!" I yell, interrupting him.

"Oh, he's most definitely dead. I set off several bombs in that mansion. It would be a miracle if anyone survived."

I shake my head at his admission. He's underestimating Luca and his team. Dante isn't a trained killer. Sure, he's probably killed in the past, but he's not an expert in homemade bombs. He could have messed something up. Maybe they weren't as strong as he thought they would be.

Or maybe they were stronger.

I grimace against the horrible thought in my head. I can't think like that right now. I need to believe that Luca is alive and is coming to save me. He's the only hope I have left. And if I let that go...I'll have absolutely nothing.

CHAPTER 59

Luca

"FASTER," I TELL Benito from the front seat. The SUV is almost to the gas station, and Aldo still hasn't provided me any more information. "What is taking him so long?" I hiss in anger.

"I'm sure he's trying his best," Benito says in an attempt to calm me down.

My phone rings, and I answer it on the first ring. "Where is she?" I demand.

"I'm not sure, sir," Aldo says. "They stopped on a back road. There is nothing for miles. The only thing I can see on the satellite images is an old fishing cabin in the middle of a huge lake."

"Send me the location."

"But, sir, it's abandoned. I don't think —."

"He took her there. I know it," I tell him, trusting my gut. "Now, give me the coordinates," I demand.

Aldo rattles off some directions, and I relay them quickly to Benito before ending the call.

"You really think they're in the middle of a lake?" he asks me.

"He knows she can't escape from there. It's surrounded by water," I say grimly. Verona must be terrified out of her mind. And the moment I get my hands on Dante, I'm going to watch the life drain from his eyes as I squeeze my hands around his fucking neck.

"Hurry, Benito." *Before it's too late.* I don't say the last words out loud, but I feel them deep down in my soul. Something bad is going to happen. I just don't know what yet.

THE WATER IS cold as we slowly and silently swim across it. I have a team of ten men including Benito and me. Who knows what the dark water is teeming with, but I don't care. All I care about is seeing Verona and making sure she's safe. And I won't stop until she's back home, with me, and in my arms.

When we reach the shore of the small island, all of us work on a system of hand gestures and signals. Tall trees and overgrown shrubbery line the perimeter. We slowly move through the brush and towards the cabin that sits in the middle of the land.

Benito stops suddenly beside me. "Solar trail cams," he whispers, motioning to small cameras and solar panels mounted on nearby trees.

"Motion activated?" I ask even though I already know the answer.

Benito nods in agreement. "Definitely."

"The son of a bitch had this all planned out for a while." And the thought of him planning on kidnapping my wife right from under my nose and taking her here to do god only knows what makes my fucking blood boil. The urge to kill him is what keeps my feet moving. "The element of surprise is gone, my friends," I announce to the group. "We need to get to that fucking cabin. Now!"

CHAPTER 60

Verona

"DANTE, PLEASE, LISTEN to me," I beg him for the millionth time.

He's been sitting at his laptop, staring at the screen for what feels like over an hour. I don't know what he's looking for, but it can't be good.

As time ticks by and Luca doesn't show up, I fear the worst. Maybe he is dead.

No. No, I can't allow myself to think that way.

Luca is coming for me. I can feel it deep down in my bones.

I just need to keep Dante distracted and away from that laptop. "I'm really thirsty," I tell Dante. It's not a total lie. I am thirsty, but I'm willing to do anything to get him away from whatever he's keeping track of.

Dante glances up at me, frowns, and reluctantly rises from his chair. He goes to the kitchen and pulls a bottle of water out of the plastic case. He unscrews the lid as he walks towards me.

My entire body shakes the closer he gets. I have so much pent-up fear, anxiety and hate towards him that it's seeping through my pores. I can't even pretend any more. *I hate him.*

When his fingers sweep across my chin, I pull back like I was just bitten. His frown deepens as he gauges my reaction to his touch. Then, more roughly, he grabs my chin, pinching it between his thumb and index finger as he brings the top of the water bottle to my lips. "Drink," he instructs.

I open my mouth as he pours a little bit of water into my mouth. I swallow quickly. He doesn't try to drown me, ironically. No, he's gentle, patient...and kind. And it makes me hate him even more. After what he did to my mother, how could he possibly be so nice to me?

"Enough," I tell him after the third sip. I can't bear to have him touching me any longer. And it hurts me to think that soon I might not have a choice in that matter. "How long are we staying here?" I ask, curiosity getting the best of me.

"Not long," he says cryptically. "We'll head out in the morning. I have a flight already booked for us."

"A flight to where?" I demand, panic setting in. If I get on a plane, Luca will never be able to find me.

Dante screws the lid back on the bottle and returns to the table, his attention back on the laptop. "You'll see," he says cryptically.

I hang my head, tears threatening to spill over, and I let them. I silently sob when I think about never seeing Luca again and spending the rest of my life with the man who murdered my mother.

Suddenly, Dante stands up, knocking over his chair in the process. My head snaps up just as his eyes meet mine. "How the fuck did he find us?" he demands. He reaches for something on the other side of the table. *A gun.* "Did Luca implant a tracker on you?"

I stare at him and refuse to answer. I know how they found me. The phone. Luca tracked the phone call. But Dante doesn't know about the phone. He never saw or heard it. He's assuming they found me by some other means.

Elation fills my body as I realize Luca is coming to save me. But that feeling is instantly crushed by the sight of the gun in Dante's hand. He'll never let Luca take me. This can only end badly and in bloodshed. Dante will make sure that someone's not going to make it out of this cabin alive.

Dante hurries over to me, untying the ropes holding me down so fast my head spins. Then, he hauls me up and out of the chair, pressing the gun to my temple. "He can't take you from me," Dante says hurriedly. "I won't let him."

And then I do the only thing I can do. I fight back.

CHAPTER 61

Luca

MY MEN ARE all getting in place, surrounding the cabin when a gunshot suddenly goes off. I check with the rest of the team to make sure one of us didn't fire first. When they all check in with me and relay it wasn't them, I realize the shot came from inside the cabin.

"Fuck!" I cry out, my legs carrying me fast to the front of the house. I have to get to her. *Before it's too late.*

"Luca, wait!" Benito calls after me, but I don't stop.

Relying on brute strength and adrenaline, I put all of my weight into my shoulder as I run full force into the front door. The old hinges creak and break, and the entire door frame crumbles around me as I fall inside the cabin.

I'm quick to get on my feet, but it's too late. Dante already has the gun trained on me.

My eyes instantly go to Verona, who Dante is keeping a death grip on. I search her body for injuries, and I blow out a sigh of relief when I realize she wasn't shot. Dante's face is scratched and bleeding, so I can only assume my little hellcat gave him what he deserved.

"Look at me, asshole, not her!" Dante shouts, shaking the gun in his hand to get my attention.

Reluctantly, my eyes meet his. "You really thought I wouldn't find her?" I ask him. "I would burn this fucking world to the ground just to find her."

That earns me a smirk from the bastard. "She's mine now. She was always mine."

My teeth grind together in anger. The fact that Dante even thinks he earned the right to lay claim on *my wife* makes me want to scoop his eyes out of his fucking skull with a spoon for even looking in her direction.

"There's no way out of this, Dante. Let her go," I tell him slowly, calmly.

Dante grips my wife tighter, crushing her body to his. "Never," he simply says before turning the gun on her, pressing it firmly against her temple.

"All it's going to take is one signal from me, and the ten guns trained on you will kill you on the spot," I inform him.

"Are you willing to bet I won't pull the trigger first? That she won't die first?" Dante threatens.

The answer is no. I don't want anything to happen to Verona, not even so much as a scratch. "Let her go, and I'll make your death a quick one." Even though I would love nothing more than to torture him and make him slowly pay for the crimes of murdering our mothers, I can't put a price on my wife's safety. On her life. That sweet, sweet revenge is simply off the table if it puts her at any kind of risk.

"Please, Dante." Verona's soft, melodic voice suddenly fills the tense room. "Please don't let it be like this. If you love me, you won't do this."

I swallow hard at her words. I know she's trying to pull at his heartstrings, if he even has a fucking heart or a conscience.

He looks down at her, kissing the side of her head. "I love you more than anything in this world, V. We're going to be together. Forever," he vows.

Verona's teary honey-colored eyes meet mine as she says, "I'm pregnant. I just found out this morning."

Her words have an effect on Dante. He stiffens, and his grip suddenly loosens. "Wh-what?" he demands, shocked.

Taking the opportunity, Verona pulls out of his grip and runs to the other side of the room, a few feet away from me.

"You're pregnant with his child?" Dante practically screams, waving the gun back and forth from me to Verona and back again.

He's unstable, erratic, unpredictable.

"Well, then...if I can't have you, no one will," Dante cryptically says before raising the gun in Verona's direction.

"No!" I yell.

And then everything happens in the blink of an eye, even though it feels like it's moving in slow motion. I jump across the room, right in front of Verona just as the gun goes off.

I can feel the burn of the bullets as they rip through my shoulder and forearm right before I fall to the ground.

More gunshots ring out, and then I watch as Dante falls to the ground, a bullet hole right in between his eyes. He stares at me as the life drains from them and blood pours out of the wound.

"See you in hell," I tell him before I roll to my back, groaning in pain.

"Luca!" Verona cries, collapsing to her knees on the wooden floor beside me.

I reach up with my good arm and cradle her beautiful face in my palm. "I'll be okay," I tell her. I don't know that for sure, but I don't want her to worry about me, especially in her condition.

Benito rushes inside. "Where?" he asks.

"Shoulder and forearm," I tell him.

"How bad is it?"

"Hurts like hell," I tell him with a dark chuckle. I try to lift my arm but fail miserably. Benito is quick to realize what I'm trying to do and carefully checks me out. "Exit wounds?" I ask, hopeful.

"We need to get you the fuck out of here," he says instead of answering me, so I'm assuming the answer is no to my question.

Fuck.

Benito motions for the men to help me while he speaks in Italian over the phone to who I'm assuming is the doctor we keep on staff for emergencies such as this.

Verona moves away from me as two of my men haul me up to a standing position. The quick movement coupled with the fact that I've lost a lot of blood already has my head spinning. I reach for my wife, but the world around me is already turning black.

"I love you," I tell her before I tumble headfirst into the darkness.

CHAPTER 62

Verona

"KEEP PRESSURE ON the wounds!" Benito yells at the men attending to Luca in the back of the SUV.

Luca's team has been working together like they've done this a thousand times before, and I'm thankful for it. They managed to get us on a boat and back to the mainland in no time. I didn't even freak out about going across the water. I was too busy being worried about Luca. He's been passed out for several minutes now, but Benito assured me it was okay.

I'm in the passenger seat, and Benito is driving. I can't tear my eyes away from Luca, though. I'm turned the whole way around in my seat. It took everything in me to let go of him, but I knew that I wasn't going to help, only get in the way.

His face looks pale, and the tears in my eyes blur his image. I quickly wipe away the tears, needing to see him. I need him to be okay.

"It's all my fault, Benny," I blurt out.

Benito glances at me and shakes his head. "Don't say that, Verona."

"It's true! Luca never liked Dante. He had suspicions about him, and I never listened." I sob in my hands. "He killed our mothers. I let a killer into Luca's home!"

Benito reaches over and grabs my hand, squeezing it gently. "It's not your fault. No one knew what was going through that fucker's head."

"I can't lose him, Benny," I cry.

"You won't," he assures me, and I find the strength I need from the confidence in his voice. "Our doctor is good. He'll fix him up. You'll see."

"How much longer?" I ask, staring at Luca's brutally handsome face as he starts losing even more color.

"Not long. We're almost there."

∼

We pull up to a large house in the outskirts of the city. It looks like a normal house, and I'm instantly confused. I thought we would be going to a hospital, not someone's home!

I start to say something to Benito, but he begins barking out orders to the men in the back.

Suddenly, everyone is clearing out of the van, four men carrying Luca's unconscious body towards the back of the house.

My legs move quickly, walking fast to keep up.

The doctor turns out to be an older gentleman, probably retirement age, with a weathered face and friendly, blue eyes. He ushers everyone inside the basement, clearly having expected us.

I anticipate a normal basement with furniture, a TV and such, but I'm blown away by the fact that it looks like we just stepped into a hospital. There is medical equipment everywhere, a few hospital beds and IV stands, medicine cabinets and pretty much everything you would expect to find in a functioning hospital.

The doctor instructs the men to carefully place Luca on one of the beds, and they quickly do. Luca looks pale. So pale.

"He's lost so much blood," I say, and I can hear the panic building up in my voice. "He's so pale. He needs blood."

Suddenly, Benito steps in front of me. "You need to calm down, Verona. This isn't good for the baby."

I stare up at him, and it takes several moments for his words to sink in. The baby. Yes, the baby. I nod emphatically. "Okay, okay, okay," I whisper.

Benito directs me to a chair in the corner of the room and gently coaxes me to sit down. "He will make it through this," he says assertively, and his confidence alone fills my heart with hope.

I lean around Benito's large frame to get a glimpse of Luca in the hospital bed. He's already hooked up to an IV with a blood bag hanging from a metal stand. The doctor is shouting out instructions to the men as he washes his hands and forearms in a big industrial sink before drying them and slipping on a pair of latex gloves.

"Time to operate," the doctor announces.

My feet are stuck to the floor like glue as I watch the doctor grab some surgical instruments from a tray. The moment he cuts into Luca's flesh, I nearly black out from all the blood gushing from the wound.

My stomach turns, and I barely make it to the trashcan before throwing up. Tears cloud my vision as I dry-heave repeatedly. Benito comes over and gently places a hand on my shoulder. "Let's go get some air," he suggests.

Shaking my head, I stand up and wipe my mouth with the back of my hand. "I'm not leaving," I decisively tell him.

He nods. "Okay. Then we'll stay. But, uh, maybe I should put your chair next to the garbage can."

When I hear the *clink* of the first bullet hitting the metal tray, my stomach twists again, and I tell him, "Yeah, that might be a good idea."

CHAPTER 63

Verona

HOURS PASS UNTIL the doctor finally announces to the room that he's finished. I slowly stand on wobbly legs and go to the older man. "Will my husband be okay?" I ask him, my voice trembling.

The doctor turns to me and says, "There are always risks of complications and infections, especially when you're dealing with gunshot wounds." He carefully takes off his mask and gloves and throws them in the nearby trash. "But I did the best I could, and I'm confident that he'll make a full recovery."

I sigh with relief. It feels like I've been holding my breath for such a long time.

"He'll need time to rest and recuperate," he explains.

"Yes, of course."

Benito comes up behind me and asks the doctor, "When can we move him?"

"He should stay here for a day or two at least. I'd like to monitor his progress anyway, check for signs of infection and keep him on some IV fluids and antibiotics."

"Thanks, Doc."

"You're welcome," the older man says before ascending the stairs to his home, no doubt going to bed after the long, arduous night he just had.

"How much will you pay him?" I ask Benito.

"A lot, but he's always on retainer. We pay him enough that he won't mind doing this again when we need him to."

The fact that they have to keep a doctor on retainer because situations like this can arise at any moment makes me feel queasy again. I don't want to ever go through this again with Luca, but I know it's just part of being in the mafia. It's a dangerous and sometimes cruel world. But I hope that the love Luca and I have for each other will trump all the bad things that come our way.

I walk over to Luca's bedside. He looks so peaceful lying there. Some of the color has returned to his face at least. I hope he's not in pain, and I hope he's dreaming of something good.

"I love you, Luca Vitale," I whisper to him before placing a kiss on his cheek.

Benito brings me a chair, and I sit down and hold Luca's hand, afraid of letting go. My eyelids grow heavy, but I refuse to sleep until exhaustion finally sets in and I don't have a choice. My dreams are filled with visions of Luca and I...and our baby. And they bring me peace.

CHAPTER 64

Luca

I WAKE UP slowly and in stages. First, I wiggle my toes...and then my fingers...and then I carefully open my eyes, which feel swollen, for some reason. It takes my brain a little while to process where I am and what I'm seeing right now.

I stare up at the familiar tiled ceiling and groan. I know I'm in the doctor's basement. Fuck, I think at one point I counted every single tile in this room from total boredom as I recovered from numerous gun and knife wounds.

My left arm feels heavy, and when I try to move it, a sharp pain has me hissing through my teeth.

"You were shot," Benito's voice comes from across the room.

"It's all coming back to me now," I say with a grimace. I remember the cabin in the middle of the lake. And I remember that bastard, Dante, trying to kill Verona. It was a split-second decision that I made in that moment to take a bullet for her. One that I would make a thousand times over again. I never want Verona to have to suffer through pain. And the thought of possibly losing her...well, it would completely and utterly gut me. I wouldn't want to live in a world without Verona in it.

"Is he dead?" I ask Benito.

"Yes," he assures me. "Bullet between the eyes. And then I knocked over the kerosene lamps for good measure before we left."

I relax back on the pillows behind me. "I wish I could have seen that place burn with his corpse inside," I spit out. I would have rather tortured the bastard for what he did to our mothers and what he did to Verona, but I'm glad he's dead. The fucker didn't deserve to breathe the same air as her, and he sure as hell didn't deserve to live another day here on this earth. I hope he's rotting away in hell where he belongs.

I glance around the room, searching for the one person whom I need the most right now. My eyes finally settle on the chair beside the bed, and my heart skips a beat as I see Verona's petite frame curled up, sleeping softly.

"She finally fell asleep about a half hour ago," Benito says. "She fought it for so long. And I know she's gonna be pissed that she missed you waking up."

I chuckle at the thought of her trying to stay awake for so long. "Let her sleep. She needs to rest." I stare at her, searing her beautiful face into my brain. Fuck, she's gorgeous. Like some kind of ethereal creature. She doesn't even seem real to me right now, but she's my wife, and she's mine.

"When do you want to move out?" Benito asks, breaking me out of my thoughts.

"As soon as possible," I tell him. Then, I glance over to Verona. "But let's let her sleep for a little while."

"All right," he agrees, and I can hear the hesitation in his voice. But Benito knows better than to argue with me. I watch as he walks over to the sink and fills up a cup of water before bringing it back to me. "Thirsty?"

"Fuck, yes," I tell him before gratefully taking the water with my good arm. I gulp down the cool liquid, and it feels like heaven on my sore, dry throat. "Tell the doctor we're leaving soon and to pack me what I need."

"Of course," Benito says before walking up the stairs to the main house.

Reaching over, I grasp Verona's hand in mine. She stirs, but doesn't wake, and I hold my breath until she falls back into a deep sleep. "I'll never let anyone hurt you," I promise her. And I intend to keep that promise until my last dying breath.

CHAPTER 65

Verona

WHEN I OPEN my eyes, I see Luca standing a few feet away from me. He's dressed in a black suit with his back turned towards me. I blink rapidly, trying to get rid of the hallucination, but he stays there. And when he turns to look at me, I realize he's real and not a figment of my imagination at all.

"Verona," he says my name, his voice gruff and strained.

A sob rips out of me as I jump up from the chair and run towards him. That's when I notice that the one sleeve of his jacket is merely draped over his shoulder, and that there's a sling, holding his injured arm to his side. "What are you doing out of bed?" I ask, confusion and panic setting in all at once.

"We're going home."

"But the doctor said you needed some time to recuperate," I argue.

He reaches out with his good hand, and I take it without hesitation. He pulls me to him, holding me tight and breathing in my scent. "I'm okay. I promise. I've taken bullets before and spent less time than this in bed."

I hate that he's been hurt in the past, and I hate that he finds it necessary to always be so strong when he doesn't need to be. Not with me.

"Let's go home," he tells me before kissing my crown.

Benito opens the basement door, and tells me as we walk through it, "Don't worry. We have a nurse on staff at the estate. She'll keep an eye on him."

That makes me feel better, but only slightly. I don't think I'll be able to fully relax until Luca is one hundred percent recovered. And even then, I'll still continue to worry about him. We live in a dangerous world, and Luca has many enemies. But at least one of them is dead now.

CHAPTER 66

Luca

I'M WATCHING VERONA out of the corner of my eye as the nurse gives me a sponge bath. I can practically hear the thoughts in my little naughty wife's head. Her honey-colored eyes are staring daggers into the nurse. I know Verona is too nice to say anything to deter the nurse, who is just doing her job, but the jealous little green-eyed monster that is my wife right now is amusing to watch, to say the least. I don't think I've ever seen her jealous before. And despite my injuries, it's turning me the fuck on.

Before the nurse can go any further down my stomach and discover my growing hard-on, I quickly tell her, "That's enough. I think my wife can manage the rest."

The young brunette nods and quickly leaves the room.

It's been a couple of days since we arrived back home. Unfortunately, I haven't recuperated from my wounds as fast as I would have liked. Maybe I'm getting too old for this shit.

My eyes meet Verona's as she crosses the room, still fuming. A smirk forms on my lips as I watch her angrily pick up the sponge, wet it, twist it to get rid of the excess soap and water and gently run it over my lower stomach.

"I've never seen you jealous before," I tell her.

The shock on her face makes me chuckle. She didn't think I would figure out her internal thoughts. But I can read Verona like a book now. She's not just my wife. She's my soul mate, my other half.

I watch her carefully as I say, "You know, in Greek mythology, humans were originally created with four legs, four arms and a head with two faces?"

Verona stares at me for a second before cocking her head. I've clearly confused her. She quickly presses the back of her hand to my forehead, checking me for a fever. Chuckling, I take her hand and bring it to my lips to gently kiss her vanilla and honey-scented skin.

"With a strike of his lightning bolt, Zeus split them into two separate beings, condemning them to spend the rest of their lives searching for their other halves, their soul mates."

Verona is barely breathing, hanging on to my every word at this point.

"I found mine. I found you," I tell her softly before kissing her hand again.

Tears fill her eyes. I'm not sure if my words have affected her that much or if it's the pregnancy hormones. She's been so up and down as of late — laughing one second and crying the next or sometimes both at the same time — but I wouldn't trade it for anything in the world. I've never been so fucking happy in my entire life.

"I love you, Verona."

"I love you too," she whispers before leaning in for a kiss.

Wrapping my good hand around the nape of her neck, I pull her in, my mouth claiming her. God, it feels like forever since I've been inside of her. My cock grows painfully hard under the blanket; and when she accidentally brushes against it with her elbow, I let out a hissing sound.

"I'm sorry! Did I hurt you?" she asks, pulling back quickly.

"No," I tell her with a shake of my head. And then, I pull down the blanket, allowing my cock to bob free.

Verona's eyes widen as she stares down at my arousal. "Luca...we can't. You-You're hurt."

Her protests are weak to my ears. "I need you, Verona. Please. I need to be inside of you."

I pat the bed beside me. She hesitates, but eventually climbs onto the edge on her knees. Her short dress rides up her creamy thighs as she positions her knees on either side of my hips.

"Touch yourself for me, honey," I tell her. Moving her thong to the side, I watch in awe as Verona strokes her clit with her fingertips, biting back a moan.

She looks like a sexy goddess, and I'm completely entranced. When she begins to get close, I stop her. "Enough," I rumble. With my good hand, I grip my cock and stroke it through her wetness. Every time I run it over that little bundle of nerves, she cries out, making my cock impossibly harder.

It's practically weeping for her, precum dripping over the crown, before I beg her to ride me.

Lining my cock up with her entrance, Verona slowly sinks down on my cock, taking every single inch of me until she's fully seated. A growl erupts from the back of my throat. Fuck, she feels like heaven every damn time.

Slowly, she impales herself over and over again on my hard length, taking her time and driving me up the goddamn wall. I watch my cock disappear into her sweet pussy so many times I lose count. I'm mesmerized by the sight, and all I can do is moan in pleasure as she sinks down on me again and again.

Verona falls apart on my cock as she has a powerful orgasm that makes her entire body shudder. She desperately tries to continue to ride me, losing her rhythm as she cries out. Grasping her hip, I slam her down on my cock until I erupt inside of her, moaning deeply.

I close my eyes and savor the feeling. Fuck, that's better than any medicine that they could give me.

Verona collapses onto my chest, and I hold her to me with my good arm. I never want to let her go again. "I love you," I whisper in her hair.

"I love you too," she whispers back.

She raises her head and looks at me with those familiar honey-colored eyes. "You're going to be a great daddy," she says, making me smile.

"And you're going to be a great mommy."

Tears fill her eyes, and she leans up to place a sweet kiss on my mouth. "I can't wait to hold our little son or daughter."

A lump forms in my throat, and I swallow hard. "Me either."

I don't know what the future holds for Verona and me, but I know that our love will conquer anything life throws at us. Together, we're unbreakable, unstoppable, and nothing will ever tear us apart.

EPILOGUE

Verona

Three Years Later

THE WAITING IS the worst part. And I'm not talking about just waiting in Luca's office, staring at a computer screen and waiting for something to happen. I mean the past three years that we've been waiting for this very moment. Constantine Carbone's empire has finally fallen. He was arrested two weeks ago; and thanks to Luca's drone video surveillance, we've managed to locate yet another group of captives who were about to be sold into human trafficking.

Constantine Carbone's arrest came on the heels of years of investigation by the FBI that Luca and I were involved in. Luca submitted everything he had on Constantine, anonymously, of course. He still dabbles in some illegal activities that he doesn't want to draw unwanted attention to, but I think he's slowly coming to the realization that doing things aboveboard is a lot easier...and safer. And lately that seems to be the only thing he cares about — keeping our little family safe.

We watch patiently from the drone footage as women and children are freed from shipping containers at the abandoned warehouse that Constantine kept them in. If it weren't for Luca's anonymous tip, who knows if they would have ever been found. Constantine certainly wasn't admitting to anything since his arrest and definitely wasn't willing to spill any information that could lead to more charges.

"You're their guardian angel," I tell Luca, leaning over to give him a kiss on his cheek.

He doesn't say anything in response, but I can see the smile creeping onto his face. I know he'll never admit to it, because he still has a reputation to uphold, but my husband has a heart of gold. Luca has donated a lot of money to help fund the shelters that the women and children go to after they're rescued. He not only saved their lives but made sure they had the extra help and care they needed afterwards.

Luca turns off the footage. "That should be the last of them," he says, and I can almost feel the relief coming off of him in waves.

It's been a long and arduous process, but Constantine is finally behind bars where he belongs. And the people he was trying to sell are finally rescued. We did as much as we could, and now it's the judicial system's turn to lock Constantine away and throw away the key.

The office door suddenly bursts open, and Nico charges through it with Benito quick on his heels. "Mommy!" he cries.

My little toddler waddles over to me with big, fat tears rolling down his chubby cheeks. He runs straight into my arms, and I scoop him up and squeeze him tight. "What's wrong?" I ask him. "Did you miss Mommy and Daddy?"

He nods his head, and his tears instantly start to dry up. I comb my fingers through his dark hair as he looks up at me with intense, gray eyes. He's a total miniature version of his daddy. "Thank you for keeping him busy while we dealt with this, Benny," I tell him with a smile.

Benito looks out of breath as he walks over to the desk. "I tried to keep him occupied as long as I could, but he said no to everything I suggested," he says with a huff. "I liked it better when he was a baby and slept all the time," he admits.

I can't help but chuckle. Benito has been the best godfather we could ask for. He's so protective of his little godson, never letting him out of his sight. Who knew he would be so great with kids? Nico and him are best buddies, and I often hear Benito reading books to my little man when he thinks no one is around. Benito doesn't want anyone to know he's a big softie when it comes to our son, and I think it's so cute.

Nico squirms in my hold, and I gently put him down on the floor. He runs straight for Benito and grabs onto his leg, mimicking wrestling moves against the big man. Benito plays along, and Nico squeals with laughter as Benito lifts him high up in the air before carefully bringing him back down to his feet.

"You don't miss the crying and sleepless nights, Benito?" Luca asks.

Benito is distracted with Nico, but he shakes his head. "No, I think I prefer that over the terrible twos."

"Good. Because Verona is pregnant."

Benito's eyes bulge out of his head as his gaze snaps up to meet Luca's. "Wh-what?"

"We're hoping for a girl this time, but another boy will be just fine too," I say while rubbing my flat stomach. I'm not far along, so I'm not showing just yet.

"Maybe it will be twins," Luca suggests.

"Oh, god. Can you imagine?" I ask.

"No!" Benito blurts out, and that makes us laugh. Even though he loves Nico, I don't think he could handle two of him at the same time.

"Whatever we have, they will be loved," Luca says, placing his hand over mine.

"Yes, they will," I agree.

Nico runs over to us, and Luca lifts him up in his arms. "Love you, Daddy," he says sweetly.

"I love you too," Luca says.

I like to think that Nico and I together have taught Luca that loving someone is the easy part. It's getting their love in return that is hard. But Luca never has to worry about us not loving him back. We love him unconditionally, and I know he loves us just the same.

THE END

ABOUT THE AUTHOR

Thank you for reading! If you enjoyed reading *Keeping My Bride*, please consider telling your friends and posting a short review on Amazon. Word of mouth is an author's best friend and much appreciated. Shouts from rooftops are great too.

You can find all of my books exclusively on Amazon and free for Kindle Unlimited subscribers: http://amazon.com/author/angelasnyder

And please sign up for my newsletter to be notified of all of my new releases, giveaways, sneak peeks, freebies and more: http://eepurl.com/cNFoo5

ALSO FROM THE AUTHOR

If you enjoyed reading Keeping My Bride, please check out my other books on Amazon.

KEEPING HER: BOOK 1 OF THE KEEP ME SERIES

To say I had a rough start in life would be the understatement of the century. My uncle may have saved me from my abusive childhood, but he couldn't save me from the neurotic and compulsive obsessions I would develop in my adulthood.

I deal with some of the worst criminals in the seedy underbelly of the world just to get what I want. What I need.

And what I need is the perfect woman. Perfect and pure in every way possible. And I'm willing to obtain that perfection…no matter the cost.

So when I make my newest purchase, I expect Adeline's fate to be

ALSO FROM THE AUTHOR

like all the others before her --- taking what I want and then never seeing her again.

But she's different.

Her beauty is disarming.

And even though I promised to let her go after I took what I wanted...I slowly come to the realization that I can't.

I have to break my promise to her, because she's mine now.

And I'm keeping her.

Find Keeping Her on Amazon here: http://myBook.to/KeepingHer

CLAIMING HER

In a world with no rules, you claim what you want...
And they all want her.

The new flu vaccine that was supposed to save lives turned humans into bloodthirsty zombies instead.

For the past two years, Trinity Sanders has found herself fighting for her life in an apocalyptic world she never imagined would exist.

After she's suddenly caught in someone's trap, Trinity thinks her fate is sealed. However, when she wakes up in a strange house and in a warm bed, she's surrounded by other humans, not the ravenous monsters she was running from.

The four handsome men who saved her are rough, rugged...and wild.

They've lived on their own since the apocalypse, surviving on the land and claiming whatever they capture in their traps, which now includes Trinity.

In a world with no rules, you claim what you want...

And they all want her.

Claiming Her is a 44,000+ word standalone reverse harem romance. It contains adult situations for mature readers.

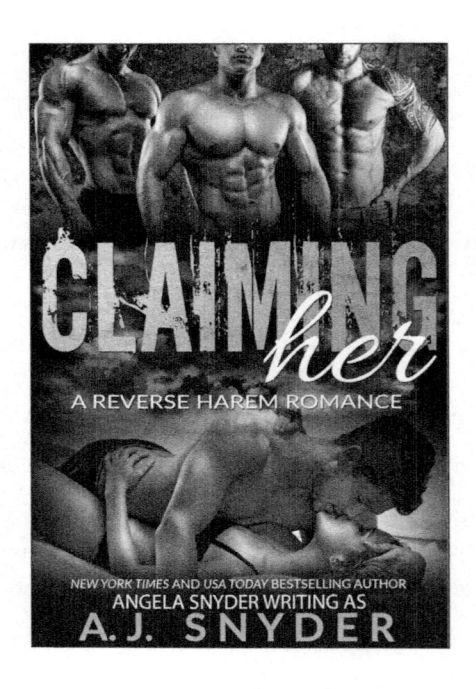

Find Claiming Her on Amazon: http://mybook.to/ClaimingHer

WRECKED

Shipwrecked. Stranded on a deserted island in the middle of the Pacific Ocean.

After a year of isolation, Gunner, Finn and Jamison never expected to be rescued.

And they certainly never expected a beautiful woman to crash-land into their lonely existence.

Rose is the only ray of light in their dark storm, and they'll do anything to protect her.

But can the four of them survive without becoming completely wrecked?

Wrecked is a standalone reverse harem romance. It contains adult situations for mature readers.

Find Wrecked on Amazon: https://viewbook.at/Wrecked

Printed in Great Britain
by Amazon